Burning Old School Ties

FOSSEWAY WRITERS

ISBN: 9781072962915
Independently published, available as paperback or e-book.
1st edition.

www.fossewaywriters.wordpress.com

Cover design by Ric Millen
Edited by Maria Dziedzan, Linda Cooper,
C.L. Peache and N.K Rowe
Formatted by N.K. Rowe

Foreword

As with many creative projects this book had its genesis in its predecessor, *Gobstoppers, Shrimps and Sour Monkeys*, a collection of poetry and short stories from Fosseway Writers over the last twenty years. In the process of pulling all of the content together I was struck by the different narrative voices that tumbled out. Clearly, they were all telling their own stories across a disparate set of unrelated pieces, but what if they were *linked* somehow?

Initially this wasn't even a consciously developed thought, more of a vague observation. It wasn't until the summer was over (with a very successful stint at the Newark Book Festival) and we were about to have our September AGM to plan the next twelve months that I began to mull the idea over properly.

The topic of 'what do we do next' was raised and I threw onto the table the idea of a party or event viewed by a bunch of different people. Each character would narrate the evening from their own perspective and have their own agenda and story arc, but they would all interweave to an extent with a larger evening narrative. To be frank, I thought it would be shot down in flames as too ambitious and complicated but to my surprise/horror/delight everyone seemed really up for it with Maria Dziedzan being particularly taken with the idea. I asked what kind of turnaround people had in mind (thinking Christmas 2019) and when everyone plumped for Newark Book Festival (which meant a window of nine or ten months) the 'delight' disappeared to leave me feeling just the surprise and horror.

After further discussion on what the 'event' should be Ric Millen hit the jackpot when he suggested a school reunion and we set about thinking up characters, back stories and story arcs. From quite an early stage (probably five minutes in) a possible death or murder was being added to the overall story; a nice bit of historical trauma was going to be useful to tie some characters together and we weren't discounting further death and destruction 'on the night'.

In the end, eight of us sat down and working individually created primary characters along with a cast of other ex-pupils. These secondary characters proved particularly useful as a means of developing plot and character as well as introducing new information. Our main objective was for each primary character to narrate in first person, present tense, so that the reader experiences everything first hand from that character's perspective. The hope is that because each story is literally written by a different author the thoughts and tone will be clearly unique to that character.

We calculated that to get a novel-sized book we needed to write somewhere in the region of 8-10,000 words each, possibly three or four chapters of around 2-3000 words. Jackie Leitch was the first to get a chapter completed and her story established a framework that the others could work around and add to.

Being a group based in Newark, it seemed appropriate that we should set the story in a local secondary school, but for the purposes of fiction it is an *alternate Newark*. Imagine there is no Grove, or Magnus school; no new-fangled Academy. We've taken elements from some of these places (there was, for a brief period in the 60s, a Hercules Clay Secondary School down Barnby Road), mangled them up with our own childhood institutions (mine is the posh school from the film *Nativity*) and plonked the result down where the Highfields junior school sits in "Real Newark". Hopefully, there's enough detail to convince the reader that it feels real; we went to the trouble of visiting schools to get a sense of what a school in 2019 feels like to someone who may not have been in one for a couple of decades (or more).

The vehicle for handling all of the content and suggestions was, along with email, an internet forum to which all Fosseway members are granted access. These are fairly easy to set up and often free of charge – we use freeforums.net hosted by www.ProBoards.com. Files containing chapters, maps, photos and so on can all be uploaded for others to view and refer to.

Extra material was posted to give background information on particular aspects of key secondary characters, locations and past events that would be common to all. Finally, once everyone had completed their individual stories, a lengthy process of editing and assembly began which threw up a few inconsistencies and timing issues. If you're actually reading this, it means that we've either resolved everything to our satisfaction or decided that we're past caring.

The whole process has been fascinating, particularly in relation to developing interactions with other characters that had authors and agendas of their own. It's similar to discovering that your own characters are deciding how a story is going to develop and adjusting accordingly, but with the added complexity of asking another writer if you can borrow one of theirs or, just as likely, someone else's character waltzing off with one of yours. The initial ideas for our stories were generally standalone plots but the more we saw of the others the more they flowed into each other; Helen Yourston went after one of Jackie's characters with a vengeance, Linda Cooper and Maria both focused on trauma at the hands of a shared character while Janey Harvey and C.L. Peache developed a particularly wonderful joint storyline. Ric's character is probably the most fun, showing a different perspective on some issues and blundering into several conversations and interactions.

As a writing project it has been really interesting and fun, as well as a little stressful and complicated! We hope that it's as enjoyable to read as it has been to write.

Nick Rowe
Chair, Fosseway Writers
June 2019

Acknowledgements

Fosseway Writers' informal gatherings run on tea, coffee, cake and alcohol so our first thanks go to our regular mid-month evening haunt, The Organ Grinder pub on Portland Street, Newark. We've also made use of a few cafes, notably Carriages, Gannets and Sweet Vibes – thank you for giving us some space to work through our issues!

We would like to thank Dave Scott, Annabelle Reilly and Becky Sims for arranging and showing us around the Magnus Church of England Academy and allowing us to see what secondary schools are like these days.

Thanks also to fellow Fosseway members Anne Howkins and Barbara Stewart for being our beta readers.

Final group thanks to Maria and Linda for exhaustive editing, Nick and Clair for sequencing the eight outputs to work as a coherent story with a functioning timeline, Ric for the cover design and all contributors for seeing it through to the end with good humour and cooperative spirit.

In addition, there are some special individual thanks:

From Jackie – My thanks to Fosseway Writers' group, especially Diane, Kirsty, Brenda and Peter; to Bob (my husband) who encourages me to keep writing even when I get bad-tempered because it won't go right! And to my sons and sisters whose love and support is always much appreciated.

From Maria – I would like to thank Nawal Duddles for her invaluable help with the issue of safeguarding the vulnerable.

From Nick – Special thanks to my wife, Sue, who encourages me and helps pack me off to meetings, without whose help I would be arriving *seriously* late. Thanks also to my daughters, Tegan and Natalie, for not laughing at my writing (although this isn't so good when it's supposed to be funny).

From Helen – Thanks to Victoria Cozens for some inspiration from her school days; Nick Rowe for tirelessly putting up with me; Alan, my husband for listening and helping me believe I can do this.

Fosseway Writers

We are a long-established group based in and around Newark, Nottinghamshire (itself situated on the old Roman 'Fosse Way', which is mostly now the route of the modern A46).

The aims of the group are to:
- provide a welcoming and stimulating environment for local writers;
- engage with, support and encourage local people who would like to try writing but don't know where to start;
- help members to improve and develop their writing skills;

...all through meetings, workshops, friendly socials and online interaction.

www.fossewaywriters.wordpress.com
fosseway.writers@mail.com
Find us on Facebook and Twitter via @FossewayWriters

To Sara

Characters and Authors

Gemma Robinson   *by Jackie Leitch*

Julia Forest   *by Maria Dziedzan*

Helen Walcott   *by Janey Harvey*

Iain Wilson   *by N.K. Rowe*

Hannah Parker   *by C.L. Peach*

Pam McPherson   *by Helen Yourston*

Amanda Shaw   *by Linda Cooper*

Phil Morris   *by Ric Millen*

Tuesday 6 October 1992
SCHOOL BLAZE HORROR
Hercules Clay Comprehensive School in Newark was the scene of a horrific fire yesterday when 14-year-old Daniel Griggs of Hawtonville, Newark was engulfed in flames during a science lesson.

Headteacher Mr Brian Billings said: 'At around 2.30 pm, the fourth years were in their science lessons when, unfortunately, one of our students was seriously injured. We are, of course, co-operating fully with the police in their investigations.'

A pupil, who claimed to be present when the incident took place said: 'We were busy doing an experiment with bunsen burners when I heard a shout, some screams and chairs being knocked over. I looked up and saw a huge fire and realised it was a person. I'm not sure where our teacher Mr Hendry was but he wasn't in the room when it happened.'

Mr Hendry has been suspended from the school pending investigations and was not available for comment. Daniel remains in a critical condition.

Wednesday 7 October 1992
HUMAN TORCH PUPIL DEAD
Daniel Griggs, 14, died as a result of severe burns yesterday following a fire at a Newark school on Monday 5th October. Police continue to investigate and Local Education Authority solicitors are in consultation with school staff and parents.

Thursday 23 September 1993
HUMAN TORCH KILLER GUILTY

A Newark youth, who we can't name due to their age, has been found guilty at Nottingham Crown Court of manslaughter. The case relates to the death of Daniel Griggs, a fellow pupil of Hercules Clay Comprehensive, in October 1992. The defence claimed that the accused had not intended to harm the victim and had been merely playing a prank that had gone terrifyingly wrong. There were mixed testimonies to the extent to which the accused had either helped or hindered the attempts to douse the flames that engulfed Daniel. The defendant was sentenced to 18 months in a secure establishment to continue their formal education.

Gemma Robinson, *pupil* – October 1992

THERE'S BEEN A lot going on. The school is seething with rumours. Pregnant girls, dodgy teachers, bad boys getting into bother. I keep my head down and work towards my exams. I can't afford to get sidetracked. It's not like we haven't heard the same stories going around before. Who knows how much is true and how much is just spiteful gossip? It's nothing to do with me anyway. I don't know any pregnant girls or dodgy teachers – although there are a few bad boys – Karl Stamford for one, but I don't move in his orbit, except sometimes in class, and I keep well out of his way, so it doesn't affect me. My focus right at this minute is my Chemistry class. I really need to pass all my sciences if I'm to go to a good university and Chemistry is not my strongest science. Talking of Karl, there he is baiting Danny again. Why does he do it? It's not like Danny is a threat to anyone. I wave to Liza and Ashley.

'Hi. I've saved our places.'

We claim our usual spot together, leaving room for Michelle when she gets here from her gymnastics class.

'Liza,' I implore. 'Change places with me quick – I want to be by Lee.'

We swap so that she is next to Danny, who's keeping as far from Karl as he can. Liza says something to Danny that I don't hear and he nods, shooting a quick glance towards Karl. There's something going on, but I don't want to know. I can't help thinking Danny's acting like a bit of a wimp. Why doesn't he stand up for himself? He's not usually so laid-back. Turning away from Danny's end of the bench, I try to think of something clever to say to Lee. I really, really fancy him but he doesn't seem to know I exist.

As we settle down, Mr. Hendry writes up some formulae on the blackboard. While his back is turned, something seems to be going on further down the room where Liza and Danny are. Oh, okay. It seems to have settled down now. We get our equipment set up and the Bunsen burners alight. So, we're all ready to put theory into practice.

Glancing at my watch, I see we still have half-an-hour to go before... freedom and lunch. What is going on down there? Where's old Hendry? Stuck in the supplies cupboard by the look of it, deliberately ignoring the pushing and shoving going on at the other end of the bench. It seems like there's a fight or something. I can't see what's happening and I don't really want to. I turn away. Mr H should sort it out, he's the teacher. That's the last coherent thought I have for some time, as the lab turns into a scene from hell.

M UM RUSHES INTO the hall and grabs me. 'Are you all right?'

I can't answer, it's too horrible.

The whoosh from the aerosol as Karl sprayed it towards Danny - too close to the Bunsen burner. The screaming - everyone screaming! And Danny blazing – fire everywhere. Karl just standing there, doing nothing, and, oh God, Liza! Her face flaring and melting as the flaming spray catches her. I don't want to keep seeing it but it fills my head like it's on a loop. And my nose is full of the terrible smell of Danny and Liza burning. I'm coughing but the smell just keeps filling my lungs.

'Mum!' I'm crying so hard I can hardly breathe. 'Danny was alight, they rushed him away in an ambulance. I could see he was... oh it was awful, he was *burning*, mum. And Liza. She... she's really badly hurt. Oh God, it's my fault. I changed places with her. It should be me.' I collapse against mum's shoulder, coughing and crying, my nose running all over her suit jacket.

She cuddles me close anyway, not seeming to care about her clothes. 'You didn't know what was going to happen. It's *not* your fault. It's that maniac Karl. They should have expelled him long before this.'

'But... what'll happen to them? Danny won't die will he? They'll fix him – and Liza? They will, won't they?'

I leave it a day before going to the hospital to see Liza. She's full of tubes and her face is covered up with some kind of cloth stuff. She's asleep – it's the drugs apparently. I know she can't hear me but I whisper to her that I'm sorry. Mrs Chastain tells me Liza's going to be moved to a specialist burns unit. She'll be scarred for life. The burns hospital is too far away for me to visit her regularly. It's a horrible thing to admit, but I'm glad. I don't think I could stand to keep visiting her knowing it's my fault she's the one who got injured, just because I wanted to flirt with Lee. Danny died in the hospital, they couldn't save him. I'll never be able to get the picture of the fire seething all over him out of my head. How could something like that happen? It took just seconds and now Danny is dead and Liza is disfigured. Mum says I should try not to dwell on it and concentrate on my exams. She tells me that I must make the best of it and work hard to get into university.

'Ruining your own life won't help anyone, Gemma. You have your future to think of. Liza's getting wonderful treatment and they can do marvels with plastic surgery these days.'

Julia Forest, *pupil* – Summer 1995

LOOKING BACK, I don't know why I went to watch our lads play football. I had no interest in the sport and, although some of the team were fit, I didn't fancy any of them. Well, not then, anyway. It might have been because they'd made the semi-final and it seemed that everyone in school was in a frenzy because we might actually win the cup. I cheered along with the others and leapt up and down when we scored. I grinned like an idiot when eleven muddy and sweaty teenagers strode off the field, finalists at last.

Helen and I linked arms and followed them to the changing room doors.

'Which one would you have?' she asked as we milled about with the rest of the team's adoring fans.

'Dunno. Haven't given it a thought.' I looked closer at my best friend. 'You have, though.'

'Yes, I have.' She blushed faintly.

'Who?'

'Dave.'

'Dave? You do know that every girl in the school fancies him, don't you?'

'There's a reason for that.'

'Of course there is. He's the handsome captain of the football team...' I didn't add that I thought in his case beauty was only skin deep.

Helen sighed. 'I know he probably won't pick me...but I can dream.'

'Come on then, dreamer. Let's walk home.'

'But they'll be out soon.'

'And going to celebrate with Butterford.'

Helen grimaced.

Mr Ross Butterford taught PE, but no one would have guessed it from his appearance. For a man in his early thirties he gave a good impression of a decrepit dirty old man. He was short, fat and always out of breath. The combination of his smoking and his asthma allowed him to give anyone a wheezy warning of his approach. He might wear a tracksuit to work, but he never put it to its proper use. Rather, the elasticated waist only expanded with his hairy belly. He seemed to have no vanity except for his shoulder length hair and even that was unimpressive. Long, thin and lank, it was a statement from another era. Somehow, his "lads", the fit gods of the football team, saw past all of that to the exclusivity of their relationship with him. The elite, travelling in the school minibus to matches, having the odd illicit pint with "Ross" on the way back. Ross who had a tongue like a nettle for everyone else, teachers included, but who could do no wrong in the Head's eyes while his lads continued to gain glory for the school. Ross, who had deigned to let his boys address him by his first name. Oh, the giddy heights.

So when the final came around, Helen and I were on the side lines again, yelling ourselves hoarse. We only had one opportunity to leap up and down with glee as Butterford's lads won the cup, one nil. Oh, the cheering, the celebration, the glory. It was at the school disco that I, too, was touched with some of the fairy dust when Mark, a midfielder, asked me to dance. He was tall, dark and sort of handsome and I didn't need to look far over his shoulder to see his team-mates grinning.

'Yeah, okay,' I said.

'You've been coming to the matches, haven't you?' he asked later as we cooled off in the courtyard.

'Yeah. Well, the last couple.'

'What did you think?'

'Great.'

He looked disappointed.

'Well, you won.'

'We did.' He brightened.

'Is that what you want to do with your life? Football? Sport?' I asked.

'Yeah, I suppose so. What about you?'

'I don't know yet. Uni first. Then I'm not sure.'

'Oooh, "uni first",' sneered a voice behind us. 'Getting your end away with a brainy one, Marky?' asked Butterford.

Mark blushed and laughed. 'Yeah.' Then he looked at me. 'I mean, no.'

I didn't help him. Anyone who wanted to please Butterford needed sympathy for their poor choice of hero, although Mark had been sweet to me.

'Well, I'll leave you to it,' said Butterford. 'Treat him well, girly,' he added, wagging his finger at me.

I didn't reply. I just watched him waddle away to embarrass some other girl.

'He's a charmer,' I said to Mark.

'Oh, he's alright. He really looks after us.'

'Good,' I said. What else was there to say? But we were overcome by the strains of Blur, so I grabbed Mark by the hand and rushed him back to the dance floor.

After that night, we became a couple. Mark relaxed into the post-season lull. He would walk over to my house in the early evening, watch some sport and chat with my dad while I finished my homework, and then we'd hang out together. It was a sweet time.

Having won the cup for the school, it seemed that Butterford could do no wrong...however he behaved. On a hot afternoon as Sports Day was coming to a close, Mr Hessle, the conformist leader of the PE department, was giving out the prizes with the Head. Butterford was fooling about with his footballers, having received their Team of the Year Award. They were in a guffawing group at the back of the crowd of pupils and teachers. One of them had clearly made a suggestive comment and they all roared with laughter, looking in the same direction.

They were looking at Stacey Grey who, despite having finished her GCSE exams, had come back for Sports Day. Not that she was interested in athletics. Well, not the running, hurdling kind. She was wearing a pink boob tube and the tiniest skirt known to man. I was trying to decide who she'd come for when I saw her walk over to the footballers, the forefinger of her right hand twisting a lock of her blonde hair. She was chewing gum and I couldn't help wondering whether she spat it out when she was busy.

As she reached the boys, I saw Butterford crook a finger at her. She ducked her head sideways and, smiling open-mouthed, sidled up to him. I couldn't hear what he said but he put his hand on the nape of her neck under her hair while the boys grinned at them both. Whatever he'd said caused raucous laughter and then he moved away with her, back towards the school.

I felt a shiver up my spine. *How could she let that creep touch her*? I was thinking, but Helen broke into my thoughts.

'She's fancied him for ages.'

I looked at her in surprise and saw she was looking exactly where I was looking, in all that crowded field. 'Stacey Grey and Mr...?'

'Yep.'

'Why?' I asked. She couldn't be short of offers with her small, slim frame and her large breasts.

'Alpha male,' said Helen.

'Alpha male? That fat fart?'

'Well, look at the lads. Leader of the pack.'

I nodded and remembered how nothing seemed to tarnish Butterford's image in the eyes of his boys. 'Did you know...' I began.

Helen linked arms with me as I paused to reflect on whether telling the story was wise.

'Go on,' she grinned.

'He has a blow-up doll.'

'What?'

'A sex toy.'

'I know what a blow-up doll is. How do you know?'

'Mark told me.'

She looked at me, eyes wide with mischief. 'Tell me.'

'The lads were all at his one day after a match and he was on the phone. So, for a laugh, they went into his bedroom, apparently to leave him a porn magazine. One of the lads opened his wardrobe and the doll fell out.'

'Oh my God! What did they do?'

'Not much. He came upstairs to see what the noise was all about and found them.'

Helen just stared at me, breath held.

'He laughed it off. Said he used it if he had to make do. When the Staceys of this world weren't available.'

'And those fools thought he was a hero,' said Helen.

'Yep.'

Helen shook her head and sighed. 'Let's call it a day.'

'Okay, I just need to pop into the Common Room to pick up my stuff. Coming?'

We walked back towards the school buildings and took the outer path past the Design Department to the Common Room. As we walked past the art room, Helen hissed, 'Oh my God! Just look in there.'

I turned my head to see Stacey Grey perched on the edge of a table, her knees wide apart to accommodate Butterford's bulk. He had inserted one chubby hand with its dirty fingernails up her tiny skirt, while the other held the back of her head in a tight kiss.

I felt the bile rise up in my throat and grabbed Helen's arm as we hurried past.

When we were out of sight of the windows, Helen let out a loud laugh. 'What a performer!'

I shook my head. How many girls might there be, whom he had bullied or manipulated?

AWAY FROM THE lads, Mark continued to seem different and our sweet time went on through the summer holidays and into the autumn term, when Helen and I became focussed on our uni applications. Too many days of worrying about making the grade caused us to escape from school one Friday, ostensibly to scour the market for smart blouses for interviews.

'Look at these,' said Helen, stopping at a stall piled high with cheap underwear.

'We're not looking for knickers,' I protested.

'Yes, but these are cute.'

'Cute or not, I'm assuming no one at university is going to care what our knickers are like.'

'You never know.' Helen grinned and began to look through the stacks of patterned cotton knickers.

I joined her, hoping she wouldn't be long.

'These are definitely you,' she said, waving a pair of knickers decorated with tiny figures which looked suspiciously like Tank Girl.

'They are cute,' I laughed.

'Go on, buy them. They'll make you feel invincible at interviews.'

'They will!' and I bought five pairs, just to be sure.

But invincible or not, a battle was coming, and it wasn't for a place at uni.

'Come on, Julia. Don't be tight,' said Mark.

'I don't want to,' I said. 'I can't get pregnant. You know that.'

'Why can't you go on the pill like everyone else?'

'Because I'm not everyone else,' I said. 'Besides, how do you know "everyone" is on the pill?'

'That's what the lads say.'

'How do they know?'

He shrugged.

I sat up and pulled my skirt down. We were lying on my single bed, which, I suppose was asking for trouble, but Mark had been happy with the limits I'd set so far.

'No, how do they know?' I persisted.

'Well, they know who they're shagging, don't they?' said Mark, irritably.

'Who they're shagging? And I suppose you've told them you're shagging me?'

'No. I haven't said that.'

Then the penny dropped. 'You've told them how far we've gone and they've told you not to put up with it and to make me go the whole way.'

Mark had the grace to blush.

'Jesus, Mark, I thought you were better than that.'

He hung his head.

'You'd better go. Tell them what you like but don't come back,' I said.

And he had gone.

Some weeks later, I was running my fingers along the spines of the stacked copies of *Wuthering Heights*...eight, nine, ten...and a second pile...twenty-one, twenty-two...and making a note of the number on Miss Summerfield's typed sheet. I moved my hand across to the next dusty pile of Bronte novels and understood why Miss Summerfield wasn't keen to do her own stock-taking. It was a dull and grubby job. However, I didn't really mind. She'd given me plenty of help with my university application. I made a note of the number of copies of *The Tenant of Wildfell Hall* and then came down the stepladder and moved it along to the Dickens novels. They were along the narrower back wall of the English Department stock cupboard and were just as dusty as the poor Brontes. I was climbing up the ladder again to count *Great Expectations* on the top shelf, when I heard the stock cupboard door opening.

'Eighteen, nineteen, twenty,' I said aloud to warn Miss Summerfield that I was counting when I felt a clammy hand close around my bare ankle. I gasped and turned to look down on Mr Butterford's greasy head.

'Oh!'

'Oh!' he mimicked while tightening his grip on my ankle.

I was instantly aware of my bare legs, my short skirt and my cotton knickers with their ridiculous Tank Girls...just as Mr Butterford was. There he stood, smirking up at my crotch.

I tried to tug my foot out of his grip but he held on to it. I realised it was too high to jump down from my perch and besides, if he continued to hold my ankle, I'd land on my head. I thought of kicking him but my shoes were flimsy.

I swallowed and said, 'Let go of me, please. You'll make me fall.'

'Oh, you won't fall, Miss High and Mighty,' he said. 'You're fine where you are, up on a pedestal,' and he began to slide his free hand up the inside of my leg.

I caught a glimpse of his dirty fingernails and the glint of the signet ring on his pinkie. Then they both disappeared under the hem of my skirt.

'No,' I said and tried to move away but there was nowhere to move to.

'Just keep still and you won't hurt yourself.'

'No,' I said hoarsely. I thought about screaming but my throat had closed up. As I bent down to push his hand away, he took it out from under my skirt, only to slap my face with it.

'Now don't be silly and keep still. You're not turning a boy down now.'

I clamped my knees together realising this was how I was going to be made to pay for blowing Mark out.

Butterford began to grope his way up my thigh towards my bottom. His fingers found the leg of my knickers and just as they began to insert themselves between the fabric and my skin, the door flew open.

'Mr Butterford,' said Miss Summerfield. 'What are you doing?'

He turned to face her, smoothly withdrawing his hand from beneath my skirt, all innocence. 'Oh, there you are. I've been looking for you.'

'Really? What can I do for you?'

'I wanted to pick up those group lists,' he said.

'Fine. If you come into my office, I'll give them to you,' and she stood back to let him precede her out of the stock cupboard. While his back was turned, she flicked me a look which said, 'Make yourself scarce,' and then she followed him out onto the corridor. I heard them talking as they walked towards her office and then I descended the ladder on shaking legs. I peered out of the door but, seeing no one, I hurried towards the girls' toilets. I could have joined the students in the Sixth Form Common Room but I wanted to recover first. Besides, I couldn't be sure that he wouldn't come into the Common Room and find some way of humiliating me in front of the others.

So I went into the toilets and locked myself in a cubicle. I put down the lid of the toilet and sat on it, hunching forward over my knees. I rubbed my ankle where I could still feel his clammy fingers. What I really wanted was a very hot shower.

I heard the door open and Miss called out, 'Julia, are you in here?'

'Yes.'

'Come out. It's all clear.'

I unlocked the cubicle and stepped out.

Miss Summerfield looked at me. 'Are you alright?'

I nodded.

'What was going on in there?'

'He just came in and...' I spread my hands then raised one of them upwards.

'Did he touch you?'

'Not quite.'

'But he would have done if I'd not come in?'

I nodded again, knowing I might cry if I had to speak.

'Will you come to the Headteacher with me and report this?'

I shook my head.

'You should,' she said.

'I can't. It would only make it worse.'

'Has he done it before?'

'Not really.' How could I explain the way he smirked whenever he saw me, even across the crowded hall in Assembly? The way he addressed me as "Miss Forest" whenever he passed me on the corridor. The way he seemed to be everywhere in my school day, with the blessed exception of my lessons.

'But he's making you feel uncomfortable?'

'Yes.'

'Do you know why?'

'No...only that it began when I broke up with Mark.'

'Did you finish it?'

I nodded. I could see she'd understood. That Mark, as one of Butterford's star footballers, could not be humiliated and so the man was taking revenge for one of his boys.

'Has Mark...'

'No. He ignores me completely.'

'Well, that may be a blessing.' She paused. 'Are you sure you don't want to take it further?'

'Yes. I'm sure.'

'Then be very careful. Try not to be on your own. Do you have someone you can walk home with?'

'Yes,' I said. 'I usually walk home with Helen.'

'Then make sure you're with her until this settles down. And try not to be on your own around school.'

I looked at her. So that's how it was going to be? Constantly looking over my shoulder for a short, fat man with long, smelly hair.

'I know it's not easy,' she said. 'You can come and see me whenever you want to.'

'Thank you.'

'Where are you going now?'

'The Common Room. Helen should be in there.'

So we walked along the corridor together and were almost deafened as the bell rang for the end of the school day. I ducked into the Common Room to avoid the onslaught of younger pupils who, it seemed, could only respond to the signal by hurling themselves from their classrooms out into the freedom of the late afternoon. I caught sight of Helen at her locker and went over to her.

'Walking home soon?'

She turned and smiled. 'Yep. Are you?'

'Yes.'

'Then let's get out of here,' and we set off across the playing field to the main road.

I considered telling Helen what had just happened but I wasn't ready to put into words how dirty Butterford had made me feel. It wasn't as if he was a lad, someone I'd chosen and liked. Someone who had my permission.

It seemed my permission wasn't relevant at all. Some weeks later, I had my head down in the school library, desperately trying to learn quotations from *Othello*. Miss Summerfield had been on at us to learn two or three quotes every day and I had thought it would be easy to do as she asked. It wasn't. It was the easiest thing to skip on the homework list and now a test was imminent. Eyes closed, I tried to remember what the text on the page looked like but my usually reliable photographic memory failed me. I opened my eyes to sneak a look at the book and saw Charlie sitting opposite me, a wide grin on his face.

'What?' I asked him.

'Are you wearing them?'

'What?'

He just kept on grinning.

'What do you want, you creep?'

'You'll have to leave the library if you want to talk,' came the stern voice of the librarian.

Charlie mouthed two words at me. 'Tank Girl.'

My heart sank. So Mark hadn't been able to keep quiet after all. I looked at Charlie and mouthed, 'Fuck off!'

He leaned over me and whispered, 'Well, that's what Butterford said.'

'What?' I yelled.

'Out!' said the librarian. 'Out you go. Julia, I'm surprised at you. I expect better of you.'

'Sorry,' I mumbled and followed Charlie out of the library. He was going to walk away from me but I grabbed his skinny arm. 'Oh no, you don't. Explain yourself.'

He stopped and leered at me. 'Butterford says you wear Tank Girl knickers.'

'What do you mean, "he says"?'

'Well, that's what he told us last team practice.'

'Why would he do that?'

'Duh! Because he's seen your knickers.' He guffawed. 'And the rest.'

'What did he say exactly?'

Charlie looked at me with a patronising smile. 'He asked Mark how Tank Girl was.'

'What did Mark say?' I asked as my stomach did somersaults.

'Well, as it happens, he didn't say anything.'

Relief welled up in me...

'He blushed bright red though.'

...and sank down again.

'So what was it like?' asked Charlie.

'What was what like?'

'Sex with Butterford.'

Oh my God, the fat bastard! He had damned me as surely as if the whole school had seen us doing it.

'Why don't you find out for yourself? You might enjoy it,' I spat at Charlie and went back into the library.

I chose the furthest corner and, picking up my books and folders, went to sit with my back to the rest of the room, seething. How could I plead my innocence without appearing guilty? The only thing I could do was to keep my own mouth firmly shut and carry on trying to prepare for my exams, my passport out of this small town.

And so much for Butterford protecting his boys, I thought. He had deliberately humiliated Mark to destroy me. I almost felt sorry for Mark, but I couldn't help feeling a bit sorry for myself too. Helen had disappeared into the wide blue yonder of teenage pregnancy leaving me only a goodbye note, so even if I'd wanted to confide in her, I couldn't.

But my own humiliation did not end there, of course. Over the next few days, I found myself receiving many appraising looks and "nicer" girls avoiding me until finally Miss Summerfield took me aside.

'Is everything alright, Julia?'

'In what way?' I asked. 'I'm up-to-date with my work.'

'Yes, you are and I'm very glad to see it.' She paused. 'But there have been some worrying rumours.'

Ah, I thought. *Here it comes. Will she ask me straight out if I've had sex with Butterford?* 'Have there?'

'Did Mr Butterford...has Mr Butterford been pestering you again?'

'No,' I said. 'But you remember Iago's "Ha, I like not that..." and Othello, on no evidence at all, believing Desdemona has been unfaithful...'

She stared at me. 'Are you saying he's pretending to have had sex with you?'

'Yes.'

She continued to stare at me. 'The bastard,' she murmured.

'Yes, Miss.'

We looked at one another for a long moment.

'What are you going to do?' she asked at last.

'There's not much I can do. Whatever I say will only add weight to whatever he's already said.'

'The Head...' she began.

'There's no point in going to him. He thinks the sun shines out of...'

'Yes, he does. More's the pity.' She put her hand on my arm. 'I'm so sorry, Julia. I really wish you didn't have to deal with this. Now of all times.'

'Me, too. But it's happened and I'm not going to let him destroy my chance of university.'

'Good, but I still wish there was something I could do to help you.'

'You can,' I said.

She brightened at once.

'Just keep teaching me and girls like me. He won't get away with it forever.'

Helen Walcott, *pupil* – 18th December 1995

THE BUS MOVES slowly past the frozen fields on its way back to Newark. My swollen stomach is hidden by an over-sized jumper. I feel constantly queasy. I've only been on a boat once and I hated it, I felt so sick. I feel like that all the time now. I open my bag to find a mint to suck and I see the pregnancy test inside that I've been to Nottingham to buy. I don't really need the test to confirm what I already know, but I do need a miracle. I was so scared of someone I know seeing me buying one that I've gone further afield and taken money from mum's savings jar so that I could afford the bus fare and the kit, but I'll deal with that later. The bus pulls into the station and I get off, trying not to breathe in the diesel fumes that make the nausea even worse. Head down, hands stuffed in my pockets against the cold, I hurry home, but when I get there, mum and dad are sitting waiting for me, arms folded, an air of tension and I know without them saying a word, that they've already guessed what I'm going to tell them.

Mum's crying; really sobbing and dad just looks sad. I don't know what to do, so I do nothing. I just stand before them, their disappointing daughter in an oversized jumper that's not doing a very good job of concealing the mess I've made of my life.

Dad clears his throat and then speaks and his voice doesn't sound like his voice, it sounds broken. 'Who is it, Helen? Who? Is it a lad from school?'

I shake my head.

'Don't you know? Is that it?'

I'm still silent. I made a pact with myself not to tell. It's not his fault. It was a quick fumble and I got caught out. I don't want to bring him into this.

'Jesus Christ, Helen! Have you no shame? Did we bring you up to open your legs for just anyone? Well, did we? I'm disgusted at you. You've let us down, Helen. You've let us down.' And he shakes his head and looks at the floor, his hand rubbing his face.

'I... I...'

'You what? Well, spit it out. You must have something to say for yourself! Please don't tell us it's that waste of space Karl Stamford. Now that really would be a kick in the teeth.'

'It's not him! It's not!' I cry. 'Why would you think that?'

'We don't know what to think, Helen. We didn't ever think we'd be in this situation.'

'I'm sorry,' I wail wanting him to stop, wanting mum to stop weeping which is breaking my heart and annoying me simultaneously.

'Whose is it? Who, Helen? Will he support you?'

I shake my head.

And then mum wipes her face and speaks and her voice is calm, determined. 'How far gone are you?'

'I've missed three periods.'

She breathes in sharply. 'Will you have it? The baby?'

I nod.

'Then I think it's best that you leave.'

'Mum, I...'

'Auntie Joan says you can go and stay with her until you decide what you are going to do.'

'I'm going to keep it.'

'You think that now, Helen, but when it arrives you might change your mind. It's bloody hard work looking after a baby and it never stops. It's all day, every day, it's relentless. She'll take care of you away from the gossip.'

'I don't want to...'

She shrugs. 'Pack a bag and your dad will drive you down tonight. Oh and Helen, you can pay the money back you stole when you get a job - if you ever get a job.' Then she turns her back and walks away from me.

'YOU READY?' Dad stands at the already open door, car keys in his hand.

I move towards mum. I want her to hold me so badly it hurts, but she just nods at me curtly and takes a step back. 'I'd say take care of yourself, but no, that was all in the past and better left there,' she says grimly. 'Tell Joan thank you. Drive safely, Jeff.' And she doesn't even wait to see me off. I choke back tears, close the door and follow dad to the car. The air is frosty between us as he takes my bag from me, putting it into the boot.

'Alright?'

I nod. 'Dad, I just need to put this,' I pull an envelope from my pocket, 'through Julia's door. Please.'

He nods, 'Be quick though, we've got a long journey ahead of us.'

We pull up outside Julia's house and I hurry from the car, push the envelope through the letterbox and look up at her bedroom window. It's dark, there's no light on and I wonder if I'll ever see her again. I hope she'll understand. I hope she won't judge me like everyone else, and I hope one day I can make amends. I haven't told her who the father is. I've just tried to explain that I know she's been having a tough time at school and that I'm only going because I have to and that I'll write soon. I also tell her how much I love her, my gorgeous friend, and I want to tell her that things will be alright, but at that moment, it feels as if nothing will ever be right again. I turn back to the car and dad waiting for me and say a silent goodbye.

Helen Walcott, *Proud Single Mum*
– May 2019

WHEN I'D FIRST seen the Facebook post, I'd only glanced at it – *Reunion, Class of '89 Hercules Clay Comprehensive School* - but for a brief second my hand had paused over the mouse as I stared at the photo of my old school on the screen. The memories had come flooding back and flicked fast through my mind like cards being shuffled: fleeting pictures of people from another life, forever frozen in their skinny teenage bodies and pimply skin. Karl Stamford arrested for manslaughter; beautiful Julia Forest, my old friend who I hadn't seen in years; Iain Wilson, with his floppy fringe that fell over his eyes, quiet and unnerving; Amanda Shaw who only ever wanted to be liked and was always, always kind to me when everyone else pointed the finger; know-it-all Phil with his acerbic tongue and knack of locating everyone's Achilles heel; and him... always him. I didn't need a reunion to remember his face. It was burnt into my memory and my heart and it still hurt to go back there. So I wasn't going to. I'd made a life for myself and my daughter. Why on earth would I open up old wounds after it took so long for the scabs to heal? Why would I want to spend time with people who had gossiped about me behind my back when I needed them the most? No, that ship had sailed and I was better off in the present where I was a success.

I scrolled on to more interesting posts from real friends travelling the globe or celebrating birthdays and anniversaries with their spouses and children. But...I kept being drawn back to the Reunion post. Before I knew it, I'd had a second and then a third look and was about to go in for a fourth when my mobile rang: Chloe. We chatted a while about uni and what she'd been doing and her plans for a trip to Edinburgh to see her boyfriend and then I told her about the Reunion.

'So why don't you go, mum? Could be fun.'

'I'm not sure. It's already freaked me out, you know, thinking about all of those people that I haven't seen in years. It's such a long time ago.'

'It is,' she agreed, 'but there must be someone you'd like to catch up with. What was that friend you've told me about before? You know, Julie someone?'

'Julia Forest.'

'Yes, you said you were joined at the hip at one point.'

'We were,' I murmur. 'Thick as thieves.' And I think back to how confused she'd been when I started to let her down, cancelling plans and not answering calls. I'd been so sick when I was pregnant that it was all I could do to get out of bed in the morning, but of course, she never knew that because I'd never confided in her and I know she would have been there for me when all around my world was crumbling. I wonder if she has a family of her own, if she's had a happy life... I hope so.

Chloe interrupts my thoughts with her chatter and we finish the conversation with me promising to think about the Reunion and I do. I can think of little else. Of course, I've been back to Newark to visit the folks, but I spend as little time as possible there. I normally drive up from Bath where I've lived since I had Chloe and stay one night and one night only. The place doesn't hold many good memories for me and makes me anxious, so I keep away like I was told to all those years ago.

I had left school and gone to live with my auntie Joan on the outskirts of Bath, had Chloe and made a life for us both away from the bad memories. I never did get round to writing to Julia. My life was so different and, I don't know, the fewer links I kept with my hometown, the better. I thought of her often though and hoped things had improved for her and the gossips had moved on. She would have loved Chloe, I was sure. She always had been wonderful with children.

There were moments I thought about how different it could have been, if I'd told him, if we'd tried to make a go of it, but I knew they were pipe dreams as unrealistic as finding a pot of gold at the end of a rainbow and I knew that I wouldn't have it any other way. It had been me and Chloe against the world and we did a pretty good job of taking care of one another. But recently the questions about who her father is have become more frequent and then when the Facebook post appeared it just sort of seemed like a sign that maybe it's time to tell the truth. Maybe I owe her this and then it will be up to her what she does with it. I still don't know whether to tell him though... Will he want a grown-up daughter in his life? Does he already have children? A family? A wife? I would hate them to see her as a cuckoo in their nest. I have often wondered if he guessed... He wasn't the brightest boy though, not back then; often pre-occupied with himself, introspective, self-absorbed and would occasionally reveal a mean streak, but I liked him. He was handsome in a delicate way and had the most beautiful hands. I painted his nails with varnish one time and he loved it, admiring the shiny finish and gloss.

I'd had an argument with mum and run out of the house one evening and ended up on the Sconce Park- not a place you want to end up alone after sunset and he'd been sat on the swings, by himself and he looked so sad. We'd chatted a bit and I'd told him that things weren't great at home and he'd said the same.

'My dad is a macho guy with tattoos and an 850cc Ducati and I don't think I'll ever be good enough for him. My mum's just interested in the bingo and *Dynasty*. They drive me mad!'

He'd walked me home that evening and we'd begun to spend a bit of time together - never planned - and then one night back at the park, not long after the new term had started, it had just sort of happened. We'd been fooling around drinking cherry brandy which I'd nicked from the drinks' cabinet at home. It tasted disgusting but lent us a warm glow and before we knew it, we were kissing.

'Are you sure you want to?' he'd breathed as he fumbled with the zip of his jeans.

I nodded a yes and told him to be careful, 'It's my first time.'

'Me too,' he said grinning. And so we did it on the hard grass in the Sconce with the stars twinkling above us in the clear autumn air. That was the last time we spoke and he avoided all eye contact with me at school. I wasn't angry with him, I felt sad. It hadn't been the greatest experience and had lasted all of thirty seconds. A teenage fumble and I'd lost someone I thought was a friend. I never breathed a word to anyone, not to Julia or any of the girls at school. And when the gossip began to grow like my stomach, it was easier to let them think they knew the truth rather than make trouble for him.

31 August 2019

Iain Wilson, *"Legitimate Businessman"* – 8:07 am

I LET OUT AN exasperated sigh. 'Jesus-shitting-Christ. What do we know about his condition?'

The voice on the end of the phone mumbles something about 'critical but stable'. I run a hand through my hair and think. 'Okay, you know the drill, get those two apes out of the city, quietly and quickly. And give them a proper bollocking.'

'How long should they stay away?' asks the voice.

'I'd say a month, but if he dies then it's clearly going to be a lot fucking longer.' I'm annoyed and I'm venting my anger at Simmo, but I know he can take it. He's my hard man, my lieutenant, my strong right arm. He also lacks guile and that's why I call the shots. But apparently my call was not sufficiently clear and what should have been a simple punishment beating with a side-serving of painful terror has turned into a coma case. The victim, some shit-for-brains lad from Sneinton who tried to shaft one of my dealers, suffered major head trauma in the wee hours and is now lying in the Queens Medical Centre on the grey line between being and not being. And this is not a Good Thing.

There are various criminal networks operating in Nottingham, as with any town or city in the country, and the police have their prying little snouts snuffling into almost all of them. The saving grace is Saint Austerity who has taken resources and manpower away from the boys and girls in blue meaning that they have to focus on the main priorities. My intel on their activities tells me that they run some kind of risk matrix to decide what to concentrate on and who to nick. Murder trumps the lot so I have been at pains to express to my lieutenants and captains that we, as an organisation, do not kill people. This is simple common sense, self-preservation. Do not give Plod a reason to come sniffing around. We have a policy on guns and knives and that information has been cascaded down to the grunts on the street, although how much of that is taken in is debatable. We do, of course, have some lovely guns and knives, but their use is strictly controlled on a carefully analysed case-by-case basis. So far, the most we have had to resort to is the odd buttock slash, a shotgun blast to the knee and some cheesy pantomiming to deter those who think they can muscle in on our business.

The key thing is to avoid attention. We should not be the Big Bad Wolf that the heroic woodsmen of Sherwood Lodge hunt down. So we have rules. Even though I am, in the words of Fat Tony from *The Simpsons*, 'a legitimate businessman', I do not want to become the biggest crime boss in the city because that will have both sides of the law literally gunning for me. We have our markets and we explore some of society's margins but we don't go toe-to-toe with the baby-faced crews in St Ann's nor the old families in Bestwood. It's not about the glory or the fun or the 'respect'. It's about the money. Easy money that's there for the taking. We focus on being the slickest operation, small and nimble but with enough bite to deter any empires with expansionist ambition. We are, I suppose, the Switzerland of Nottingham crime gangs.

And even though it's about the money, we don't go for the showy bling. I sat a few of my trusted lads down and explained POCA to them – that's the *Proceeds Of Crime Act*, if you didn't know. *They* didn't and they're in the bloody business. So, no conspicuous wealth. And no sodding social media either, although that's hard to enforce; I sometimes do a sweep to see what I can find out about their friends and their posts and after a few serious discussions in front of a baseball bat we've managed to keep a lid on that potential pot of shit. We keep a low profile organisationally and we insist on the same values at an individual level. There are only two people who know who I really am in the organisation and another four or five who just know me as 'The Accountant'. The remaining half a dozen are ultimately unaware of who pulls their little strings although I am kept up to date on who they are. And because I don't agree with extravagant wealth I don't need massive Rolex watches or gold plated Bentleys, and so I can afford to pay my lads well. And to ensure they don't buy some tasteless, blingy Plod-attractor, I suggest they invest a good proportion of their hard-earned in sensible, mainstream accounts that will help detract attention from the large volumes sitting in investment portfolios in various tax havens.

It's all about risk mitigation in a fundamentally risky business. And that gives me pause for thought; clearly, the route of least risk would be to Go Straight. You can't lose the game if you don't play it. But then, where's the fun in that approach?

Did I say fun? At the moment I am not having fun. It's just gone eight on a Saturday morning and my weekend happiness dangles on the thin thread of a nineteen-year-old in a coma. If he pulls through we may get away with some half-arsed investigation that ultimately fizzles out due to lack of evidence. If he carks it we're up to our necks in CID officers who fancy themselves as Gene Hunt from *Life On Mars*.

There's not a lot I can do about it now, other than ensure the pair of dickheads who went too far are spirited away to somewhere clean and quiet. Ideally, we'll get them doing some manual labouring to pay for their accommodation and living costs while in exile, otherwise it'll be a case of raiding the contingency fund and getting them to repay it once they're back in circulation.

My usual morning visit to the gym has gone out of the window thanks to Simmo's call and, frankly, I'm not really in the mood for it. I put some Radiohead on and mooch about the flat, gazing out of the windows at the rooftops, tower blocks and churches of Nottingham city centre. The views are good from up here, one of the reasons I chose this particular luxury apartment. The others include decent underground parking, concierge service and excellent security. And although it's fancier than some of the boxy cells you find in the new student accommodation springing up in cities across the country, it isn't an ostentatious mansion. And I rent it – you never know when you have to up and leave. Having assets tied into immovable concrete, steel and glass isn't ideal for someone who may need to disappear overnight. And in case you're wondering, I do have an exit plan.

I look around my gaff with an appreciation for the fact that nothing lasts for ever. If I had to go, would I miss all of this? All of... what, exactly? A nice kitchen, an arty yet comfy sofa, plenty of discrete tech and gadgets. A large bookcase full of business texts, crime fiction and psychology (all read). The rug Becca picked out. The prints that Sophie spent days choosing. Neither of them are around anymore; they moved on when they couldn't uncover the real me. It's not a persona that I introduce to other people. A handful of select colleagues know the real Iain Wilson; to everyone else I'm just a successful business consultant. I do have some genuine, straight-up clients that have no idea about my other activities and, again, this is the cover I need to keep the show on the road.

Some show. It has a very small cast; a miserable one-man show, spinning plates for the sake of a few quid. Okay, perhaps I'm feeling sorry for myself, or maybe the Radiohead songs are getting to me. Technically, I'm spinning some very valuable plates for huge sums of money and – this is the clever bit of the analogy – *without anyone actually seeing me touch anything.*

I decide I ought to do something useful with my day and so check on the local news website about the QMC's latest coma patient. Nothing much being reported at the moment, just the basic injuries and location of the assault. Request for witnesses, that sort of thing. Nothing yet to make me worry even more, but nothing to calm my anxiety either.

I need to do something mundane to take my mind off the waiting (I hate waiting). I could clean up my laptop, run a defrag, clear out temp files, the usual dull admin. Maybe reply to a few emails. Actually, I haven't been in to a few old email accounts for a couple of months so it's probably worth checking those out first. I have several email addresses spanning the past two decades or so, the oldest being a Yahoo account from when I was a kid in the earliest years of the World Wide Web. It's generally full of spam and adverts these days so I don't tend to pay much attention to it.

I click through the login screen and look at the number of unread mails sitting in my inbox. I could just delete the lot but you never know when you might get something from an old friend or distant relative so I scroll down the list to check if there's anything interesting before binning them all. Nope, nothing worth... hang on. A message from Hercules Clay Comprehensive School:

'We are holding a thirty year reunion for those pupils who joined our first year in 1989...'

A reunion? I snort a small, derisory laugh. Go back to school and meet up with a bunch of ageing, bitter ex-acquaintances with greying hair and expanding waistlines? Jesus, who would go to such a painful, awkward event? Not me, that's for sure. I've left Newark well behind. Sure, it wasn't all bad and I came out of it with enough qualifications to do Business Studies at the local college, but some of the kids in my year were absolutely mental. *Shit! What if they invited Karl?* No, there's no way he'd be there, not after what he did. I wonder where he is these days. Probably either dead or in prison.

Mind you, there were some good times too. I smile as I remember our lunchtime games of football, jostling with mates in the lakeside supermarket after school, trading in illicit fags and porn mags behind the boiler block. I wonder if Matt's going. He was my best mate but we lost touch once we left school. That may have been down to some of my college activities. Not my best few years but it gave me an insight into street-side supply and demand that has served me well.

I wonder if Katy Greeves is going.

Sometimes my own subconsciousness surprises me. I haven't thought about Katy in years. Not properly, anyway. She smiled at me once in class and I was captivated. I never quite plucked up the courage to ask her out. And then I left school and... just... never...

Radiohead's *Fake Plastic Trees* oozes out of my speakers and I'm lost in time, remembering missed opportunities and heart-rending teenage angst. I was such a pathetic nobody. I feared the truth then and my forty-year-old adult self points a finger back down the years and confirms it. *You didn't deserve her, Iain. She would never have been interested in you. Scrawny, dull, gawking waste of space.*

Not like now. I'm involuntarily flexing gym-toned muscles.

I carry on reading the email. '*... hope you can attend on the evening of Saturday 31st August...*'

My heart thuds. That's tonight.

I'm not going. Of course I'm not going. I've got... things. It's for sad losers. Small minded, small town, small people.

Katy might be there.

So what? She's probably aged horribly, wrinkled beyond belief, chained to some dead end job with a fat husband and a mortgage and whatever.

But she might be there.

I delete the email.

I sit back and scratch my hand over the morning stubble on my chin and stare at the screen.

Hannah Parker, *was a proper Charlie* – 2:00 pm

'I DON'T KNOW WHAT to wear tonight, I'm so nervous,' I say to Lucy.

As I perch on the bed, with my phone cradled next to my ear, I look around my bedroom. Not an inch of space is free from clothes, including trousers, skirts, dresses, leggings, jeans and tops. I've tried on everything, everything. What am I going to wear? This has always been a problem for me, boy or girl, I've just never had any fashion sense. My slim frame would seem easy to dress, but it never has been. I envy Lucy's curvy frame. My boob job has done something to change that, and the fat I've had transferred into my backside; not too much, just enough. I can now acknowledge that I have a shape, but even after all these years, I still find myself shocked when I catch a glimpse of myself in the mirror. Sometimes the feelings are still there, even though my reflection tells a different story.

'You're starting to make me nervous,' Lucy says, 'although I'm also so excited. I've never been to a school reunion before, even though it's not mine, I think it's going to be so exciting for you to see how everyone has changed, and you will need to tell me about everyone as we meet them. All the school secrets, I can't wait. Especially the one that involved that fire in the classroom. Nothing like that ever happened at my school, oh, and point out that creepy teacher, I will make sure I stay away from him. What about that dress you bought last week, the emerald green with the silver streak across it? That looked stunning, you will knock them dead in that. I can't wait to get to the free bar. This has literally never happened to me, never, ever had a free bar before. Someone must be really loaded to be able to sponsor a free bar all night.'

Lucy is a talker. The girl barely comes up for air; she changes from one subject to another without taking a breath. I'm always in awe of her lung capacity. She is right about the dress though, as soon as I'd walked into the shop, I knew it was the one. It fitted perfectly.

'But, what are people going to think? I'm so different from the school days. I'm not sure this is a good idea after all,' I say.

In more ways than one I think. Will Helen be there? And Philip? What would he think about me now? The times we would sit and slag off everyone in the school, picking apart anyone that was different – the difference often being someone wearing cheap school clothes from the charity shop. A person that wanted to alter their gender because it wasn't who they were, was unheard of when I grew up and the times we grew up in. That's one of the reasons I'd moved away to a bigger city. You could almost blend into the background if that's what you wanted.

My counsellor told me it would be a good idea for me to confront my past. I'd mistreated some kids, goaded on by my mate Phil, but it was kill or be killed at Hercules Clay. Any form of weakness and someone would strike – kids were so cruel. I'd felt angry at school, and was always ready to take it out on someone. I feel embarrassed thinking about it now, I know it's my own insecurities that made me like that at school, and it wasn't as if I was the school thug. Sarah Greene was the real bully. I'd got carried away when I got wound up, usually because Philip had gone on one of his rants. Although it wasn't Philip's fault, he was one of a kind.

Could I wipe away this leftover guilt by saying sorry to people now? Even though many years have passed since the 'good old' school days. People's lives were ruined after being bullied at school, and I would hate to think I'd affected someone's life that badly. If I could say sorry, maybe it would help.

Also, I couldn't spend my whole life making up excuses not to return to Newark. I'd only returned once because there had been a course for work I couldn't get out of. I'd found a love of working out over the years, and had joined the local gym while I was there; unluckily for me a couple of the old school gang worked there. They hadn't recognised me to begin with, but the unwanted attention at the small gym had meant I was glad when the four-week course was over, and I could go back to my real life.

The usual excuse I used to my parents was that work was busy and I couldn't find the time. It's only an hour and a half on the train from London after all. I suspected they'd never told their friends I'd transitioned to a woman, although they were supportive of me when they realised this was who I was, but they have never really understood why I've taken this path.

Dad had walked in on me once when I thought I had the house to myself. I'd been wearing one of mum's dresses and her make-up. He'd closed the door without saying a word. We'd never spoken of it. But consequently, they weren't surprised when I told them my decision to live as a woman.

I come back to the conversation and realise Lucy is still talking. She hasn't even noticed that I've been reliving my past.

I tune back into her voice, 'Don't we all. My whole body pretty much points to Australia nowadays. I've got on so many pull–up pants, push-up bras and pull-in tights I feel like I've done a full work out by the time I get dressed.'

I laugh, Lucy has the natural ability to lift my mood no matter what. Lucy is one of those upbeat people who is always happy and enthusiastic about everything. Nothing matters to her; she never judges anyone. She doesn't care, as long you're nice, that's all that matters. Lucy hadn't treated me any differently when she'd found out I'd been born and lived as a male until I was eighteen. I'd started the transition as soon as I'd got settled in London, it had been a tough time getting all the money together and the endless medical appointments. Back in those days you couldn't just surf the internet to find out the information. I considered myself as one of the lucky ones that had fallen into a supportive group that had helped me through all the NHS appointments and hospital stays, all the confusing and conflicting information. Lucy had just shrugged, and said, 'Cool – you can tell me what kind of boys to avoid, and what they're thinking.' That had been it, we'd been firm friends ever since.

'Look, Hannah Parker. I'm telling you,' says Lucy, bringing me out of my memories again. 'Wear that dress. You look fabulous in it, and who gives a stuff what the others think? We'll turn up, say hello and then get plastered on free booze. We'll dance until our legs give way. Deal? Now, sod off and get ready. I need to apply my next layer of make-up before we catch the train.'

'Okay, thanks, Lucy. See you at the station in thirty minutes.'

Lucy hangs up. I put all the clothes away, and take Lucy's advice. The dress looks beautiful. My slim figure had never seemed to fit as a boy, as a woman I know I look stunning if looking through someone else's eyes. I pack my high heels, grab my overnight bag and leave the house. No going back now, it's time to face the music. I hope my counsellor is right and that it will help me to take the final step to accept my past life. To make amends for my behaviour to some of the kids, explain that wasn't me. I hadn't known back then that the body I'd been given at birth was not meant to be my lot in life, that a better life awaited me as a woman. The gender doesn't really matter in a way, in some ways I don't feel it is all about that. It's about how happy I am in my own skin, the fact that I belong to this body. I thought people that felt that way from birth were lucky, it's taken me years to feel this way. All the counselling, drugs and procedures have been worth the time and money to get where I am today.

Pam McPherson, *Coordinator of Events* – 4:30 pm

ALIGHTING FROM THE train at Newark it was nice to get out into the fresh air. The journey took over five hours from Perth and we were ten minutes late getting in. Trains are a great way to travel providing they perform correctly. It's nice to enjoy the scenery, hook into wi-fi and do all sorts of things on the way. The food is pretty crap but then I made sure I had a holdall full of goodies before boarding. Thank goodness there was a taxi outside which I grabbed.

'The Bellranger Hotel please,' I ask the driver. Yes I could easily walk the distance, which was really bad but all I want is to get into the hotel and relax before the evening.

An invitation had dropped through my door about two months ago. It was a bit of a surprise to see a group were organising an official reunion at my old school in Newark. Showing it to Sam, my husband, he glanced at it; passing it back he asked if I wanted to go.

I wasn't at all sure, thinking part of me wanted to find out what everyone had done with their lives and part of me just thought that I hadn't kept in contact with anyone, my life was great so why would I want to go? I just smiled at Sam and shrugged my shoulders.

I'm still not sure if my decision is right, but here I am in the bath with my clothes laid out while I try to work out in my head, which is the best outfit to wear. Back in the bedroom surveying it all, my first thought is jeans and a top. No, I want to be slightly smarter than that. *Bloody hell what am I going to wear?* I look at the image in the mirror at my first attempt – God I look awful. I always hate the way I look, although I still have to admit my figure isn't bad, tanned because I spend so much time outside and shoulder length hair. I made sure my hairdresser did her magic before coming down. Why are women so vain, I wonder? For me it was all about not accepting getting to the big 4-o. Mind you the grey has been coming through for some time. I chose a colour that was natural to me – light brown – really interesting! Forcing a smile into the mirror I now see myself in terracotta jeans. *Ha that's a contradiction but these do look good. That will do otherwise you will be here all night trying to be someone you are not.* I have never been a showy woman, you have to take me as I am.

Sighing and saying to myself, 'Right, make up - check; hair - check; bag – check,' I decide not to take a coat as I walk out into the evening. It is quite warm so I take the long route to Hercules Clay. Always thought that was a ridiculous name for a school, but then I suppose he was a very important person in his day and deserved some recognition being the Mayor of Newark during the Civil War. The walk encompasses some of the great houses of Newark, so solid and symmetrical where carbuncles of extensions haven't been added.

Iain Wilson, *"Legitimate Businessman"* – 6:42 pm

O F COURSE I'M not going. Just because I'm now sat in the McDonalds in Newark does not mean I'm going to the school reunion. I had things to do. Seeing mum and dad, mainly. I've not been up in a couple of months so, you know...

Dad was moping about the state of Notts County and how he ought to switch allegiance to Lincoln City and to be fair Sincil Bank is fractionally closer to his house than Meadow Lane. There's only so much anguish a fan can take, so I'm not surprised. But he won't consider following a Premiership team. It's funny how he prefers the painful end of the football league, even shunning the faded glory of Forest. I remember getting carried away as a ten-year-old when Forest won the League Cup twice in succession. Dad never really accepted that I'd gone to the red side and that season in the early 90s when our two teams were both in the top flight was full of (mostly) good natured banter. He was still crushed when they were relegated at the end, though. The fairy tale was over; for County and, as it turned out, for Forest – that last appearance at Wembley in the 1992 FA Cup Final was the high water mark before it all drained away. It was also the point when reality came and shat on the family good and proper.

We all changed that year. I suppose it was hardest for mum and dad, but they tried to keep things together for my sake. Bless 'em. It didn't last that long, though. Dad moved out and we sold the family house in Elm Avenue next to the cemetery and then I was facing the prospect of triangular travel between mum's two bedroom terraced house in Grove Street, dad's first flat on Barnby Gate, and school.

I make an involuntary harrumphing noise as I stare at the remains of my chicken wrap. To make sure no-one sitting nearby thinks I have some form of Tourette's I cough and clear my throat, then swig down some orange juice. The pale fries scattered on my tray look like corpses, fallen soldiers cut down as they exited their landing craft, the survivors huddling towards the back of the bag not daring to come out. I take another bite of wrap.

Mum fussed over me when I popped in, as usual. Said I wasn't eating enough, but isn't that everyone's mum? It's weird when my life suddenly phases into a stereotype. I am clearly not a stereotypical business consultant, nor a stereotypical drug dealer. I never thought I was a stereotypical son. I'm not sure if my visits to the old hometown and my parents are a blessing or a curse. On the one hand I get a fleeting sense of normality, a calmness that whispers to me that everything is fine and there's nothing to worry about except eating home-made cake and talking about football.

But of course, nothing is normal and there's everything to worry about. I don't really belong here anymore. I don't think I belong anywhere.

After mum's I went to see Ella. It was the usual combination of numbness and gut-wrenching sadness. Mum's flowers from last week had dried up in the late summer sun and a dandelion was arrogantly leaning over the side of the headstone. I had ripped it out and chucked it behind me. The dates, chiselled out in black stone and highlighted in fading gilt paintwork, pounded in my head along with the words that always made me swallow. *Devoted sister*.

And now here I am in McDonalds, wearing a crisp lime green shirt and expensive grey suit, surrounded by teenagers and families. I finish my orange juice and glance around, looking for the ubiquitous divorced-dad-and-child weekend treat. Been there, done that – as the kid, not the dad; I wonder if I will ever experience the reverse. I'm faintly disturbed by the fact that the guy trying to engage in conversation with his sullen phone-obsessed ten-year-old is clearly younger than me.

I wipe my hands, dump the trash and head back to the car. It's a nice car. But it follows my doctrine of not drawing attention. A dark grey BMW 320i. Respectable. Capable.

Anonymous. But... I'd really, really fancy a bright red Alfa Romeo. Or a Maserati.

I slide into the Beamer's driving seat with a sigh and the door closes, giving an efficiently refined soft Germanic thunk.

My hands grip the steering wheel and I stare at my knuckles. I'm not going.

But perhaps a drive past is in order, for old time's sake.

I head down Lincoln Road, back towards the town centre, past the fancy new cop-shop, then the college (where I spent a couple of years getting some useful qualifications and some interesting acquaintances) and then on to London Road. As I'm approaching the bridge over the old railway line my palms begin to sweat and I slow the car.

There's the entrance to the school with the driveway extending round to the front of the old red brick main building.

I grimace, lips tight. I can feel an impulsive thought about to explode into action.

'Shit shit shit.'

I swing the car left and into the entrance, along the drive and up to the visitors' car park where I reverse into a space, looking back down towards the main road. 'What are you doing?' I murmur to myself.

It's fine, my internal consciousness tells me. *We're not actually going in. Just gonna sit here and watch the sad bastards as they arrive.*

And from somewhere else, perhaps my hidden Jiminy Cricket conscience, I hear the response. *Yeah, sure. You know you didn't need to be in Newark today. You've planned this all along. Stop kidding yourself and just be fucking honest about who you are and what you want.*

Wow. I don't recall Pinocchio having such a blunt conversation with *his* conscience.

Amanda Shaw, *Woman Reborn*
– 7:05 pm

I PULL THE BRASS handle of the heavy door and step tentatively inside. There are things I instantly recognise, though obviously there've been a lot of changes. Not as many as my own however. The flashy reception area painted in bold colours appears a lot more welcoming than the insignificant secretary locked behind glass panels in my time. Positive phrases and words are displayed on walls and notice boards. The words I'd use to describe school for me back then would be immediately erased and banned.

I pray we don't have to wear those sticky name labels, but have strategies in place should that situation arise. All eventualities are hopefully covered; I've been planning this for a long time. I'm pretty sure no one will recognise me and I'd prefer it that way. I make my way to the hall, a little unsteady in my high heels as nerves kick in. Thankfully there's no queue or anyone patrolling the entrance doors at present so I remain inconspicuous. Judging by the amount of people in the carpark, I've timed my arrival perfectly. Surprisingly the hall is pretty much as I remember it. I clock some familiar faces straight away; the years have been kind to some and punished others brutally. It's early yet so I anticipate a lot more arrivals will be filling any empty spaces before too long and then I can consider my options.

I'm not particularly interested in socialising, but all these years of counselling and attending self-help groups have improved my acting skills dramatically, if you'll excuse the pun, so I can circulate and ooze charm along with the rest of them. The confidence I lacked during school years has grown significantly so I can put on a show of interest while biding my time.

No one's noticed me yet which suits me fine. Gives me time to study the surroundings and the guests. I can see Bony Tony is still as gaunt and vile as ever though his partner could give him a run for his money. Well matched physically, but I wonder if her character is equally perverted. I notice Smelly Kelly is unaccompanied and still looking decidedly unkempt. I'd wager she didn't shower before she turned up, but everyone will be too polite to say anything just like they were at school. They felt sorry for her because of her poor background and dysfunctional family so always treated her kindly. No one did that for me, but then the details of my home life were not something I was prepared to share with anyone.

You probably think I'm heartless giving people such disrespectful nicknames, but at least I've always kept them to myself, unlike the ones they bestowed on me. They probably won't remember, but I'll never forget.

I approach the so-called bar and order an orange juice. Hard to believe how easy it is to resist alcohol now after years of being out of control and almost permanently in a drunken stupor. I had my reasons, though no one cared or showed much understanding. I wasted opportunities at school by being wasted too often myself, but now I'm a totally different person. Sober, in control, physically and emotionally healthy despite all the hell I've been through, but still struggling to forgive myself or others for the past.

The lighting is subdued and my contact lenses are probably not as up to date as they should be, but as I peer around the dim room I can make out a male figure approaching me. I think I remember him. Bike shed or changing rooms? It doesn't really matter; their faces all merge into a hazy blur of memories I'd rather forget, but sadly cannot. I force a friendly smile and mentally prepare the responses I've been rehearsing for a long time.

'Hi,' he arranges his own false smile and offers his hand. I have no desire to make physical contact with any of them, but needs must. I shake his hand firmly, remembering all the hands I allowed to venture into places I shouldn't back then.

'You need a name badge.'

Good. He doesn't know who I am. His name I recognise. Martin Pearce. One of three Martins in our year and I'd sampled them all yet recall little of the fumbled couplings. Unlike the one that almost destroyed me.

'I'll get you one...it's...erm...'

'Sandra,' I lie. 'Sandra Goodwin.'

Actually, it's not a huge lie. Not to me anyway. Sandra and I are so close now we almost meld into one person. All this was her idea and she's fully aware I'm planning on pretending to be her tonight. She received an invitation months ago and we were both aware how unlikely it was I'd get one. Not just because I'd moved away either. They'd have found me if they'd bothered to research, but I doubt there's anyone here who'd have wanted my company. Amanda Shaw? School bike and drunken head case. No way would she be welcome at a school reunion. At least they're not aware how close Sandra and I have become. She's not seen any of them since leaving so they won't know about us and hopefully won't suspect anything as long as I can keep my cool.

Martin returns with the name badge. I swiftly take it from him to avoid any contact. Strange how the mere thought of a man's touch repulses me now when I was quite willing to oblige anything with a penis back at school. Not that I enjoyed the encounters, but I guess I thought or hoped it was the way to be accepted.

'Oh, I remember you now.' Martin interrupts my thoughts. 'You were President of the Dramatic Society weren't you? Didn't you play Cordelia in *King Lear*?'

'That's right. Must have been quite the performance for you to remember. Or was it so bad you've never forgotten it?' I resurrect Sandra's schoolgirl giggle.

'God, no. You were great. I really envied your confidence and acting skills. Bit of a shrinking violet myself in those days. I hated the thought of making a fool of myself.'

Me too, but I was the biggest fool of them all. What happened at home convinced me I was just a vessel to be used for the pleasure of the male species. No self-worth, unaware of how wrong everything in my life was yet blaming myself for it. I believed the only way I'd be liked was by allowing them all to exploit me.

'Do you remember that Christmas special when whats-her-name fell off the stage?' he continues. 'Pissed as a newt she was. Amanda wasn't it, though she was always Randy Mandy or Shaw the Whore to all the lads.' He smirks and my insides twist. A good job I had my Chamomile tea and Valerian tablets before setting off, otherwise I might just throttle him.

I pause slightly, searching deep for a suitable response.

'Well, I guess living in a pub the temptation might have been a bit much for any of us back then.'

'Oh yes, that's right. Her parents ran the local didn't they? Great people. Always turned a blind eye when we went in for a drink.'

Oh yes, they turned blind eyes alright and made sure everyone else was kept in the dark about their after closing time activities.

'Yes, they knew you were all underage, but were quite happy to provide.'

'Bet they're retired now. Probably living the life out in Spain on the profits.'

No, they're both dead and no one is happier about that than me. I wasn't a daughter, just an inconvenience to be ignored until they felt the urge to use or abuse.

'Do you ever see her?'

*Only when I look in the mirror, but even I don't recognise the slut I used to be in my school days. S*andra has been a saviour in more ways than one, helping me to change not only my appearance, but my whole outlook on life. Although there's one thing I'll never fully recover from, but hopefully I can seek some solace this evening.

His expression can't hide the fact he'd love to hear some juicy scandal or news of a gruesome demise, but I'm giving nothing away.

'No. She moved away and I went to university in Sheffield. '

He can't hide the disappointment, but is obviously unsure of how to continue that line of questioning.

'What did you study?' he enquires disinterestedly. His eyes are already scanning the room to find a reason to excuse himself.

'Medicine and psychology, though I now run my own clinic of holistic treatments with my partner.'

'Oh, nice. Did you bring him along tonight? '

People make such stupid assumptions even in these liberal times. *'I'm a lesbian,' I want to yell.* No, I wasn't aware of it at school and I'm not convinced I was born that way. Maybe life experiences turned me. Memories try to engulf me, but I snap the box lid shut and lock it. Sandra isn't sure when she realised she was gay either, but we agree boys just didn't cut it back then. Sandra's experiences were limited, but I think I'd hold the school record for intimate encounters of all kinds, with all sorts, in all places. A shame there were no prizes or 'A' stars for that particular achievement.

'No. I thought it better to come alone so I can have a good catch up with old friends.'

'Anyone in particular?'

Oh, yes. Primarily the one who totally wrecked my life for years. But no way am I discussing that with him or anyone else at the moment. Maybe by the end of the evening they'll all know what happened to Amanda Shaw and I hope they'll feel guilty for the way they judged me.

'Okay. Time to circulate a little I think. It's been a pleasure talking to you Sandra. Catch you later.' He walks away before I can answer, leaving me to shake off memories I'd rather bury.

Hannah Parker, *was a proper Charlie* – 7:10 pm

THE TAXI ARRIVES at the school. The driver nearly crashes; he's spent way too long looking in his mirror at our low-cut dresses than at the road. I wonder if I've made the wrong choice after all. We'd touched up our make-up and got ready at the hotel, having decided that I didn't want to stay at my parents' house. Lucy's pull-up, pull-in garments are doing their job. She looks stunning with her long blonde curly hair cascading down her back. She will certainly turn a few heads. Hopefully, that will give me the time to get my bearings before I have to reveal myself to anyone. Although my long red hair is a bit of an attention grabber; maybe not the best idea when I want to blend in.

Oh well, too late to dye it a softer colour now. I love it though. It's odd how much confidence hair can give you. I'd always envied girls with long hair at school, how many different looks they could have. How some used it to hide behind if they were shy, or the confidence it gave them. I'd started growing mine as soon I'd moved to London and Lucy and I were regulars at the salon getting hair extensions. It cost a fortune, but was worth it.

I look up at the school building, and the memories come flooding back. The times Philip and I had bunked off school. I was the only person that could put up with him for any length of time. He was a know-it-all of epic proportions, he knew everything or thought he did. He had an opinion on everything, and even when he was proved wrong he didn't care – he could talk his way out of anything, and eventually, you would forget what you were arguing about. The constant drone of his words was mesmerising. I don't know why I'd gravitated towards him at school. Probably because I was angry all the time and spending the day slagging people off was a good way to vent that anger. It sometimes involved getting physical with other kids, but not often. I wonder what Philip will think of me now? He's the most opinionated person I've ever known, but for all that he is harmless. It is difficult not to like him, even though he is annoying – will Philip have changed with time? I doubt it.

'Bloody hell, look at the queue,' Lucy exclaims. 'I thought there would only be about thirty people, there must be about forty in the queue alone. I loved the drive up to the school, by the way, I feel like a celebrity. You never told me you went to a posh school.'

'It's not posh, Lucy. I will admit the tree-lined drive is impressive from the main road. But, I think it is more to hide us away from the general population than anything else. The place looks like a prison to me.'

Lucy laughs. I'm secretly pleased that there are so many people here, it means I will be able to blend in a little easier. I'm also surprised by the number of people that have turned up – amazing what free booze will do for a reunion. I'm not quite sure who is paying for it all. The invitation stated that someone had sponsored it, but they obviously want to remain anonymous. It appears everyone has brought a plus three, never mind a plus one. Surely these all couldn't be from our school year?

The school looks the same. Glancing over to one of the doorways I can see a figure in the shadows. I wonder who it could be. Maybe someone worried about being seen? Perhaps they are watching to see who turns up before they go in. I couldn't blame them. Now I'm here I don't know why I've bothered, why I let Lucy talk me into this reunion. Facing the people from my past doesn't seem such a good idea anymore.

'Ooh, we're moving. Come on, Hannah, you were miles away then. Good job it's a warm evening. Oh, look at him further up front. He looks like a right knob. What's he wearing?'

I strain to see past the other people, but I cannot make out who Lucy is talking about until the person shoots out of the queue and makes their way to the side entrance. Sneaky. I recognise him – it's Philip! Fancy him being the first person I see tonight. I don't recognise anyone else so far. Maybe it is going to be harder than I thought to make amends. Perhaps the people I want to see haven't come.

No turning back now though. Lucy will not leave with the prospect of a free bar. Time to do this. I'm pretty sure no-one will recognise me, that should give me the time to brace myself for the difficult conversations. The make-up, dress and general look are not one they would remember as Charlie – my now 'dead name'. As we get closer to the check-in point, I realise that people are queuing up to hand in their coats and receive a name sticker. Oh, God, I hadn't thought about that.

Lucy had seen the reunion on Facebook and told me we were going. She'd arranged everything. She worked at the same recruitment firm as me and had contacts all over the country, nothing happened that Lucy didn't know about. I swear she would give any celebrity a run for their money with her friends and Instagram followers or whatever they call them. I don't bother with all that social media stuff. It holds no interest for me, so I'd been happy to let Lucy do everything. I hope I'm not going to regret letting her talk me into this.

I know Lucy has arranged this because she knows I have demons I need to exorcise. I tell her as much as I do my counsellor, maybe more. I owe it to Lucy to make this night a success.

My chest feels tight. I wonder what name Lucy has given to the school? Will I have to walk around all night with a label saying, 'Charles or Charlie' for God sake. That name is my past, a person that has nothing to do with me anymore, with Hannah, it isn't who I am now. Deep down I know I shouldn't have come. As we get nearer to the table, I turn to get out of the queue and bump straight into Philip sneaking out of the caretaker's door. Obviously, he's taken a shortcut to avoid the queue. Great, this is all I need. Of all the people to bump into first.

Phil Morris, *The Man, The Legend* – 7:10 pm

THE OLD SCHOOL is just around the next corner and I feel a twinge of trepidation. I haven't kept in touch with any of my old crew and wonder how they have fared since schooldays. I expect I'll be greeted with enthusiasm, but maybe they will be nervous. People hate it when their friends become successful, as the great Morrissey sang. Well, I look pretty sharp in the BOSS chinos and Dior Homme shirt combination I found at the Barnardo's shop, and my Air Max 270 copies were the 'biz' – thanks to TrainerGuy on eBay.

As I approach the main entrance, I see there's a queue. Sod that, I hate queueing, and I don't want to get caught up in small talk with people I don't know, don't remember or don't like. I slip between the bushes and make my way to the caretaker's entrance; that was always open when there was something going off. With a bit of luck – yeah, the handle turns, and the door creaks open. I walk past the mops and buckets and through the inner door into a fairly busy entrance foyer. A couple of people are looking at me, but I just smile – I don't know them and for all they know it could be my office I have just left. I join a crowd of bodies at a row of trestle tables and pick out my name badge from the alphabetically sorted rows.

I turn to step away, peering down at my chest as I stick my ID badge in place, then walk straight into a good looking bit of stuff.

'Ooh sorry,' I say, backing up a little. 'I, uh, didn't mean...' Our eyes meet. I study her face. 'Umm – do I know you? You look...'

She blushes, in fact her face reddens considerably. It's glowing, almost as if somebody has flipped a switch. Red alert! A hint of a nervous smile.

'Hello, Phil, you used to know me,' she says with a shy, nervous smile. 'My name is Hannah, I...'

'Fuck me! Charlie? You crazy bastard, you came in drag? Damn, I missed the bit where it said fancy dress! Jesus, you look good mate, brilliant makeup job and you smell great.' My hand automatically moves up to cop a feel of the rolled up socks, or whatever it is simulating the pert boobies. I'll make a "honk" sound – it will be hilarious.

But in a flash, his hand comes up ninja style and slaps mine to the side. 'NO, Phil,' he says in a strange, hushed but deeply assertive tone, 'NO!' and then the stern look mellows and an equally gentle voice explains, 'I am not in "drag", Phil.'

'But...' I nurse my bruised hand and stare at him. Slowly the proverbial penny rattles down the rickety chute and comes to rest.

'My name is Hannah now. I am a woman. I have been a woman since the day I was born. It just took me time to realise it.' Then after an uncomfortable pause. 'Are you okay with that, Phil? I'm sure it's a bit of a surprise, but I hope it's not gonna be a problem. I hope you can accept me as I am now.'

'Uh – yeah – of course – wow!' I say in theatrically hushed tones as if I had been let in on a big secret that I must keep to myself and never let slip. I step back and look her up and down, examining my old friend's body in a way that would have been wrong previously, when he was a bloke. 'You're a – tranny? Part of the LG-PDQ, gender fluid craze?'

'Oh, Phil, there's so much wrong with that question! For a start, "tranny" is a pejorative term for transvestite and I am certainly not that. If you must be clinical about it I am transsexual! The acronym is LGBTQ, and gender fluid is a whole diff– but never mind that, I'm a woman now, and I hope you are okay with that, Phil?' he says hopefully.

I shrug, 'Oh sure, if that's what you want, mate. Whatever floats your boat. Good for you,' I grin, looking down pointedly at his chest, 'So – are those puppies real? Did you get silicon whatchamacallits? Have you had a proper boob job? They look amazing, mate.' Then after a moment's thought, I nudge his arm with my elbow and wink, 'Something extra to play with in bed!'

'Hey, eyes up here, you are embarrassing me. Never mind all that, Phil, it's really none of your business. I just want you to be cool with me as I am now. Are you?' The practiced soft feminine tones seem to be slipping as he gets a little agitated.

'Oh sure,' I grin, and my eyes widen. 'Ooh, what about – have you still got your meat and two veg? Remember when you used to turn them inside out in the changing room? Shit – were you thinking about it back then? Did you always want to be a girl? Wow, have you got a...'

'Jesus, Phil, forget the body! It's personal. Yes, I have transitioned completely. I am a woman. I have always been a woman on the inside and for the last twenty years the outside has matched! It took a lot of courage to come here tonight, and I hoped you would be one of the people that would accept me the way I am now.'

'Of course, mate,' I tap the side of my nose in a conspiratorial manner, 'our secret.' I turn to the "eye candy" on his left and grin.

'And please don't call me "mate" anymore, Phil, it's really not appropriate.'

'Oh, sure, okay Charlie – Hannah – but what do you want me to call you? Lovey? Babe? Sweetie? Sugar tits?' I grin at the last one. 'It's not gonna come natural, mate.'

'No, please don't! Hannah works for me – it's my name – maybe Han if you want to shorten it, in a friendly sort of way.'

'Cool, like Han Solo!' I grin.

After a significant pause and a rather obvious eye-roll, 'And this is my best friend, Lucy.'

I turn to Lucy, 'Princess Leia, I presume?'

Lucy proffers a hand. 'Nice to meet you, Phil,' she says, ignoring my joke completely. I take her hand and give it a long, gentle squeeze and a slow shake.

I look her up and down, in a discreet sort of way then turn back to Charlie and whisper, 'Is she one too?' Then with a "knowing" wink, 'Are you scissor sisters?'

'Fuck off, Phil!' He snaps as he pushes me away with the flat of his hand. He grabs Lucy's arm, and pretty much frog marches her along the corridor toward the main hall. She turns to look at me as she is being led away. Lucy smiles and shakes her head a little, obviously apologising for how rude Charlie has just been. Oh well, it was probably the hormones. I will give him another go later – if he wants to be a girl that's his choice, and I'm cool with that. I smile, Lucy was super cute. Maybe, if she's a proper girl, we could get together later. If Charlie isn't shagging her, I could definitely give her one.

Iain Wilson, *"Legitimate Businessman"* – 7:13 pm

A FEW PEOPLE I'M not sure I recognise are walking down the path towards the entrance, dressed up in smart-casual attire. A silver Audi A4 oozes past. Someone struts across the front of my car but my eyes are drawn, as they walk away down the side of the building, to the fact that they've matched their chinos with some truly terrible trainers. And that's probably what encourages me to get out of the car; even given some of the seriously dubious life choices I've made, at least I'm not him.

I straighten my suit and check my phone for the fiftieth time today. Still no news from Simmo on the coma case. There's not a lot more I can do about it so I guess I just need to forget it and concentrate on the present. But that's getting harder the closer I step to the main entrance. It's like the past is spooling back at me from an old VCR that's been fired up deep within my head. I haven't been back here since, what, 1995?

The people in front of me clear the main entrance door and I follow them into the reception area. New carpet. New lighting. Paintwork. An actual reception desk. A guy sweeps past from down the corridor on the right, stops at a table full of name badges and then moves on. I realise it's the guy with the trainers. Still can't place him, though.

I wait patiently as people shuffle past the name badge table and the attendant sixth formers. I acknowledge a faint stab of resentment over the fact that I never stayed on to do A levels. It was vocational computer and business courses for me, down at the college. The place where I learned all about supply and demand. The point where I lost touch with old friends. You can't find me on social media (I'm there, but not as Iain Wilson) and few of my schoolmates knew my old e-mail addresses. The whole Friends Reunited thing passed me by. And when I moved to Nottingham in 1999 I pretty much left the old faces behind.

'Hi, what's your name, please?'

I am jerked back to the present. 'Sorry. Miles away.'

'Miles... sorry, is that your name?'

'Oh, shit, no, sorry; it's Iain.'

'No problem,' says the girl behind the table, face reddening as she scans the printed sheets of sticky labels. 'What's your surname?'

'Um, well, the truth is I haven't actually, you know, kind of let you know I was coming, sorry.' *Christ, two minutes back inside a school and I sound like I'm fourteen again. Get a fucking grip.*

'Oh,' says the sixth former, momentarily confused. 'Well, we can make you a name tag easy enough. Do you want to put your name down as a sponsor as well? It goes towards the drinks and stuff.'

I pull out my wallet and slide a couple of notes into her hand. 'Here's a fifty for the booze and a tenner for you and your colleague, as recompense for the hassle I'm causing you.' She starts to object but I smile and close her hand around the cash. 'I insist.'

She blushes and stammers something about finding a pen. I consider using an alias but, frankly, what kind of idiot goes to a school reunion and uses a different name? Plus, it's not like the City CID are going to be raiding the place. And even then, I'm just a Legitimate Businessman. I take the sticky label from her and press it on to the lapel of my Paul Smith jacket (whilst hoping the adhesive isn't going to make a mess of the fabric) and walk down the corridor to the hall.

There aren't that many occasions these days that I find myself on the back foot, unsure of how to handle the situation in front of me. It must be the fact that I haven't been here since I was a teenager and every doorway I walk through peels away another layer of adult shell surrounding the kid I used to be. I'm glad there's nobody here that knows the real me, whatever that might mean. What is the true nature of someone's personality? Is it the young, undeveloped but untainted lad these people might remember? If they remember him at all. Or is it the worldly-wise bastard I am now? I suppose there's a bit of the young me still in there, even if it's just my taste in music. Talking of which, what is this DJ playing? *Chirpy Chirpy bloody Cheep Cheep*? I glare at the guy on the turntables on the stage. He must be all of twenty-five, which means that a room of forty-year-olds falls into his 'oldies' set. We grew up on Oasis, Blur and 2 Unlimited, not something from God-knows-when. I had planned to head for the drinks first but this is important. I stride up the steps onto the stage and see that he's cueing up the next 45. A glance at the sleeve by the side of the decks tells me he's going to play *'Tie A Yellow Ribbon Round the Ole Oak Tree'*, a song I have heard a grand total of twice and I still have the scars. I need to stop this now. I tap him on the arm and point to the deck as he turns to look at me.

I stare right into his eyes and say very clearly, 'No. Do not play cheesy shit.'

He starts to protest but I clamp a firm hand on his shoulder and move my mouth close to his ear. 'We are not pensioners. You will not play anything older than the 80s, do you understand?' Another squeeze on his shoulder. I don't usually do 'menacing' (I have people for that) but I've spent enough time around the experts to know the basics.

He swallows and nods. 'Um, Fat Boy Slim?' he asks warily.

'A good start, I guess.' I remove my hand and gesture to him to scrabble amongst his box of antique vinyl. Instead, he turns to a laptop and with a few clicks has pulled up a selection of tunes. I peer at the screen. 'Yeah, that one,' I say, pointing to Freak Power's *Turn On, Tune In, Cop Out*. I watch as he cues it up and presses play as *Chirpy Chirpy Cheep Cheep* draws to a close. The intro keyboard hook begins to pulse around the hall and by the time the drums come in there are a few whoops coming from the happy throng. I see a thumbs up from a guy with a bald head and I can't help but smile. We're definitely not the same people on the outside but the old personalities are still locked up within, waiting to be freed by the right key.

I turn back to the DJ who is now scrolling through new options for the evening's entertainment. I pick up the single that's still cued on the deck, wonder if this 'Tony Orlando and Dawn' were ever allowed near a recording studio again, and skim it like a frisbee to the far end of the hall. I hope it breaks. I edge nearer to the DJ and his laptop, curiosity getting the better of me. 'Do you have any Catherine Wheel?' I shout.

He looks around at me with a blank look on his face.

'How about Slowdive? Adorable? Ride?' Still nothing. *Really*? I sigh. Okay, I need to go a bit more mainstream. 'Oasis? Blur? Shed Seven?'

He gives me a thumbs up and gets back to his computer.

I'm just leaving the stage when a couple of women brush past me on their way up to the DJ chanting 'I'll tell you what I want, what I really, really want...' It's good to know that he's going to be kept on his toes.

Helen Walcott, *Proud Single Mum*
– 7:15 pm

I'VE BEEN NERVOUS all day. Chloe arrived last night. She's coming for moral support. I can hear her music now, some dance track I don't know the name of that thumps through the wall like a heartbeat. We're staying with mum and dad for a couple of days, but thankfully, they are away visiting Uncle Frank who had a fall and is in hospital up in Newcastle. I don't think I could cope with their questions. I know there'd be many, there always are. They've never been able to let it go. I sip the glass of wine I've poured to steady my nerves and look at myself in the mirror. I'm still slim, that's the gift of having a baby so young. I sprang back into shape almost immediately and I've always exercised and tried to take care of myself. I glance at the dress hanging on the wardrobe door: emerald green with a lightning bolt of silver shimmer streaking across the bodice. I wonder if it's a bit over the top but when I saw it, I knew I had to have it, despite the expense. I suppose I ought to start doing my face if we're going to be on time. I definitely need to present myself in the best way possible tonight, just in case I do decide to tell all...

I wonder who will be there and whether I'll remember them. It's so long since I moved away, but the ghosts of my past are flickering and indistinctly hovering at the edges of my memory like faded watercolours that I can't quite make out. Briefly, I wonder why we place so much emphasis on our school days when actually it is such a short time in our lives and often miserable. I apply primer and blush, shade my eyes and lips and think I don't look too bad for an old bird when Chloe's head appears around the door.

'You ready, mum?' She looks beautiful. She is beautiful and bright and I feel a swell of pride at my girl, not at all sure I want to share her now or ever.

'Almost.' I look at myself in the mirror, the flowery wallpaper that's seen better days providing a nostalgic backdrop to my appearance. I stand up, slip into my dress and turn for Chloe to zip me up. 'Will I do?'

'You look great, mum. Have confidence.' Chloe smiles at me. I sink my feet into my shoes, take a deep breath and we leave my old bedroom, a Rick Astley poster still blu-tacked to the back of the door, a cushion in the shape of a rabbit slumbering on my old single bed.

In the car, Radio 4 is soft in the background, the voices barely audible. Chloe sits beside me scrolling through her messages on her phone, her long hair falling in front of her face.

'Ready for the new semester?' I ask.

'Yeah, I'm looking forward to my linguistics seminars but some of the others sound a little dull.'

'Dull?'

She nods. 'It's fine, mum. Honestly.'

'Jack okay?'

'He's fine.'

We're quiet for a while, the silence comfortable between us like a cosy blanket.

'Do you ever wish you'd gone to university, mum?'

'Me? You're kidding!' I laugh. 'Don't forget I left school at seventeen to have you.'

'I know, but you could go now.' She looks at me.

I laugh again. 'Now? I don't think so. It's that long since I've learnt anything, I'd be bottom of the class.'

'There's loads of mature students at my uni. Women and men whose kids have grown up and they want to do something for themselves.'

'Really? But how do they pay their mortgages and bills?'

'You can get loans to help, mum. There's ways.'

'Right, this is it.'

The school looms in front of us like a malevolent boil. It was never a pretty place; architectural design seemed to get left behind in the sixties and the original Victorian building is hidden by the newer monstrosities.

'Christ! It looks like a prison!' Chloe says.

'Yep, you're not wrong. Now, keep your eyes peeled for a parking space.' I turn into the school carpark, still the same after so many years and feel my body tense at the memories that come flooding back and park in a vacant space next to a silver Merc. 'Someone's done well for themselves,' I murmur.

'What?' Chloe lifts her head from her screen.

'Oh, nothing. Talking to myself again.' I grab my bag, lock the door and we walk towards the double doors, the sound of *Tainted Love* spilling out into the night time air reminding me of life a long time ago.

'Good evening,' says a bright-eyed girl, obviously drafted in for the evening and eager for her minimum wage. 'Can I take your names, please?'

'Helen and Chloe Walcott.' I look around nervously. There are only a few people milling about in the foyer where we are, but I can see the hall beyond is already quite full.

'Great,' she says, eyeing a printed page, her pen moving down a long list of names, 'Ah, there you are!' and she ticks us off, a big smile on her face. She is unbearably cheerful, like a too-pleased with itself terrier. 'Now, if you'd like to put these on you can go and enjoy yourselves.' She hands us our sticky name labels. 'The bar is through there - it's free! Have fun!'

'Thank you,' says Chloe and smiles at me. 'Okay?'

I nod. 'She obviously thinks we don't get out much,' I murmur and she laughs. I take a deep breath and swallow the lump in my throat. I don't know if he'll even be here and even if he is, it's over twenty years ago, we're different people now. What the hell am I doing?

Julia Forest, *Tank Girl to Child Protector* – 7:16 pm

I INDICATE TO PULL out of the slip road onto the A46 and head north for Newark. It won't be many miles until I see the spire of St Mary Magdalene beckoning me to the place I escaped at eighteen. It seems a long time ago, but I wonder if the years will fall away when I see the people I once knew. The person I most want to see is Butterford, of course. Well, "want" is perhaps the wrong word, but I would like to finish the business between us. I try to work out how old he might be. He must be coming up to retirement and I wonder, yet again, whether it will be worth calling him out or not.

I have survived him. And I have survived the malicious rumours. I am happily married with two daughters studying for their exams. I love my job teaching English, seeing understanding blossom in teenagers. And I like my new post of responsibility as the school's Child Protection Officer. The last of which makes me wonder, how many of us were there at Hercules Clay that he interfered with? How many girls did he damage? I know that I won't be able to make a case for myself because I was adamant that I would not make a formal complaint against him. So I know that in the case of historical sexual abuse, I'm not going to have a leg to stand on. No one in any kind of authority knew about what he did to me...except Miss Summerfield and I have no idea what happened to her. I hope I might see her tonight but it would be a very long shot to have him convicted on my word alone and on Miss Summerfield's corroboration of my story. She didn't actually witness anything very much and nothing was ever written down. I don't plan a witch-hunt in the manner of all aged, long-haired men wearing tracksuits and a bit of bling. And I'm not sure revenge is what I'm seeking...which is why I'm travelling alone.

Mike offered to come with me but I put him off with promises of boredom. I love him but I have never told him about how thoroughly Butterford managed to cut me down, how his toxic presence proscribed my actions during my last months at school. Mike would be shocked to know that his confident and competent wife was once reduced to a humiliated silence in front of her peers. Perhaps I'll exorcise the monster tonight.

That's also why I'm driving myself to the reunion. I want to keep a clear head if I see him. I don't want to confront him as a shrieking drunk. He can't have that satisfaction. After all, he didn't ruin my life. He simply made me too wary and too cynical for an eighteen-year-old, which did prove to be a useful shield at uni. I wasn't the wide-eyed ingénue the third year men enjoyed picking off in Freshers' Week. Later, I made sure I did some of the choosing, and Mike was my prize. A good husband and a good dad.

I wonder who else I might see as I overtake a heavy lorry. My lovely Helen? Mark? I'd like to clear the air with Mark. We never spoke again after the knicker rumour. But Helen? I would love to know what happened to her. I really missed her when she left, not least because I had such need of a confidante myself.

The journey from Nottingham doesn't take long. I race across the years to Newark where I've not had to go "home" before now because mum and dad took advantage of me leaving school to fulfil a lifelong dream of living beside the sea. I tell myself it's only another arrangement of bricks and mortar but I can't help seeing my younger self looking over my shoulder at the lads who took such pleasure in shaming me. They're going to have no chance now. I've perfected the raising of the sardonic eyebrow to an art form and if I can quell a roomful of fifteen-year-old boys, men approaching middle age are going to be no threat at all. Besides, I have taken great care with my appearance and I've learned that women, and men for that matter, can wield their attractiveness like a weapon. Scare the bastards off, I will, if necessary.

I take a deep breath before I step out of the car and turn to look at the old place. The car park is almost full. As I lock my car, I see I've parked beside another Volvo estate. An attractive woman gets out of the passenger seat. She smiles at me.

'Your kids going to uni, too?'

'Yes. Getting ready to transport everything she can't live without in September,' I say.

'We're the same. Glorified taxi drivers.'

I nod and smile across at her husband. 'Mark!'

He's heavier, but not in a bad way. Still handsome. But he blushes as he recognises me.

'Julia.'

'How are you?' I ask.

His wife is still smiling.

'I'm well,' he says. 'This is Megan, my wife.'

'Yes, we've met,' I say.

'No husband?' Megan asks.

'He's at home, supervising teenagers.'

There's an awkward pause and I decide this might be my only chance. I plunge in. 'Have you heard of upskirting?' I ask Mark.

'What?'

'Taking photos up girls' skirts,' says Megan.

'Photos?' he asks.

'Well, in our day, a male could find out what a female was wearing by looking up her skirt. Especially if she was up a ladder.'

'Up a ladder?' he repeats.

'In the English stock cupboard.'

'What? Did he...' begins Megan.

'No. Mark was far too nice to do that, but he knew someone who would.'

Mark looks at me, still puzzled.

'Think about it,' I say.

'So he lied,' he says at last.

'Of course, he lied.'

'The fucking bastard,' he says slowly.

'Now, we're not going to have any trouble are we, Mark? Meet up with old friends is what you said.'

'Yes, yes. I mean, no. It's fine. Don't worry,' he says to her. He turns to me. 'It's a bit late in the day...but I am sorry.'

'There's nothing for you to be sorry for,' I say. 'We're all grown-ups. We all survived.'

'Hey, Marky!' yells a new arrival.

'Well, I'll leave you to it,' I say. 'Have a good evening.'

'You, too,' he says.

Megan smiles with what might be relief to see the back of me.

I walk towards the hall. One down, two to go.

Gemma Robinson, *Business Queen* – 7:20 pm

I'VE SPOTTED A few familiar faces. The most immediately noticeable being that of Sarah Greene, now married to Ascot Thomsett, son of Gil Thomsett, owner of a string of used-car garages across the Midlands. It's hard to miss her. As is Ascot, who looks like he's embraced the good life a little too enthusiastically. Well cut suit, but it still doesn't hide the bulge round his midriff. And no number of good suits will ever detract from his florid, puffy face. Then again, he was always fleshy. Yuk! Not a memory I wish to revisit. No, it's Sarah who is the focus of my attention. Sarah the spiteful, Sarah the bitch. Not a good person back in the day.

In contrast to her indulged husband she looks positively skeletal, and, if I'm not mistaken, she's had some cosmetic work done round her jaw and eyes – not that successfully judging from here. It's hard to ignore them, although I would if I could. Crossing the room towards where they're holding court – they regard themselves as akin to royalty in this small town - I catch a glimpse of Ryan chatting to Jamie. Ah, Jamie – the effortlessly coolest boy in the sixth form. I'm a little surprised to see him and Ryan getting on so well. Perhaps the passage of time has seen Ryan come out of his shell sufficiently to be able to hold a conversation with Jamie without blushing, stuttering and generally making a complete arse of himself. There's a knot of people standing near the DJ who seems to think that school kids in the mid-90s were listening to music from the 70s. Really? *Chirpy, Chirpy, Cheep, Cheep*, anyone? Before that I'm sure we were being regaled with Robson and Jerome. He must have asked his Gran what she was listening to back in the day.

There's another familiar face hanging around near the DJ: Iain Wilson. I had some dealings with him when I first started up the business, but didn't like his approach or his friends. I'll steer clear of him, he's not someone I want to be associated with.

I make my move. 'Sarah! Goodness me, I hardly recognised you.'

She turns towards me, tacks a hard, false smile to her face and gives me an air kiss. 'Gemma, dear. What a surprise. You haven't shown up at either of our previous little "get-togethers". How lovely that you've made an effort this time for the official reunion.'

So, not much change in Sarah then. Still got a nasty mouth. Well, two can play at that game.

'I know,' I reply, with a false smile of my own. 'The business keeps me so busy, I don't have time for much else. You know what running a successful, global business is like. I'm afraid attending school "get-togethers" hasn't been a priority. But I thought I'd pop in this year as it is, as you say, an official reunion and see how everyone else is doing.' And if the Thomsetts have a successful, global business I'm Richard Branson.

Sarah takes Ascot's arm. 'Look who's here. Wonder girl herself.' She turns towards me again. 'Ascot is the main sponsor responsible for the free bar, you know. He has such fond memories of being at school and wanted to support the reunion.'

I ignore her comments. Several of us were approached about sponsoring the food and drinks, so Ascot certainly isn't the "main sponsor" any more than I am. I wave a dismissive hand. 'Not a wonder, nor a girl for that matter. Just a hard-working woman succeeding in a male dominated industry.'

Ascot holds my upper arms and brushes my cheek with a warm, wet kiss. I have to steel myself not to wipe it away in front of them.

'I hadn't realised you were so attached to Hercules Clay,' I say.

'Mmm, I felt I should do my bit, y'know. I saw you on the old telly box last week,' he splutters. 'Thought you did very well. Convincing performance all round. You must be coining it!'

Ascot likes to give the impression he's been to public school, rather than failed all his exams at a comp. Pretentious twit.

I look at him and raise an eyebrow. Does he really think I give a damn about his opinion, or his approval? Patronising idiot – he probably didn't understand a word of what I was saying anyway. I don't think hi-tech is his thing – clapped out cars is more like it.

'Thank you,' I say producing another insincere smile. 'So good to know that the second-hand motor trade is keeping up with the complexities of the computer industry.'

As I speak I realise that a number of ex-classmates have wandered closer. I hear one or two sniggers as Ascot's face registers confusion at my remark.

'Yes, I was reading about your company in the FT.' Jamie's joined us. 'One of the best, according to their analyst. And, you give a tithe on your profits to charity. That all sounds pretty wonderful to me.'

'Just putting my principles into practice,' I reply. 'It's good to see you Jamie.' I look him up and down. 'Still cool, I see.'

He laughs and gives me a hug. 'You're not so bad yourself.' Looking around, he comments, 'Ryan's here somewhere, we were talking just now.'

'Yes, I saw you. How is he?'

'Great. Look there he is, come and chat.'

We move away from the Thomsetts and find Ryan standing by the so-called bar, apparently trying to decide between the too-warm boxed white and the too-cold boxed red. Lidl's best, I see.

'Look who I've found!' Jamie slings his arm round Ryan. 'Gemma's here.'

As we stand chatting, Ryan's keen to know my thoughts on the damage Brexit is doing to the British economy.

'Oh, I'll give you my opinion, Ryan, but not tonight. I'm off duty and I really don't want to talk about it. Some other time maybe. And, I promise to tell you all about how I beat off the competition to win that very lucrative contract from HM Government.' It will be a heavily censored version, of course.

'All the sordid details, I shall enjoy that. I know what,' says Jamie, giving Ryan a significant look. 'Why don't you come to dinner one evening? Ry does a great stuffed, baked sea bass with Mediterranean roast vegetables. Stay overnight. It'll be fun to catch up properly.'

Ryan gives an enthusiastic nod. 'You can give us the inside story then.'

Seeing my startled look Jamie laughs again. 'You didn't know – well, why would you? We stayed in touch after school and both came out at uni. Then we lost touch during the early noughties but met up again in 2015. We've been together for nearly four years and are planning our wedding next year. We'll send you an invite.'

So that's what's behind Ryan's more confident manner, I think. *I'm really out of touch with what's going on in the lives of people who were once good friends.*

'Sounds great. I'd love to come to both dinner and wedding. I don't live locally now, and work is pretty demanding, so I'll need a fair bit of notice.'

I'm aware that I might be coming across as somewhat aloof. It's a failing of mine, developed over the years to help me keep my distance from work related people. Yet, as I smile at Ryan I can see he and Jamie aren't offended.

'No problem,' says Ryan, putting my phone number and address in his mobile. 'While I've got my phone out, let's have a photo of the three of us. Then I can impress everyone with my high-powered friend!'

The music seems to have improved and the evening's getting well under way when I see Elizabeth Chastain coming towards me. From a distance she looks pretty good - considering. It's a few years since I last saw her and her figure remains slight and girlish. Her fine, long blonde hair is worn with a heavy fringe, continuing to provide the "curtain" she hides behind when she's feeling vulnerable. And, as before, her dark brown eyes glimmer with a hint of sadness. As she comes closer though, I have to try hard not to stare at her. It's always like this for me. I can hardly bear to look her in the eye. The work she'd had done after the incident in the lab when we were fourteen, had done marvels given the circumstances and she is obviously good at camouflaging her scars but I still struggle.

I smile, 'Hi there, Liza, how's things?'

She gives me a brief hug. We'd been part of a small group of girls interested in the sciences so had known each other well at one time, close friends in fact. Since the day everything went spectacularly wrong I've only seen her occasionally at business events and so on, and I still can't get past feeling guilty. If I hadn't swapped places with her, just so I could stand next to a boy I fancied, it would have been me with the scarred face and her trying not to keep looking away.

'Yeah, okay thanks.'

'Business good?'

'It is, thanks for asking. I've increased the range again recently, which has worked well. I get orders from all over the world. It's amazing how many scarred people there are out there.'

Liza had set up a restorative make-up company with the compensation money set aside for her in the aftermath of that day, and through hard work, determination and bravery, she now has a successful business which is still growing.

As on the other occasions we've met up, I wonder why we don't stay in touch. I like her and admire what she has done with her life. I guess I just can't get over the "what if". Maybe she can't either. With a tentative smile, she walks away in the direction of the bar. Yet again, I've not been able to renew the connection we once had.

This must be one of the best turnouts for a school reunion that Hercules Clay Comp has ever had. I guess there are around 80 or more people in here now. The noise level has increased again. People are milling around so I can't always be certain if I recognise a face or not and, in any case, most of us have changed, one way or another. I can see a woman on the other side of the room, standing listening to her friend who is talking and waving her hands around. There is something familiar about her, but I can't put my finger on exactly who she is. I feel I should know her yet I don't think she was one of the girls in my class. Oh well, it's a mystery. I'll try to catch up with her later and read her name label.

I spot Mr. Bloom near the door to the corridor. My God! He looks so old. He was a great teacher – English Lit – one of my favourite non-science subjects.

'Gemma! What a pleasure to see you here.'

I can't decide whether to go for a kiss on the cheek or a hug. In the end I do neither. It seems too weird to kiss a teacher and a hug seems equally inappropriate. I settle for a warm smile of genuine affection and a brief touch on the arm of his shabby old jacket – surely not the same one he used to wear when he taught me? Actually, I think it is – or it's a clone! I ask if he's retired now.

'Goodness me, yes. Years ago. I usually come to these things but increasingly find fewer ex-students to chat to. I'm so glad you've come tonight. I hardly recognise any of the people here.'

'Me neither. Just the odd one or two. Mr Bloom, do you know who that woman is?' I gesture towards where I saw her last. 'Oh no, sorry. She's moved and I can't see her now. I feel I should know her but just can't place her at all.'

'Ha! That's exactly how I feel at these reunions. Although I did see your friend Liza earlier on. She came quite early. I haven't had a chance to talk to her yet, but I will before the night is out. Despite the terrible times she has been through she's made a wonderful life for herself.'

I agree, and Mr Bloom and I chatter on while I keep my eye out for the woman I can't identify. As we talk, Iain Wilson crosses my eyeline and I turn slightly away. He looks – I don't know – haunted?

This wine is bloody terrible. I wish now I'd brought a bottle of something reasonable with me. On my wanderings in search of a decent drink, I stop for a quick chat with Pam who seems just the same as she was when she was fourteen.

Surely someone has smuggled in something decent to drink. I should have known! Jamie and Ryan are pouring out what looks like a very nice Cotes du Rhone. 'I'll have some of that,' I say, holding out the plastic beaker for a fill-up. It is as good as I'd hoped. Thankfully, Jamie has brought several bottles so the small group of us is reluctant to leave the steady supply of quality alcohol.

When I spot a shifty looking bloke hanging around outside in the courtyard, I do a double-take. It can't be! Shit, it is, it's Karl. I look around, unease making my stomach gripe. Where the hell is Liza? She really mustn't see Karl. The fallout would be nuclear. I put down my plastic beaker - quality glassware not being in evidence this evening. I keep eyes on Karl, he's skulking around, his expression a combination of anxiety and contempt. Why is he here – who the hell invited him? What does he want? Knowing the Karl of 20 plus years ago, he's up to mischief. The question is what kind of mischief is he up to? I tap Jamie on the arm, 'Look out the window, don't make it obvious. Is that really who I think it is?'

Jamie glances around with a casual "Wow, look at all the people here" air. 'Yup, it's Karl. How did that bastard get an invite?'

'Don't know. But... Liza! How do I keep them apart? If she sees him, she will either go mental or go to pieces. I don't want either to happen. I need to find her.'

Jamie nods and I leave the group happily swapping life stories, partner changes, job successes, or failures, and tales of their amazing kids. My mind is boiling. I can't see Liza anywhere and now Karl seems to have disappeared from view. What the hell is going on with me? I put this all in the past years ago. Why do I feel so responsible for Liza?

Iain Wilson, "*Legitimate Businessman*" – 7:25 pm

AND THEN SUDDENLY I'm looking at Gemma Robinson. Probably the most successful ex-pupil Hercules Clay has ever produced and not someone I expected to be here tonight. I did some business consultancy work for her back in the early days, a few months before I moved to Nottingham. She'd just finished her degree in whatever sciency thing it was and had come up with some new gadget and was wondering how to get it to market. This was way before Dragon's Den or anything. No, we got together because of our mums.

You know how it is – parents who have seen each other at school gates, open days, picking kids up after parties, all that stuff. They talk to each other, pop around for coffee, chat in supermarkets. And that carries on *even after you've left school*. Conversations about what their respective offspring are doing, what university they're at, all that stuff.

Well, Gemma's mum must have bumped into my mum and mentioned that she was trying to do some marketing or something. And then my mum said how I had done my business course and had a few clients already (to be honest, they were mainly local plasterers, furniture makers, garages, that kind of thing) and suggested we get together.

Telephone numbers were exchanged and, grudgingly, we set up a few meetings, me focusing on what she wanted to achieve, what the product did, what the USPs were, all the usual. The problem was that around this time I was getting into street-side supply and demand. It was much more profitable than telling a mechanic to consider setting up a website. And one meeting I had with Gemma in a pub almost ruined everything.

To be fair, I was a bit high after a mid-afternoon spliff otherwise I wouldn't have invited Dexy to sit down with us when he shuffled up to me. He was a typical wheeler-dealer, provider of assorted pick-me-ups and chill-me-outs. He seemed genuinely interested in what we were trying to achieve but as the meeting went on I could tell that he needed to talk to me privately. We excused ourselves and went to the gents, where we did some narcotic-based negotiation. It was Dexy and his knowledge and contacts that made me interested in how much more effective supply could be with a little more forethought and organisation. With the right people I realised I could make serious money and a short while later I met Simmo and moved out of Newark to play with the big boys.

After sealing a deal to shift some tabs in from Holland, we did a quick line each to perk ourselves up and went back to Gemma who was nursing the remains of an orange juice and lemonade. I was feeling the buzz, energised and ready to go. She was stony-faced and unimpressed. She told Dexy that he could go as this was supposed to be a private meeting, and as he shambled off she turned on me with surprising venom.

'What the hell are you playing at, Iain?' I started to protest but she cut me off, gathering her paperwork together. 'I do not work with druggies.'

'I'm not a druggy. What makes you think I'm a druggy?'

'Apart from your erratic behaviour and your scuzzy dealer, the biggest clue is the white powder on your nose.'

And that was that. She swept out and I had to explain later to my mum that we'd gone as far as we could with our collaboration. It was a jolt to my easy-going life, but at least it meant that I became much more focused on ensuring a proper separation of business and pleasure. I never again went into any meeting under the influence. I guess it marked the change from half-arsed amateur to laser-focused manager of risk.

That was the last time I saw Gemma, outside of the odd television interview (the most recent of which was an entertaining demolition of James Dyson and his decision to move to Singapore). I don't think I would know what to say to her now. She's the one person here that has an inkling of what I was doing in my early twenties and may guess correctly that I'm still involved in that scene.

I pull myself together and wander over to the table that represents the 'free bar'. Looks like non-specific boxes of wine, Lidl orange juice or water. I catch the eye of another press-ganged sixth former tasked with handing out the drinks and gesture for a red wine.

'Just the one?' the spotty youth asks.

'I'll take one for my partner, too,' I say, plucking another plastic glass. He peers behind me at the space where my non-existent partner ought to be standing. I smile again and take a sip. The smile slips into a grimace. 'I just remembered,' I continue as I put one of the reds back, 'she's not coming.'

A blonde-haired woman I don't recognise stumbles past me and leans over the table, thrusting a sizeable cleavage at the poor lad. 'You got anything stronger?' she yells in a distinctly cockney accent. 'Like vodka?'

He swallows nervously and drops down behind the table and pulls out a large bottle of clear spirit. 'It's supposed to be for later, though, once everyone's arrived.'

'Well,' says the woman, grinning manically, 'the most important people have arrived, so crack it open, sunshine.'

She turns to me and looks me up and down, much as a wolf does to a small girl wearing a red hood. 'I like your shirt.'

'Thank you. I like your no-nonsense attitude to alcohol.'

'It comes naturally. A talent handed down from my granny.' She holds out her hand. 'Lucy.'

I shake it. 'Iain. You're not from round here, are you?'

'Nah, came with a friend. She said there was going to be a free bar so here I am.'

'Indeed you are.'

She beams at me and then rescues a couple of plastic glasses of vodka and orange from the lad behind the table.

'So who have you come with, then?' I ask. *Please say it's Katy.*

'Oh, it's my friend, Hannah. We met in London years ago. I'll, you know, send her your way later. Or I could keep you for myself?' She smiles carnivorously.

I raise my plastic glass in salute. 'I need to catch up with a few people first, but the night is yet young.'

She smiles and winks, 'Ciao, Iain,' and then turns and sashays into the crowd. And there, across the makeshift dance floor, stands Katy Greeves.

Phil Morris, *The Man, The Legend* – 7:25 pm

I STRAIGHTEN MY BACK and feign confidence as I walk down the corridor to the main hall. I open the swing doors and pause at the portal to elicit a little drama. Okay, maybe I am a bit early. I release the doors and saunter into the void, my trainers spoiling my entrance a little as the soles squeak with every step on the polished parquet. I pause at the drinks table. Well, it said 'bar' but a few boxes of red wine, white wine and orange juice hardly qualify. I notice the beer at the end, but decide to take a tumbler of the fancy red anyway.

I sip my red wine, not bad - I'd rather have a lager - but this is better than nothing, I think as I drain my plastic glass. I see the occasional flash of a bottle here and there. It seems that some people have smuggled in their own alcohol. God knows why. They probably didn't realise that this stuff would be supplied free of charge, I smile. Back at the bar table, a young lady refills my glass, and I take a swig. Huh, they should have supplied bigger plastic glasses.

I look around at the familiar faces. Many have hardly changed while others are barely recognisable. There's a wide selection of beer bellies, receding hairlines and fuzzy chins - and that's just the girls! Boom! Boom! I imagine how much the lads will laugh when I say that to them; I'll definitely use it when I see them later. *I must remember it,* I think with a smile. Actually, most of the girls who looked good back in the day look even hotter in their civvies.

I am relieved to recognise a couple of familiar faces, Willy and Chunk, a couple of my old mates. 'Guys,' I say, 'looking good!' They really do look good. Chunk is now slim and obviously works out a lot, and Andy is free of spots and of his infamous Pat Sharp mullet. They both smile and greet me.

Willy says, 'Hi, Phil, nice to see you. Where have you been, dude? Haven't seen you since you left this place!'

'I'm okay, mate. Hey, you'll never guess who I've just been talking to.' Then after looking from one blank face to the other I announce, 'Here's a clue, '*Ooh, I'm a lady,*' I say in a pretty good copy of the David Walliams line from Little Britain. Then, realising that it isn't actually a clue at all, I add, 'You remember Charlie?'

'Sure, but it's Hannah now, Phil, has been for ages. She won't like you mocking her like that, mate. It's not cool,' Willy admonishes.

'She came to my gym for a while, attracted a bit of interest too,' Chunk adds with a smile. 'She was a popular girl. I have a feeling that's why she stopped coming. Probably wasn't confident enough to handle the attention back then. It was some years ago now. Will be nice to see her again,' he says as he scans the room. 'Charlie was a great guy, and Hannah is a really nice girl.'

'Oh, sure!' I agree. 'She looks quite hot now, great boobs, anybody could be fooled. If I didn't know I could even fancy giving her a quick one myself. Well, if the plumbing is all right. Know what I mean?' I grin and look from one face to the other. They obviously don't understand my joke or just don't appreciate it. Have they both had a sense of humour bypass since schooldays?

'Anyway, what are you dudes into now? You still number one 'Jon Bogey' fan, Willy?'

After a faint half-smile Willy says. 'I still listen to Bon Jovi, Judas Priest, Aerosmith – all the old guys, sometimes, but not so much, you know...'

'What ya doing now? Workwise?' I ask.

'I am with the police,' he says.

'You mean, helping them with enquiries?' I grin.

Willy smiles a broad smile. 'DI Andrew Wilkins,' he says as he symbolically proffers a hand, which I take rather limply and he does his best to shake. *Fuck*, I think, *Willy Wilkins is a copper – a detective*?

'Fuck!' I say, remaining open-mouthed.

'It's just my job, Phil, it's what I do. Relax, I'm not on duty. Unless – you're not planning anything dodgy are you?' he asks with a stern face.

'No, I – uh – no, not me,' I say.

'Ha, ha – just kidding, Phil – don't be daft!' he grins.

Chunk is barely hiding his amusement as I squirm. He holds a hand out too and announces, 'DS Denis Jones.'

I slowly move my hand to accept the proffered handshake. But before I touch skin, he lifts his hand, does that silly thumb on nose wave, and laughs.

'Gotcha! I run the gym, Studio 42 on Barnby Drive, Phil, but I couldn't resist.'

'Bastard!' I say with an appreciative grin. 'And what do you really do, Andy?'

'Oh, I really am a DI,' he smiles. 'I'm based at St. Ann's, Nottingham. Not a problem I hope, Phil? I'm sure you're still an upright citizen,' he says as he gives my upper arm a firm but friendly slap. 'So what about you? What do you do to earn a crust? Don't tell me, let me think – you were into PC games, The Smiths, top shelf glossy mags - I know! You run a special interest porn site for depressives?'

'No – I, uh, I'm in the building trade – scaffolding – hire – Farndon,' I announce staccato style. 'Getting a bit busier now,' I announce as I look round at the steady movement of bodies through the double doors into the hall.

'Yeah, I didn't think so many would turn up. I guess there's nothing else happening locally,' opines Dave. 'Not that there ever was much going on in Newark.'

'Oh I don't know,' I say, 'some good pubs, cinema...' I drain my glass. 'Gonna fill this up. Can I get refills for you guys?'

'Driving mate,' says Andy as he and Denis both lift their orange juices. 'Did you come by taxi then, Phil? Or did you get dropped off?' Andy asks.

'Oh, I, uh – yeah, well I came in the motor but gonna get a taxi home and pick it up tomorrow,' I smile, pleased with my quick thinking. 'Anyway, catch you later guys!' I say as I turn and head for the bar, breathing a sigh of relief as I walk away from them.

Hannah Parker, *was a proper Charlie* – 7:30 pm

WELL, IF THAT is a measure of things to come, then this is going to be a long night. Cheeky sod. All Philip had done was stare at my chest the whole time. I could see him sniggering with a group of boys, well what were supposed to be grown men now, although you couldn't tell from their behaviour. The way they're reacting shows them up as the same immature boys. Oh well, I remind myself that I've developed a thick skin to whispered comments over the years. I glean some satisfaction from the fact he hadn't recognised me straight away. The one thing I could claim is that I look very different. Which is a good job as I've spent a small fortune over the years.

'Well, he is a complete arsehole. Were you actually friends with that knobhead? What the hell is he wearing – look at him strutting his way over there? Loser. So glad you told him to fuck off before I did,' Lucy says.

'That's Phil for you. I hope I wasn't too rude to him. He's harmless enough, but he never could filter his mouth.'

'I would have punched his mouth if we'd talked to him any longer! Scissor sisters – cheeky bastard. 'Have you come in drag?' Jesus, I forget that bigots like him exist in this world. Is that what happens when you come 'up North'?'

To Lucy, anything past the North circular is 'up North'.

'Now who's being judgemental? You've just pigeon-holed most of the country, Lucy, and really, Phil isn't that bad. Like I said, he just has no filter.'

Lucy grins. 'Well, you know I don't mean it. I love Northerners, I love you don't I? We're best friends. And I wouldn't go around telling others like your mate Phil. Anyway, enough of that loser.'

Lucy passes me the sticky name label she'd grabbed off the table. It says Hannah, I feel a wave of relief wash over me. I stick it on my dress, doubting that it will stay on. As I turn to talk to

Lucy, she rushes off to get some drinks, leaving me on my own; exactly what she said she wouldn't do. I shake my head and smile. Lucy is a good friend, but she really loses her head when it comes to the prospect of free alcohol and a party.

I take the opportunity to look around. The hall looks the same, barring an extra lick of paint here and there. I can't believe the place hasn't fundamentally changed after all these years. Then again the brain is capable of overlaying the memories, blurring the past with the present. The structure is the same, but I guess it has had more than a lick of paint over the years. Large inspirational quotes are stencilled everywhere. I wonder how many meetings the school board had to come up with those useless quotes; as if kids care about them? Maybe Ofsted would care. Ticking boxes is what Education is all about nowadays – or so my friend tells me every time we catch up for coffee. Year in year out the Education system just seems to get worse. Maybe we didn't have it so bad all those years ago.

Glancing around the room my eyes land on the sleazy sports teacher Mr Butterford; not all the rumours about him could have been lies. I'm slightly taken aback to see he's in a wheelchair, and I'm sure I recognise the woman pushing him from school. He notices me looking at him and when he looks me up and down, I feel as if I've been violated. Well, he certainly hasn't changed his ways. Horrible man. This was how the girls at school must have felt, and I played my part by teasing Julia Forest about the rumours. About her and her pants. The old anger fizzes to the surface, and I flip him the finger before walking off. As I turn, I notice a woman smiling at me. I feel a blush touch my cheeks as I realise she's just witnessed what I did. I don't need the name badge to know this is Julia, who'd been one of Helen's friends. I wonder if they are still in touch.

I take a deep breath and grasp my courage with both hands – if only I had a drink! I make my way over to her, skirting around groups of people hugging and exclaiming it's been too long. It's time to do what I came here for.

'Sorry, you saw that. He gives me the creeps, even after all these years,' I say to Julia.

'He deserves that, and more, but life is too short. Maybe, time has punished him enough,' she says, but not with the venom I expected. 'But I still enjoyed the look on his face when you flipped him the finger.'

'I couldn't help it, it just happened. I'm not normally the kind of person that flips someone in a wheelchair. Coming here seems to have transported me back to my school persona.'

She nods. I can see she is mentally running through the school years trying to place me. Without success, judging from her confused expression.

I take a deep breath. 'Julia, you probably don't recognise me as I've changed a bit from school. You would have known me as Charles or Charlie. I used to hang about with Philip, and Helen sometimes. I want to say how sorry I am for being a bitch to you at school. I was going through my own issues and didn't realise what a shit I was until I finally grew up.'

The words I've been waiting to say for years come out in a flurry. I need to say it and take the consequences, whatever that may be. I'm worried about what Julia is going to say, she's staring at me open-mouthed.

'Charlie? Jesus Christ, I wouldn't have recognised you if you hadn't said.'

'Well, it's hardly surprising. I've changed a little bit,' I say with a wry smile. I hope this first apology goes well.

'I'm sorry again, Julia. I really didn't mean to be horrible to you at school. It might not mean much, as the damage has been done. But for my part, I apologise for any rumours I helped to spread about you, and those Tank Girl comments about your pants. God, I feel so embarrassed just thinking about the way I taunted you. It wasn't fair, and I do regret it.' I hold my breath waiting for Julia to answer.

'It's okay. Look, thanks, Charlie, sorry I mean, what's your name?' Julia says, staring at my name tag. Her cheeks are flushed with embarrassment, or maybe it is anger.

'It's Hannah,' I say nervously, wondering again how this is going pan out.

'Hannah, right. Look it's okay. I know what kids can be like, and although it wasn't very nice at the time, you certainly weren't one of the worst ones to gossip about me and stir things up. Thank you for the apology though. It really does mean something, even after all this time.'

I'm so relieved. If this is the only apology I make tonight, it has been worth it. I feel all the worry about coming to the reunion is justified, just for this one moment. Saying sorry feels as therapeutic as my counsellor said it would. Already I feel like a weight has been lifted off my shoulders.

'Thank you, Julia. Your forgiveness means more than you can know.'

'I'm sure that you must have suffered your fair share over the years. What you have done cannot have been easy. I see things on social media all the time about people who transitioned and have a terrible time. Is that the right word? I never know what the right words are nowadays. Anyway...'

'You're right, it hasn't been easy, but I've been lucky enough to have supportive friends. It makes a big difference. I certainly haven't suffered as much as others.'

Julia nods, and I can see she has spotted someone in the crowd, 'Look I have to catch up with someone. Thank you again for the apology, Hannah. I promise I will try and catch you later for a proper chat. Well done again on flipping that tosser the finger. I couldn't have done it better myself,' Julia says smiling.

She reaches out and squeezes my shoulder before moving away from me.

I nod and smile at her, grateful for her understanding. I take a deep breath, and then slowly let the first breath of anxiety leave my body. I wonder if this is how religious people feel when they confess their sins.

Lucy still isn't back with the drinks. What the hell is she doing? I feel stupid standing around with no drink. I scan the crowd trying to see if I recognise anyone else. I can't believe how many people have turned up. Some people I remember from other form groups look exactly the same. It's like they have been teleported from school to here, with just a slightly more 'worn in' face. Others, I have no idea who they are.

I wonder again if Helen is here. I've thought of Helen often over the years. The brief romantic interlude – who am I kidding? It was a totally crap fumble into the world of sex on the Sconce park that neither of us will want to reminisce about. We'd been so close at one stage though, I even wondered if Helen had known about me.

Helen had painted my nails one day when we were bored. Just for a laugh we'd said at the time. But I'd loved the sparkly nail varnish and had worn gloves for days so I could keep the varnish on, taking the gloves off when I was alone so I could look at the effect. I remember the terrifying moment when Philip had tried to pull my gloves off. I'd had to punch him to get him to leave them alone. The teacher had told me to take them off in class, but I'd made up an excuse about having eczema on my hands and needing to keep them covered. I felt a stab of fear thinking how much stick I would have got if I'd had to take them off.

It was a real shame that Helen had left Newark, it was so sudden. Again there were rumours about her and the shit of a teacher. But, I hadn't believed them. I'd always felt a little hurt that Helen hadn't said goodbye. Even after everything that had happened, I thought we'd been friends.

I raise my hand from the tight grip on my bag and look at perfectly manicured nails. They'd cost me a small fortune at the salon. Not like the cheap nail varnish back at school. Somehow though, the nails of the past looked more beautiful than these. They had represented someone I didn't know I would become. I'm brought out of my trip down memory lane by Lucy finally turning up.

'Ta-Dah. Look at these I managed to get us,' Lucy exclaims. 'You look away with the fairies again. Is everything okay? Oh my God, you haven't broken a nail have you?'

I laugh at the seriousness in her voice. A broken nail! This would be a party-ending event to Lucy. 'Yes, I'm fine. Tonight is just bringing back a lot of memories. What the hell is this?' I ask, peering into the plastic pint glass.

'Vodka surprise,' Lucy says excitedly. 'I told the barman to give me the proper stuff. Not that crap they have on the so-called bar. Oh my God, you should have seen the amount he poured into it! It's like one of the measures you get abroad. This free bar is AMAZING. So glad I managed to get the under-counter stuff. Get drinking, and I will go and get us another. The queue was massive, but I managed to use my boobs to sneak in front of a couple of blokes. One of them is that bloke you were talking to. He's a right know-it-all, Jesus. I thought he would never shut up. Can talk for England that one, he's boring the arse of someone else in the queue. Was he like that at school? Also, I saw this really fit guy – I will point him out later and you must tell me all about him.' Lucy draws breath and then replaces her speed talking with a drinking straw.

Not for the first time I'm amazed at Lucy's lung capacity and she will only get worse the more she drinks.

'Yes, Phil was like that in school as well,' I say, putting the straw in my mouth. I take a small tentative sip of the drink and start coughing. It must be 80% proof vodka at least.

'Jesus Christ,' I say explosively.

Lucy is laughing hysterically, 'Hannah, your face! Get it down you, it will put hairs on your chest that will.' Lucy realises what she's said, and totally loses it. As is the norm for her, she starts to snort with laughter, some of the vile drink coming out of her nose. I can't hold back the laughter any longer. Thank the lord for the waterproof mascara. Lucy is such a tonic. Not for the first or last time, I feel grateful for Lucy's company tonight.

When Lucy has finally calmed down, she says, 'Ooh, you will never guess what.'

Before I get the chance to answer, she carries on. 'I've seen a woman wearing the exact same dress as you. Can you believe it? What are the chances? Anyway, you totally look better than her, although, I must admit she does look good in it. I would avoid that side of the room if I were you.' She points in the vague direction of the bar.

'Now start filling me in on everyone, I need to know names and all the gossip about them. Who do you want to talk to? We have a mission tonight, Hannah. You also need to take me to that science lab later so I can see where that lad got killed. But not until we've had a few more of these gorgeous little mixtures, and then we can boogie until we get chucked out.'

I sip my drink trying to process the barrage of words, and wondering what to answer first, I'm interrupted by the sound of a cough from the stage. The current headmaster looks like he is about to give a speech – oh Lord.

Pam McPherson, *Coordinator of Events* – 7:40 pm

ARRIVING AT THE entrance it doesn't seem so imposing as I remember, mind you that was around 25 years ago. God where did that time go? I'm approached by one of the present sixth formers, Karen according to her name badge, and she welcomes me in. I find my name tag sticker on the table. What will tonight bring? Karen asks me if I remember where to go.

'Unless it's changed drastically the hall is through the double doors in front of me,' I reply pointing to the doors where music and voices are filtering through.

'Yes, that's right,' she smiles.

Moving away my stomach does a somersault with trepidation. Pushing the doors, the noise has somehow ceased, there's a loud clearance of a throat and the bash of someone hitting a microphone on the top to make sure it's working. Shit, I timed that just wrong. There is what I presume to be the current Headmaster on the stage with microphone in hand.

'Good evening, ladies and gentleman,' he begins. 'I welcome you all to this first reunion of the class of 1989. Most of you have already found the bar, and you probably remember where everything else is, nothing has changed that much. Before I go on can I please ask you to put your hands together to thank our present sixth formers for giving up their time to look after you tonight?'

After one of those sickly pauses the clapping starts and subsides quickly.

'It is a long time since most of you were here, but...'

A crescendo of music comes across the speakers immediately recognisable as Pink Floyd, *Another Brick In the Wall;* one of my faves. The Headmaster's voice is drowned. He looks across crossly at the DJ trying to stop him but the DJ is in his own world ignoring everyone. It is pretty obvious no-one else wants to hear him either as the crowd has started mingling and talking once more. In a way I feel a bit sorry for him, he just looks around and says into the mike, 'Well have a good night,' and walks away but no-one is listening or can hear him properly.

Surveying the crowd as I move forward, I am surprised how many are already here as it's only about half an hour since kick off time. The bar is the most popular place as ever, quite of few of them just chatting, others queuing for a drink. Smiling to myself I think, *Bar, that's a laugh, two tables stuck together with a cloth slung over it.*

I might as well join the queue and wait my turn for a drink.

'What can I get you?' says a voice from behind the bar. It belongs to a young lad called Alex, according to his name tag.

'What have you got?' I ask.

'White, red or rose, beer, lager and soft drinks,' comes the reply.

'Just an orange juice, with ice if that's possible.'

Alex smirks, 'Ice! You have to be joking.'

I smile at him. 'Yeah I suppose I was.'

While I wait for the drink a sleek voice to my left says, 'Pam, long time no see.' That sounds like Kim, my best pal at school.

'Kim! It is you,' I exclaim as I turn towards her, beaming a smile. 'So glad you're here. Have you got a drink?' Before she can answer I lean forward whispering in her ear, 'If you drink gin then I've got some in my bag.'

'You sneak,' she smiles. 'The bar isn't very adventurous. Get me an orange and we'll make it interesting.'

'Coming up,' I reply.

Kim still has a curvy figure, and glancing across I notice that she has a wedding ring on and nicely manicured nails. We haven't been in touch since I left the area so there is likely to be a lot to catch up on.

'You look pretty good,' I comment as we move away to make gin and oranges, not the best but at least it is better than the alcohol on offer. 'How long have you been here?'

'About half an hour. Seen one or two so far. You haven't changed much either.'

Yeah, right. 'Thanks,' I reply, 'didn't like getting to the big four O this year. So fill me in. What have you been up to?'

'Hello, you two.'

As I swivel round I can see that Kim has already recognised him. 'Well I never – Scott!'

I am looking at him through downturned eyes wondering what he has done (or not done) with his life given the lines and crags in his face. Scott had been the gorgeous Adonis in our class; everyone wanted to know him, be with him or go out with him. I give him a peck on each cheek. His aftershave is strong but it still feels good to be near him. I don't think Kim knew anything about the two of us, not many did. I certainly kept it from my parents who would have gone ballistic, especially dad – his little girl misbehaving. If only he knew!

Kim breaks the silence. 'I hear you studied Architecture, did you get...'

A face catches my eye and I feel myself freeze. Sarah.

'Are you okay, Pam?' Scott cuts across Kim looking concerned. 'What's up? You look as though you have seen a ghost.'

'I suppose I have in a funny sort of way,' I say through gritted teeth, 'just the cow who picked on me. She was such a bitch.' My stomach is churning. Bloody hell. I'd forgotten all about her until now. I certainly wouldn't have bothered coming if she'd still been in my thoughts. I can't believe that after all these years she still has that sort of impact on me.

'Take a deep breath, sweetie,' Kim advises. 'She was a prize idiot at school. She did some terrible things to people - luckily I wasn't one of them - but I can remember picking you up on more than one occasion, getting you home in one piece.'

I turn so that I can't see her but I can't shake that image. Dragging a smile to my face I say, 'You were just about to say, Scott, please do continue,' as I gulp a large part of my drink in one go.

Scott is looking across at her. 'I remember her. She even tried to bully some of the boys. Anyway, yes, Kim, and yes, I have my own practice now.'

'Well done, you,' I reply. 'What sort of commissions do you get?'

'As you can imagine, with your own business you take a lot of small jobs with the hope they lead somewhere else. At the moment my claim to fame is the great mansion in Little Carlton. Do you know it? You can see it from the road.'

I look at Kim, who shrugs her shoulders.

'Sorry, Scott, I don't live here anymore. Haven't done so for quite a few years.'

He looks disappointed. 'Oh well, it doesn't matter. I am quite happy with how it's going. Here take my card, you never know when you may be wanting some work done.'

'Thanks,' I smile, taking the card. *Fat chance of that where I live.*

Kim takes one as well. 'You never know,' she says flicking the card in Scott's direction.

'See you later most likely,' Scott says as he moves away. Kim and I follow his form and then turn to each other smiling and giggling.

'He is still quite a hunk and he still knows it,' comments Kim.

'Better from the back than the front though, his face could do with a little TLC,' I comment. 'I have to pity his wife. She must have had a hell of a job keeping him in check if his past form is anything to go by.'

I take a sly look at Sarah. Turning to Kim I say, 'I see the bitch is in a crowd and looks like she is the centre of attention as always. Any idea who the guy is with her? He looks a right slimy creep.'

'It's Ascot,' Kim exclaims.

'Ascot? Crikey, I didn't recognise him. God, their wedding was such a bloody circus. I remember hearing that they acted like they were some kind of celebrities or royalty. Mind you,' I muse, 'there was a rumour that one of the wedding party got up to something scandalous.'

Kim looks quizzically at me.

'Oh, I don't have any of the juicy details, just some gossip I picked up before I left.'

Kim peers at the group across the room. 'That's Gemma talking with them, isn't it? That's odd, I seem to remember that she never got on with her.'

My stomach is doing somersaults. *Get a grip, Pam, you're a big girl now. Why should Sarah get the better of you?* It hadn't crossed my mind until just now but it would be great if she got a taste of her own medicine.

'I need the loo,' I say to Kim, 'see you later.'

Heading across the hall towards the toilet I spot Samuel, the religious guy. His parents were churchgoers, they never gave it a second thought that their son wasn't going to follow in their holy footsteps. He railed against them big time because they were so strict. I wonder if they ever knew what he got up to at school. Funny thing is he looks very monk-like now. I wonder what happened to him? Perhaps I might catch up with him later. The rest of the way I see faces I think I recognise, even after all these years.

Away in my own world, I grab the door on my way back out of the ladies. The next thing I literally bump into my nemesis.

'Mind where you're going,' comes the clipped faux-posh voice.

Looking up I blush. This can't be happening like this. 'Sorry,' but the anger rises in me. 'Oh, it's Sarah, isn't it?' My voice becomes hard, ready to do battle. *Easy girl, this is not the right time.*

'Yes', she says warily looking me up and down. 'I don't recognise you.'

'Oh, I guess not. Perhaps if you take yourself back to our school days you might. You were a right little shit then, weren't you?' I say, raising my eyebrows.

She actually looks chastened.

'Mind you, it wasn't just me, was it? Have you any idea of the living hell you dished out?'

Sarah is squirming.

'Seems you still think you're something from what I have already seen. I'll leave you to your pee. I am SURE,' I emphasise as I walk off, 'that I'll see you later.'

Letting out a large breath and composing myself, I re-enter the throng. More people seem to be turning up. Grabbing another drink, there is Gemma not too far away.

'Hi, Gemma,' I say as I come up to her.

'Pam, how lovely to see you.'

'Are you now friends with Sarah?' I ask. 'I saw you chatting earlier.'

'No, you have to be joking. Just thought I would interrupt their bunch of hangers on.'

'Glad to hear it,' I say. 'Nothing like making her squirm for what she did in the past. Anyway, congratulations, you seem to have done extremely well for yourself.'

'Thanks, what about you?'

'I don't live round here anymore. When I left I studied event management, got myself into some great places and ended up organising some high profile events.' I can see Gemma's eyes glaze over as I list some sporting events and trade shows. *End of conversation, I think.* 'Anyway I'm sure you don't really want to hear about me, Gemma. Lots more people to see!' As I move away I think that most people here, including Gemma, wouldn't believe where I am in my life now, anyway.

'I see you're not happy about someone here,' a voice says next to me stopping me in my tracks.

I recognise Alfie. 'I don't suppose you are, either.'

'No, not particularly, but *she* wasn't going to miss swanning around, was she?'

'Did you ever get retribution for what she did to your sister?' I ask.

'No, but I wish I could tonight.'

'Oh?' I say, raising an eyebrow, 'Anything in mind?'

He looks down at the cocktail stick in his hand that holds a pickled onion and a chunk of cheddar. 'I did consider attacking her with this.' He pauses as Ascot shuffles past us on the way to the toilets. 'Let's talk about something else. I don't want my evening ruined by that cow.'

'Hey, Alfie, did you ever follow through with your metalwork from school?' I ask. 'You were so artistic, you always said you felt you were being held back.'

'Yes, I did thanks. The Tanya/Sarah business didn't help. It sounds a bit daft really, I don't know if you remember but Tanya missed a lot of school after the incident. She was in therapy and all sorts, then mum moved her to another school. I was affected too. I felt so guilty because I hadn't been with her that night, so much so that I stopped my after school metalwork for quite a while. Mum tried to get me to go to a shrink as well but I refused. Mr Bolton actually pulled me to one side after our normal metalwork class and had a long chat with me. He was really cool. He really helped me get some way to being back on track. Even to the extent where he guided me towards the Blacksmithing College in Rutland. I am now a fully fledged blacksmith,' he comments with some pride. 'Thank God the horse world took a turn for the better. I have a mobile van for that and am in a community-based blacksmith's workshop where I do special commissions.' He pops the last of the cheese and onion into his mouth.

'Alfie, that really is good news! Make sure I get a card before I leave. You never know, I have some things up my sleeve that I may be able to use you for even though we are miles apart.'

Alfie is looking over my shoulder. 'Please excuse me, Pam. There is someone I would like to catch up with.' As he moves off to join some guy I don't recognise he turns with a wry smile and hands me the empty cocktail stick. 'If you get close to her Ladyship, stab her one from me.'

I smile to myself. Sarah had been with Ascot so long she probably wouldn't notice another little prick.

Helen Walcott, *Proud Single Mum*
– 7:45 pm

WE MAKE OUR way to the bar and I grab a white wine and soda and an orange juice for Chloe. I take a sip of the wine, which is, as expected, disgusting and look around. I haven't seen anyone I know yet, but then the light isn't great and my eyes weak with my contacts in. Vanity always triumphs over necessity and my usual glasses are at home.

'Do you want me to drive home?' asks Chloe, nodding towards my drink.

I shake my head and grimace, 'This will be the last. It's Dutch courage concealed as cat's piss -God knows where they got it from - and very weak. I'll be fine by the time we want to leave.'

'The offer is there if you change your mind.'

We glance around the hall. 'Seen anyone you know yet, mum?'

I shake my head. 'Not yet. Everybody is older. I probably won't recognise anyone.'

'It's early yet. Give it time.' She's sipping her drink and still looking at her mobile, scrolling and tapping out replies with speed. It drives me mad, but I don't want to bicker, not tonight. Not when I feel stressed enough anyway.

'Well, if it isn't Helen Walcott! How the devil are you?'

A man is talking to me, but I have no idea who he is. I search his face for the boy he once was, who seems to remember me and I draw a blank and paint a rictus smile on my confused face. He doesn't seem to notice and keeps talking: 'So what do you do with yourself? You moved away didn't you? Weren't you up the duff? You've still got a nice arse - even for an old bird!' He's laughing at his own appalling comments and it comes to me - Philip Morris! He always did open his gob before he'd engaged his brain. I know he's harmless, but I really don't want to get landed with him for the whole night.

'And who is this little hottie?' he says eyeing Chloe up. 'You fancy a drink darlin'?'

Chloe looks up from her phone and smiles at him, 'Thank you but it's a free bar and you're an old man so please go away or I shall scream loudly.'

I burst out laughing and Philip looks confused. 'Can't a bloke offer a girl a drink these days... the world's gone bloody mad. Bring back the 90s,' and much to our relief, he shuffles off, huffing and puffing to himself.

'What a horrible man!' says Chloe. 'Surely he wasn't a friend of yours, mum?'

'Oh, he's harmless. Friends? Not really, but this woman was. Julia!'

'Helen! Oh my God! I was hoping you'd be here!' We hug and hold onto one another in a tight embrace.

'Helen. You look amazing! How are you? It's been too long. Listen! They are playing our song!' And sure enough I hear Starship's *Nothing's Gonna Stop Us Now* and we both sing the lyrics laughing, the shit wine imbibing me with a spark of excitement.

'I've missed you, Helen Walcott!' she beams at me her eyes singing. 'We need to catch up,' she casts around for some free seats and points. 'You have a drink? Let's sit over there and you can tell me what you've been doing for the last twenty years!'

'Philip hasn't got any better has he?' Julia laughs. 'Still as blunt as a sledgehammer.'

'Julia, this is my daughter, Chloe.' I draw her near and Julia gives her a big hug.

'Gorgeous like your mum,' she smiles. 'How old are you now then? Do you know your mum was my best friend at school. Thick as thieves we were-' and she's off chatting away, walking towards the seats arm in arm with Chloe. It's like the last twenty years never happened and I feel a swell of happiness at the joy of someone knowing the young me like Julia does.

'I'm going to find the loo, mum. It looks like you and Julia have a lot of catching up to do.'

'Are you sure, love? You're welcome to join us.'

'Yes, join us, Chloe,' says Julia. 'I can tell you all your mum's juicy secrets.' She smiles at her.

'I'll look forward to that!' says Chloe laughing and wanders off while Julia and I take a seat.

'I'm sorry I just disappeared like that Julia. Did you get my letter?'

She nods. 'Yes, I did. I guessed your bitch of a mother had something to do with it. I was sad you never kept in touch though. I checked the letterbox for weeks. I did see your mum from time to time, but every time I asked after you she changed the subject.' She sips her drink. 'I had a tough time after you left. The gossips had a field day about me you know. I was called all sorts.'

'But you never got pregnant did you? I committed the cardinal sin.'

'Who was it, Helen?' Julia really looks at me then. 'Have you ever told anyone? Does Chloe even know?'

I shake my head, 'Nope and I don't know if she ever will. There's never been the right time.'

Julia sighs and pats my hand. 'Well, she's your daughter. I'm sure you know best. Have you seen that creep is here, Mr Butterford. What a perv!'

'I feel sorry for him, in that wheelchair.'

'Seriously? He destroyed me and God knows who else. I loathe him. Just because you're old doesn't absolve you from your past misdemeanours.'

'No, of course not. I'm sorry, Julia. I'm really sorry and I wish I'd been here for you. You must have been so scared of him and of coming to school.'

'Water under the bridge,' she smiles. 'I'm just glad you came tonight. Let's hope it's the first of many. Cheers.' And we attempt to clink our plastic cups when we are joined by Jamie and Ryan, two boys who had been in our form. They are hilarious and have smuggled some decent wine into the event, which, despite my protestations that I'm driving, seems to keep filling my plastic cup. Chloe is sitting at the end of the table and I can see her watching me. I'm someone she never knew in this company and I like it! I've been a mum all of my adult life and it's really, really nice to remember the girl I once was.

'It must have been hard, having a baby so young,' says Ryan. 'You've obviously done a brilliant job!' He raises his cup and toasts me - he's tipsy now - but I feel proud and I toast myself too.

'I just got on with it. I had no choice. What about you?'

'Me? Oh, after a few years of being a repressed arse, I finally accepted what everyone else seemed to have guessed and came out. The rest, as they say, is history.' And he glances at Jamie lovingly, reaches over and squeezes his hand.

We talk some more and then dance to the crap songs that mean so much to us all, that transport us to another time before we had to grow up and we laugh. We laugh a lot and I realise that despite hating this place, despite not seeing these people for more than twenty years and despite only knowing them for such a short time in my life, I have missed them. Thoughts of driving home have left my head and I want to get really, really drunk and not think about tomorrow. Jamie is holding up the empty wine bottle and asking if we think they'll let him out, so he can sneak to the off-license and buy some more wine.

'I doubt it,' says Julia.

I offer to do a bar run and tell Chloe to come and help me when I get served.

'Okay, I'm just going to call Jack and I'll come to the bar when I've spoken to him.' She leaves me squished against bodies I do not recognise, swishing the remains of the decent wine around my plastic beaker, savouring it.

Julia Forest, *Tank Girl to Child Protector* – 7:45 pm

THE SECOND ONE is also easier than I thought it would be.

In the crowded hall, as soon as I see a striking forty-something in a remarkable green dress my heart flips over and forgives Helen her disappearance from my life just when I needed her. I wend my way through the crowds to her side. We shriek our helloes but the hug we give each other absolves the past and flies across the years.

'You look great,' I say as she is joined by a young beauty who can only be her daughter.

'This is Chloe,' she says with a lift of the chin that tells me all of Helen's teenage pain must have been worth it.

We stand grinning at one another like idiots until we do the grown-up thing and sit down to catch up.

'Married?' she asks. 'Children?'

'Yes. To both. He's lovely. The girls are... well,' I shrug. How can I say they're the most precious people in my life and I would commit murder to protect them? 'They're lovely, too,' I end lamely.

But Helen's a mother and she grins knowingly. 'Why didn't you bring... what's he called?'

'Mike.'

'Why didn't you bring him?'

'Things to do,' I say.

'Like what?'

'It's a long story but I have unfinished business with Butterford.'

'Ugh, that perv!'

'Indeed.'

But before she can put me on the spot and ask me what I intend to do, we are joined by Ryan and Jamie and we clatter off into exclamations of wonder at who we've all become.

I'm not sure who I am though. Have I come back to Hercules Clay like a Valkyrie to darken Butterford's days or am I simply going to leave the past behind? I have long outgrown the agony of humiliation but am certain no girl I know, or don't know for that matter, is ever going to go through what happened to me. I know it could have been much worse. The cases I've had to deal with as the school's Child Protection Officer would harrow up anyone's soul: fathers pimping their daughters; drug dealers tempting the truants with a taste to take away their inhibitions; all the young female bodies treated as just that – bodies, not people. And all of that goes on despite the efficiency of protecting the vulnerable. It's so streamlined these days, what with the MultiAgency Safeguarding Hub and the swiftly held strategy meetings run by a Local Area Designated Officer. Butterford's feet wouldn't touch the ground now...but then, then he could do as he liked, almost with the Head's blessing.

Iain Wilson, *"Legitimate Businessman"* – 7:45 pm

BEFORE I CAN take a single step towards Katy I feel a hand clamp down on my shoulder making me flinch.

'Bloody hell, it's Iain!'

I rivet a smile onto my face and turn to see which of my old mates has clocked me. I stare at him, conscious of trying not to look at his bald head. I fix my eyes instead on the greying goatee. None of this is helping me dredge up an inkling of who this guy is. It's like playing *Guess Who* but where there's a couple of decades between the two sets of pictures. At least he doesn't have glasses on to compensate for deteriorating eyesight.

'Ha! You probably don't recognise me without my glasses! I had laser surgery a few years ago.'

I mentally flick through the options, cross-matching with rough face shape. 'Neil?' I say tentatively.

'Yeah, how you doing, mate? Bloody long time no see.'

'Yeah, good thanks.' Neil was one of the outer circle of our little clique, a group of counter-culture rebels who rejected the nauseating popularity of the Footy Lads, with their gelled hair, good looks and vacuous egotism (not to mention the undercurrent of racism and misogyny). We weren't exactly purer-than-pure either, nor total drop-out material, but we were smart enough and socially aware enough to spot a bunch of self-obsessed wankers when we saw them. We used to go around to Neil's house to watch his dad's *Monty Python* videos but he never tended to join in with our own games of footy at lunch-time, nor show an appreciation of the indie music scene, which seemed immensely important to us at the time. But he was generally a good lad.

I glance over his shoulder and see another vaguely familiar face hovering behind him. It squeezes a tight smile at me.

'You remember Sam, don't you?' says Neil jerking a thumb back at the owner of the face.

'Yeah, of course.' Who could forget? Now *that* was a family with issues. His parents were proper God Squad; fundamental creationists, for crying out loud. At the turn of the millennium? Jeez. We, on the other hand, were a blend of disinterested agnostics and supercharged atheists which of course meant that we used to wind Sam up with evidence of how bonkers his mum and dad were. And to be fair to the guy, he did develop his own views which caused no end of conflict at home, which he would then bitterly retell back at school to much shock, outrage and hilarity. Ah, happy days.

We pass a few minutes discussing What We're Up To These Days (Neil's a plasterer, Sam doesn't say), wondering if Matty Jones is coming (doesn't look like it) before moving on to the new décor, the structural changes to the old place, the signs on the corridor that profess a zero tolerance towards bullying. I know it's big news these days, especially with social media, but I can't say I recall a lot of bullying going on back in my day. Maybe we were lucky. There were a couple of rough moments that I remember but generally we were an inclusive bunch of outsiders, enough safety in numbers and enough bloody-minded attitude to cause needy dickheads to give us a miss. We also had Jason in our little gang. The PE teachers tried to get him to join the woeful rugby team because they needed someone built like a tank, but Jase was far too into his grunge scene to take up anything so elitist as rugger. I wonder what he's doing now.

'I don't suppose you kept in touch with Jason?' I ask Neil.

'Yeah, I have actually. We both go and watch Mansfield Town when they play at home.'

'Blimey, never had you down as masochists. But he wasn't interested in coming tonight? Plenty of repressed pain to be uncovered here, eh?' I wink at Sam. He doesn't respond. I get the feeling he doesn't like me very much.

'Ah, well, no, um,' Neil mumbles, 'he was going to come but he gave me a call this afternoon. Bit of a family crisis. His daughter, she's at college in Nottingham, Christ, that makes me feel old, well her boyfriend's in hospital in intensive care, so they've been down to the QMC to be with his family.'

'Ouch. Is it serious, then?' I take a sip of wine, whilst trying to show some interest.

'Well, he's in a coma. He got badly beaten up last night by some drug-pushing bastards and Jase reckons he might not pull through. Becca, that's his lass, is absolutely devastated. Jase said that, of all the blokes she could have chosen to go out with, this young Tom was sound. Well, the police are involved, obviously, and they say the usual but we don't know if we'll ever find out who did it. Bastards. I told Jase that he should go down to Sneinton with some of his mates from the gym and beat the truth out of the local druggies. But anyway, that's why he's not here tonight. Bedside vigil and everything. Are you alright, Iain?'

The blood has drained from my face. My mouth has dried up, my throat has tightened and my stomach is churning. I did this. I did this to an old mate, to his daughter, to her boyfriend. I feel sick. I've existed in such a bubble, isolated from my decisions, that I've never had them presented so starkly back into my life, into a special, personal part of who I am and where I came from.

'Uhh, yeah, just a bit of a long day. And, I'm not good with hospital stuff. Had a bad... leg thing once.' I'm wittering. I need to get away from this. 'I just need to go and get some air. I'll catch you later, yeah?'

'No worries, mate. Good to see you again.' Neil pats me on the shoulder as I leave while Sam gives me another thin smile.

I take a large swig of wine to relieve the dryness in my mouth and step outside into the courtyard beyond the hall. A new building stares back at me, occupying a space previously held by an area of tarmacked playground. I find myself wanting to rewind back to those days in the early nineties, before they built on top of my memories, before I started dealing, before I left a broken home, before my mum and dad split up, before Ella died.

Jesus. What a mess. How can I sort this out? Flowers to Jason's daughter? Construct some kind of fake retribution? I guess we've got the wherewithal to set up some low-level idiots from St Ann's or the Meadows, make it look like they were done over because they were the ones who attacked this Tom. I'm not stupid, I know that this isn't going to be as effective as sentencing the real perps (which absolutely ain't going to happen) but a bit of revenge beating helps people come to terms with things. And if he dies, who's to know that they weren't the ones who did it. And if he lives, well, everyone will be so happy that they won't care some innocent druggies got a pasting. Win win. I'll get Simmo on to it tomorrow.

A movement out of the corner of my eye makes me look down the outside wall of the school hall towards the path to the other blocks. I'm sure someone just stuck their head around the corner and then pulled it back again. Odd. Well, I'm in no mental shape to talk to more old faces right now, so I may as well go for a wander around the old place. I set off towards the edge of the building where I think I saw the head. As I turn the corner I see a figure in some kind of grey track suit, hands in pockets, head down, nonchalantly heading away from me. The nonchalant attitude isn't very convincing because he's walking at quite a rapid pace. He turns another right hand corner and disappears. I can't be arsed to follow so mooch around the new buildings, peering through windows and smiling wryly as the sight of old, forgotten parts of my life unlock memories of when I was a kid. Dropping my empty plastic wine glass into a nearby bin, I look out across the playing field where we used to have lunchtime kickabouts, the darkening twilight making them seem even more out of synch with the past I remember. I see the small grove of trees at the edge, close to the ponds and the old disused railway line and the aftertaste of the wine goes sour in my mouth. That's where Karl Stamford picked on me after we lost Ella.

I had just needed some time on my own so had gone down to the trees; he just needed some entertainment. At that time I wasn't the fit, capable exponent of mixed martial arts that I am now, and he was bigger than me. And then Danny Griggs magically appeared and told Karl to fuck off, which he grudgingly did. That's how it started. That's why Danny died.

I shudder at these memories. I try not to think about them, focus on the here and now, but sometimes they break through the wall I've thrown around them. I guess a school reunion wasn't the smartest move for someone haunted by ghosts and with several tooled-up skeletons in the closet.

Amanda Shaw, *Woman Reborn*
– 7:45 pm

I NOTICE A COUPLE of women deep in conversation. I think one is Gemma. I'd envied her at school. She always seemed so popular and well balanced. Looks like she's done well for herself too.

I move a little closer and realise it's Liza she's talking to. She's looking good despite the obvious scarring to her face after the incident with Karl Stamford in the chemistry lab. I don't envy her scars, but it hurts deeply when you know your own scars are all internal and invisible to outsiders. Only Sandra knows all the gory details of what happened to me shortly before I left school and the devastating events that followed as a result.

I often wonder if it was just a coincidence when she was allocated as my counsellor after I was sectioned. I didn't recognise her when we first met, but she remembered me instantly. Strange how we'd both eventually ended up living in Mansfield after we'd left school in Newark. She'd become a successful psychiatrist and counsellor and I'd become a physical and mental wreck. Her counselling helped tremendously and over time we became really close. So close she had to leave her job and we moved out of County where we set up our alternative therapy business. She taught me everything I know and for once I was an eager and responsive pupil. We run a very successful business and hopefully will be together for the rest of our days. I'd like to say I'm happy, but there's always that one open wound that refuses to close and fade into a soft edged scar. Unlike Liza, no one here can see or sympathise with the emotional damage I carry everywhere or the pain of being considered damaged goods for most of my life. It's taken me to reach forty before I realised none of it was really my fault at all. My parents, who started the process are long gone and hopefully the main perpetrator will get his just desserts tonight one way or another.

It's difficult to believe or imagine all these middle-aged faces were just hormone rampant teenagers back at school. We're all about to enter our fifth decade on the mortal coil and no doubt some will be looking forward with unshakeable optimism while others will be dreading whatever the future holds. Life begins at forty they say. It can also end. Both my parents were killed in a fortunate accident when they were forty and I'd be a hypocrite if I said I was sorry or that I missed them. They were never parents to me, but it was not something I talked about or even understood back when I was at school.

Only Sandra knows all the details of my agonising childhood, the grotesque events at school which resulted in completely wrecking my future and the shame I carry for the things I did while my mind was deranged. It's taken years of therapy to understand the reasons why I behaved as I did and even longer trying to forgive myself. I'm not sure I ever will completely, but at least now I can function in society and feel I have something worthwhile to offer others in the future. That's a massive turnaround and mainly due to Sandra. When I left the house earlier this evening I felt incomplete without her company, but no way could we both be here.

I remember turning thirty. That's when I crashed. I was still fifteen in my head. They say if you suffer trauma you can remain mentally stuck at the age when it happened. I think trauma started soon after I was born one way or another, but I guess I sort of got used to it and it became the norm for me. I recall little from my childhood apart from the nights when *he* came to my room and carried out what he called our secret games. Not the sort of play I defined as fun and it always left me in pain and tears. He'd bring me sweets and comics the morning after, so I thought I must be doing something good as he never gave my mother any presents, only black eyes and bruises. A broken arm once too, but she told the doctor she'd fallen over and told *him* she knew she deserved it and was sorry. I thought maybe that's what grown-ups did and never mentioned any of this to anyone.

I did try talking to my mother once about *him*. I knew she didn't like me and often bashed me about a bit if I didn't complete my chores, but I thought maybe she'd be able to stop him because I knew she liked him all to herself. She'd scream at him if he came home late or talked to women in the pub so it seemed to me she wouldn't want to share him with anyone. But when I told her what he did to me at nights, she screamed even louder, called me a spiteful bitch, a vicious liar and took a belt to me before locking me in the cellar for hours. I kept schtum after that. Convinced myself I must have got it all wrong and that must be my role in life. If I said nothing then life was easier all round, tolerable even. I was quiet in school, kept my head down and was careful with words. That didn't make me very popular or bring me many friends.

When I started at Hercules Clay it wasn't so easy to be ignored. I was an early developer and had boobs and pubes by that time. Funnily enough as I grew breasts and filled out my father left me alone and despite the relief I still felt guilty, thought I'd done something wrong and it was all my fault. Boys at school were always giving me the once over and making lewd suggestions so I just carried on doing what *he'd* taught me. I guess I thought that was all I was good for. But the thing was, even though I was out of control, it was the one thing I felt I had control over. I could allow or refuse their advances, decide where, when and how the encounters were carried out and walk away when I'd had enough, sometimes leaving them begging for more. I always insisted they use protection. I wasn't totally stupid and certainly didn't want an unwanted pregnancy or disease. But then...

I shudder as my thoughts begin to travel down a path I can't bear to revisit. I put up my mental road block as Sandra has taught me to do and head to the bar for a refill. I watch the DJ on the stage while I wait, the music evoking a multitude of mixed feelings. I've always had a passion for music through most eras of my life, but this nineties stuff always reminds me of the disastrous path I'd chosen during my school years and how it turned me into a no hoper with a catastrophic future lying ahead.

Someone taps me on the shoulder and I turn sharply. He peers at my name badge, but I have no need to do likewise as I recognise Ascot instantly. He'd been one of my first and it was a definite underwhelming experience. A ram, bam, thank you ma'am, ten second wonder encounter.

'Sandra,' he exclaims with a sickly grin. 'I didn't know you were here. Good to see you, though I must say I'd never have recognised you. You've really changed over the years.' He seems a little unsteady, slurring his words and reeking of alcohol.

'Oh, surely not, but if I have I hope it's for the better,' I manage to stutter through another plastic smile.

'So how are you? What are you getting up to these days?'

I relate the details I've practised, but sense he's not really listening. His expression is unreadable, but is making me feel a little uneasy for some reason.

'You married? Any kids?'

Just the word stabs me in the heart.

'No and no, but I am in a relationship.' I still can't decipher his expression, but sense there's some lust in there and that needs quashing immediately.

'I can't get over how different you look. If anyone had asked me who you are I'd never have guessed, though you do look familiar. You remind me of someone else from school, but I can't recall the name.'

I need to change the subject fast.

'Great turn out isn't it? Good to see all the old faces and hear all the old songs.' Blur's *Charmless Man* is the current tune and it seems appropriate.

'I'm not a fan of this sort of stuff.' He pulls a distorted face. 'I prefer the classics. I still remember your singing when you played Maria in *West Side Story*. You had an exquisite voice. Maybe you can get up on stage later and entertain us with some decent music. Can I treat you to some Dutch courage as an incentive?'

"Thanks, but I don't drink.' Admittedly Sandra has a decent singing voice, but we didn't anticipate she'd be remembered for it or be asked to demonstrate. I feel my face redden as I search for an excuse. Much as I love music, I can hold a tune about as well as a jellied eel so there's no way I'm getting up on any stage.

'I might have guessed. You always were a good, rule abiding girl. I often regret not asking you out as I really fancied you. I'd sit behind you in Maths admiring that little beauty spot on the back of your neck.'

He bends forward unsteadily, his eyes drifting towards my neck. Sandra didn't mention him in our discussions about school days. She probably didn't realise he was interested in her.

Britpop segues into the Meatloaf anthem, *I Would Do Anything For Love,* blaring from the speakers and a speck of panic stirs in my torso. I need some air and time to think.

'Excuse me. I need the ladies room.' I begin backing away in order to avoid his probing eyes searching for the beauty spot I haven't got.

'Catch you later then, Sandra. Come over and meet my wife and friends. I'm sure they'd love to hear you sing. And I'd love to get to know more about you, if you catch my gist.' He winks and breaks into a leery grin simultaneously.

I head across the hall and am relieved to find the doors to the courtyard are unlocked. I step outside, take deep gulps of the balmy night air and try to order my thoughts. My mind drifts back again to that afternoon when it happened. Yes, I'd have done anything for love, or even to be liked, accepted, but much as I was an easy lay and willing to oblige far too many boys it was always on my terms and with my permission. I guess it made me feel in charge, gave me some power I couldn't acquire through other methods. But, there were limits and lines I wouldn't cross.

Is Ascot more astute than I thought? Has he cottoned on? Admittedly, Sandra and I don't look like twins, but there are similarities these days. We have an image to live up to in our line of work, so keep our hair short and neat, our make-up understated and our clothing chic yet classy. But then he hasn't seen her since school and seems to be mentally searching for the name of someone else he remembers. I can't allow him to succeed or my cover is blown, then all hell could break out.

I have an eyeliner pencil with me so can easily create a pretty little mark on the back of my neck. I know exactly what Sandra's looks like so it's no problem. But I do need to think of a way to avoid exposing my masquerade so no one realises I can't sing a note. Maybe I need to develop a sore throat or claim a recent larynx operation. Perhaps I should phone Sandra and see if she can come up with an idea? No, I have to prove I can face things head on alone now.

I gaze around the courtyard while I think, remembering how it looked back then, all the places I'd hide cigarettes and booze to keep me going between lessons and break times. The trees and bushes that concealed my wanton activities with boys who knew they could lose their virginity or practice their technique with the easy school slapper. I don't particularly blame them or hate them for it, but realise now what a simpleton I was to believe it might make them care for me in any way.

I turn to go inside knowing I need to visit the ladies in order to acquire the necessary beauty spot and compose myself. Ascot will hopefully be too inebriated by the time I return to bother with any more interrogations or requests. I really hope the toilets have changed since school as that's where it happened and I need no reminder to stir up the events in my head.

From the corner of my eye I spot a figure cautiously lurking amongst the bushes. Definitely a male and it looks like... no, it can't be; no way would he receive an invite to a school reunion and I feel pretty sure he'd have no wish to gatecrash. I stay transfixed as he moves cautiously around the edges of the yard, then turns to face me. His eyes meet mine and my worst fears are confirmed. It is him. Karl Stamford.

Worries about Ascot, being recognised, singing on stage all fade into insignificance. Should Karl Stamford recognise me there are far more serious things to fear, especially if he's discovered the truth about the last time we met. Memories are rushing into dark places like rats in the sewers as I dash towards the doors of the nearest ladies room.

Gemma Robinson, *Business Queen* – 7:55 pm

I DRAG MY THOUGHTS back to the present. Liza seems to have disappeared. I've checked everywhere I can think of. Then I have an unnerving thought. She wouldn't – would she? I'm almost running in my haste to get to our old Chemistry lab. It's dark in the corridor. As my eyes adjust, I can see a slight movement behind the glass panel of the door. With care, I ease it open. She's standing near the windows. The lab looks different in the dim, shadowy light. I realise it's been changed again since the refurbishment after the fire damage. Liza turns around.

'It's the first time I've been back in here and nothing looks like I remember.'

'No, it does look different now. But, Liza, why have you come up here? Why put yourself through it? Surely, it's not a pleasant feeling being here where you...' I can't finish what I was going to say. For one thing, my throat is too tight and my guilt is eating away at my stomach. For another, I don't need to say any more. Of all people, she wouldn't have come here lightly. It must be something she needs to do.

'I'm killing the ghosts and trying to find some measure of acceptance. I can't go on like this, Gemma. I caught a glimpse of Karl and realised that I'm still so angry. And I've tried every kind of therapy I could find. Nothing helps in the long term. I guess I thought coming in here might... Oh God, I don't know – something. I'm desperate. Somehow, I need to put this all to rest.'

Her voice breaks as the tears take over. I put my arms around her. She is trembling so hard that I'm not sure I can hold her up, but hold her I must. What the hell is my guilt in comparison to all this pain she still carries around with her? Day in, day out, for all these years. I thought she was okay, with the business and everything, but what do I know? I never talk to her about any of it. While Liza recounts the recurring nightmares, her memories of that day, I can feel the control I'd always kept over my own recollections slipping from me. Being in the lab with her, listening to her, everything that I had locked away in a separate part of my mind is in danger of coming loose. One word was all it took to unlock the box and let all the nasties out. She says it – "flesh" – and the intervening years sweep away. I'm back in the lab with the smell of burning hair and charring flesh. The sight of Danny becoming a column of flame, as I watch. The terror on Karl's face. All in the blink of an eye. This is what I have buried deep, deep down. For one terrible moment the stink is so vivid, so real in my nostrils, that I think I am about to throw up. I start to let go of Liza, intent only on finding a sink but she clings on tighter and I have to swallow hard, the scent and taste of vomit rising up in my nose and throat.

Clutching Liza, feeling in my body the hurt she carries in hers, makes me realise that my feelings have been self-indulgent, childish. I've always put myself first, focused on what I wanted, *my* achievements, *my* business, *my* glittering career. Now, faced with Liza's agony, I see myself as I am. Someone who walks away from friends and family, people who need me, unless it suits my purpose to be involved. And it so rarely does. The charity donations and my reputation as an ethical employer are just a front. Below the surface, I'm not really that person. It is all down to guilt. Not just swapping places and escaping a lifetime of scarring and pain, although that is part of it. The rest is down to being such a bad friend, being repulsed by her appearance early on when she first came out of hospital. I disentangled myself from her when she needed me most. With shame I know it is not just Liza I have let slip from my life, other friends have been abandoned, lovers dismissed when they tried to get too close. Even mum and dad, my brother and his family, are all fast becoming strangers. I can't seem to keep any kind of relationship going without starting to feel stifled and anxious to be free of any demands on me.

As she hiccups and talks, pouring out her grief, I pay attention to Liza in a way I have never done before. She tells me about her depression, the fact that her mother helps run the business a lot of the time because Liza cannot always cope with the stresses of decision making, staff problems, the ongoing day to day minutae of keeping a business afloat.

'I'm past forty, Gemma, and I've come to believe that I'll never have the "normal" life I once saw for myself – children, a loving partner. Someone I can tell how I feel without feeling judged. Someone who won't flinch when they see me without makeup.'

I knew none of this. Why would I? I had deliberately distanced myself from it all.

'When I was burned, on top of everything else, I lost friends I had trusted, who I thought cared about me. Everything I thought I knew, everything changed. They – *you* - didn't come near me and I needed you.' Her tone is accusatory and I don't blame her. 'Since then I've found trust hard. Any men that I ever let into my life end up turning away from me. They stay for a while and then meet someone whole and undamaged and they leave me. I think it's too late for me now. Nothing will ever be the way I hoped.'

I'm not a crier. I keep too tight a rein on myself to give way easily. All that I have made of myself has been down to control. And yet, as Liza and I hang on to each other, I cry tears of my own with the realisation of how badly I have let her down and failed to be the friend she needed. All that guilt was more about how I felt rather than how she felt. I vow to her and myself to put that right: I must and will do better by Liza. She's my friend, once as close as a sister.

We sit up in the lab until we feel able to rejoin the reunion downstairs. The talk moves to less emotional territory and, at last, we are able to chat freely like the best of friends we were – and would be again. I had promised.

As we are trying to repair our smudged make-up, there is a tentative tap on the door, which opens slowly. It's Jamie, come to see if he can help. With a sense of shock, I realise that he knew we were here and has been waiting for the right moment.

'Do you need anything?' he asks, waggling a full bottle of wine and three beakers.

Liza laughs and nods. 'I think Gemma and I could do with a drink.'

Jamie has judged it just right. I sigh with relief, it seems that Liza and I have cleared the air and she believes the honesty of my promise to stay in touch, and my offer of a supportive shoulder and sanctuary when life gets too difficult. Jamie pours us a drink each, which goes down quickly. We throw the beakers in the bin, gather up our things and make our way back to the hall.

Jamie's taken Liza off to chat to Ryan, who's looking a bit lost over in a corner on his own. I see Ascot glance over towards Ryan but he makes no move to join him. Sarah is keeping her back turned. She never did like Ryan and clearly nothing has changed. Ascot catches my eye and smiles with a soppy look on his face. Jesus! Don't tell me I'm going to have to fight him off later. Ridiculous I know, given what Liza and I have just been crying and emotional about, but I badly need a smoke. I'm feeling jangled and a cigarette will calm me down, I hope. There was a small courtyard outside where the older teachers used to go for a fag – they thought we didn't know about it but we did, and it's just the place I need to be now.

Hannah Parker, *was a proper Charlie* – 8:05 pm

THANKFULLY THE HEADMASTER'S speech doesn't last very long. The interruption by the DJ after a couple of minutes is a stroke of timing perfection.

After Lucy has downed her drink during the speech, she is predictably desperate for the loo.

'Come on, let's use the short cut at the side of the hall.'

I drag Lucy through the crowd of people, our heels noisy on the wooden floor.

Some people are already half-cut and dancing on the stage this early in the night. I recognise a couple of them from my class, but they're not people I want to speak with, or care to catch up with. It's clear they haven't changed; demanding to be the centre of attention just like at school. I notice one of them is gyrating against one of the old teachers. Crikey! I spot some of the current students taking photos of them; those pictures and videos will be all over social media in five minutes. I'm thankful that I have nothing to do with the online world.

'God, Hannah I feel pissed already,' Lucy snorts.

'I'm not surprised, this drink is so strong. You do know the bar is free all night? You don't have to drink it like someone is going to start charging you. We've only been here less than an hour, Lucy.'

Lucy giggles, 'Okay, I get your point. I will just have a half of that delicious potion next time. The barman is proper fit.'

'Lucy, he is probably half your age. Please don't go hitting on the six formers.'

'What do you take me for? Anyway, I have my eyes on a few dishy men I've seen lurking around at the edge of the dance floor.' She grins wickedly.

'You little slut,' I laugh delightedly.

'Hey, I'm single. If they're on their own, they are fair game. I've checked out their ring fingers to make sure there is no evidence of a ring or a tan line. You can never be sure.' She giggles.

'You're incorrigible, Lucy Longton. Now come with me before you wet yourself.'

This earns me a few more snorts from Lucy.

I steer her to the toilets. A good-looking bloke catches Lucy's hand as she is about to pass him. Lucy giggles and lets herself be led into a twirl before he lets her go and we carry on up the corridor.

'Oh my God, he's so fit. You totally have to introduce me to him later,' Lucy says, too loudly.

'You have your vodka eyes in tonight. You think everyone is fit. I'm trying to think who it is. I recognise him. I just cannot pinpoint his name.' I turn, trying to get another look at him, but he's melted into the crowd.

'Yuk, your toilets are as horrible as the ones at my school. Why do all schools have horrid toilets? I guess it's one way of putting students off hanging around in them. Although it didn't stop me at school.' Lucy giggles.

'Lucy!' I say, not actually shocked by this revelation.

'What? Every kid has a fumble in the school toilets. It was like a rite of passage or something. You never know, I might just re-enact my school days if I get my hands on that fit bloke.'

Laughing and shaking my head, I push Lucy into the toilets. Luckily, there is no queue.

I wait outside just in case Lucy needs me. Toilets; now they are something that most people never give a second thought to. Once I'd nearly wet myself waiting for the cubicle to be free when having to use the male toilets at school. I'd never felt comfortable using the urinals. Toilets during school days was where anything went. The teachers rarely checked on them, so they were a bullying hotspot. At lunchtimes I used to go to the local shopping area and use the toilets. The issue had become a massive news story a few years back for transgender people. It is good to see that most of the coffee shop chains are mostly unisex nowadays. A much better way to avoid any embarrassing issues. Even the toilets at my friend's school are gender-neutral – all very forwarding thinking, but I bet it still doesn't stop the kids from getting bullied.

'What the hell are you daydreaming about again? Is that special cocktail making you reminisce about your own toilet experience?' Lucy says smiling, her words starting to slur.

I smile, no point dragging up the past. Some people just don't understand the hardships of others' lives. Especially Lucy. Everything is so simple to her. She wouldn't care who used the toilets, an alien could rock up, and she wouldn't bat an extended eyelash. That's what I love about her.

'Right before we have another of those wonderful drinks, why don't you take me to that room where the 'incident' happened?' Lucy's voice lowers into a whisper; well she obviously thinks it's a whisper. For everyone else it would be their normal pitch.

'Okay, come on. Better go now before you get too wasted.'

I take Lucy through the corridors and up the stairs to the science lab. A few people are milling about and peering into rooms, reminiscing about times gone by, as I have.

'This is it, the science lab or chem lab as some kids called it.'

Stopping outside the room, I think back to that day. The smell of the burning flesh, the screaming of the other students. I wasn't involved in any of that group. There always seemed to be constant dramas going on with some of the kids at school. But I'd felt so sorry for the girl, Liza, well and Danny of course. Being left with scarring was one thing – being dead was something you could never get over.

'So, this is it? The place where that boy died? Wow, nothing like this ever happened at my school. I wonder if he's here tonight. Not the dead one, of course,' Lucy snorts, 'that... what's his name that did it? Or that girl, Liza, that got burned?' Lucy says.

'Danny Griggs was the boy who died. Karl Stamford was the boy that caused the fire.' I tell her for the millionth time. I'd seen Liza and Gemma together earlier. I'm surprised Gemma has come; she is probably the most well-known figure of the school year.

I peer in through the window. The light is on, so someone has apparently had the same idea. Then again I bet everyone from those days wants to have a look. I can see two women embracing, one of them is Liza. I can see the scars, even though she clearly has a lot of make-up on. But then again so do I. It's amazing what a good mask make-up is. The other person I think is Gemma, but cannot be sure from this angle. They are having a moment, and it isn't one I wish to interrupt.

'What's happening?' Lucy says, in a real whisper this time.

'I think we better come back later. I don't want to intrude on whatever is happening in there.'

Thinking back, I'm sure I'd seen someone in the shadows when we'd arrived. What with everything that has happened, the name badges and meeting Philip it had slipped my mind. I wonder if that had been Karl? Surely he wouldn't have come tonight – wouldn't have been invited? If Liza is already this emotional, seeing him wouldn't help her. I hope to God I'm mistaken. It could have been anyone waiting in the shadows. I'm unsure if I should go in and mention it to them.

'Look, let's go and get another drink, and then we can come back to the science lab after,' I say to Lucy, deciding it isn't the right time to interrupt them, and pretty sure that Karl wouldn't want to come to this reunion, even if he knew about it.

'Sounds like a plan. I really want to see inside.'

'You're so bloodthirsty.'

'As I told you, nothing like this ever happened at my school. I must see the scene of the crime. You know I love my crime films.'

'Come on Miss Marple, let's get you a drink.'

Laughing, we make our way back down the stairs, the sound of our heels unnaturally loud on the stairway. I see Jamie make his way up the stairs, alcohol in hand. As we make our way back into the hall, I catch a glimpse of green. My dress. Lucy was right, the woman turns the corner to the toilet. That quick glimpse of her profile is enough for me to realise that it's Helen.

I take a wrong turn, distracted by thoughts of Helen, and decide to take Lucy on a quick tour of the downstairs, showing her the common room and one of my form rooms before we go for another drink. I can't believe all the things they have in there for the students. When I was at school, it was a pool table and board games if you were lucky.

My head is all over the place thinking about Helen. She is actually here. As we walk into the hall, I see Julia and mouth hello as Lucy tries to drag me onto the dance floor. I'm not quite ready for dancing just yet. Luckily, as we arrive at the edge of the dance floor, the guy that twirled her earlier – I still cannot place his name, grabs Lucy's hand and asks her for a dance. I offer to go and get the drinks. She nods and shimmies onto the dance floor. Poor bloke, I think.

I make my way through the crowds to the make-shift bar. There is no mistaking that green dress. Helen is waiting in line. I take a deep breath and stand next to her.

Amanda Shaw, *Woman Reborn*
– 8:10 pm

THE TOILETS ADJACENT to the courtyard are in the same place, but have indeed changed in one way. Unisex. How modern. I can hazard a guess at some of the logic behind that decision and can't help wondering if they'd been like this in my day would it have happened? Open fronted with clear views of each cubicle, there'd be less chance of any sordid activity going unnoticed or disturbing sounds being unheard. I can't dwell on that or the memories right now as I need to deal with how to avoid Karl Stamford if he is stupid enough to join the reunion. I'm pretty sure no one will have forgotten or totally forgiven him for what happened in the science lab, so why is he here? Does he know I lied? Would he care?

I left school at the first opportunity. Fifteen, pregnant and desperate. Desperate to keep the baby that is, despite its conception not being something I wanted to think about. A child of my own, someone to love and cherish who wouldn't judge or condemn me suddenly seemed like the answer to all my problems. By then I'd realised how atrocious, disgusting and uncaring my own parents had been and felt I had it in me to be a good mum with enough unused love to give to an innocent child. If I could only get away, set up on my own somewhere new I felt sure I could make some sort of better life for myself and my baby.

I tried to conceal my thickening waist and muffle my morning sickness, but my mother had always honed in on anything unusual in my behaviour. I had planned on trying to tell her of my condition at the best opportunity, though not the circumstances behind it and hoped if nothing else she'd be glad if I offered to move out and distance myself. I had few qualifications and no savings so finances could be a problem, but I knew she wouldn't care about that and I felt determined

I'd make ends meet somehow. But I wasn't given the opportunity to discuss anything.

She burst into my room one morning, demanded I get dressed and went off on a frenzied rant about how she knew I was up the duff and what a filthy whore I was.

'We aren't having any bastard child of yours here. Bad enough my own life was ruined when I had you, without you giving us another useless mouth to feed. All you've ever done is lie, cause trouble and bring shame. And no way is anyone going to find out about this. Get yourself downstairs pronto.'

I never did understand why she was so livid. Maybe deep down somewhere in her subconscious she thought the father might be her precious husband. It wasn't of course and I wasn't telling her or anyone else who had made me pregnant. There'd be no point and no one would believe me anyway. The thought repulsed me, but it didn't stop my longing for the child.

She took me to someone she knew who'd get rid of it and keep her mouth shut to use her own words. She didn't even care enough to make sure I saw a doctor and had the foetus removed safely. It was never mentioned again and I never forgave her. She barely spoke to me afterwards and I became more unstable than ever. With no real qualifications and my damaged mental state I had little or no chance of getting a job or doing anything worthwhile so I just became their skivvy. Every unpleasant task associated with running a pub became my responsibility. I was treated like an unpaid drudge and allowed little freedom or chance to socialise. Not that I had any real friends, but any company was better than theirs. I suppose I should have done something about it; reported them or run away, but I was too damaged and weak willed to bother, yet hating myself for being that way. Besides, I was now borderline alcoholic and at least the premises of a pub allowed me to indulge without their knowledge. I had learned a lot of cunning tricks and underhand ways to feed my habit and keep myself from being totally destroyed.

Being only fifteen I couldn't work behind the bar to start with, but it didn't matter about my age when it came to other ways of employing me. It was a rare night when a half inebriated regular wasn't sent discreetly to my room to be entertained. My parents made it quite clear that's all they considered me fit for and no-one ever discussed it or spread rumours as money changing hands kept them all quiet, though I never saw any of it.

My life was pretty unbearable, but there was no way of escaping that I could think of. Lethargy, heartbreak and feelings of defeat were my constant companions and alcohol my only means of blotting things out. But, over the years a deep rooted anger simmering in my unhinged mind began to surface and my devious, vindictive side took over. My psyche was choked by the thorns and brambles of early adversity and had now become as twisted; my macabre, destructive thoughts occupying most of my time.

A plan started to form in my disturbed brain and I concluded I would need the assistance of someone with no scruples or conscience, someone willing to take chances for personal profit, someone who'd ask no questions or care about any consequences. My mind kept returning to one name. Karl Stamford. I was pretty sure he'd have led a life of crime and corruption since leaving school and like me would probably never shake off his damaged reputation or recover from the trauma of past events.

I knew he'd moved away and his parents had divorced, but both were regulars at the pub and it was surprisingly easy to find out where he was and his contact details. After getting in touch we arranged to meet next time he visited Newark. As I suspected he was still up for easy money and agreed to arrange a fire at the pub while my parents were away in order to claim the insurance money. I told him they were in financial trouble and needed the funds and he was willing to accept my generous offer for payment. That was as much as he needed to convince him it was a worthwhile risk. He'd had plenty of experience in deviousness and unlawful practices to ensure his survival since leaving school.

The thing was I'd had plenty of experience in lying and being consumed by hatred, so he wasn't to know my parents knew nothing of my intentions, were not going away and were fast asleep in bed at the pub when he successfully turned it into a blazing inferno. I'd made sure I'd raided the safe, the tills and every hidden deposit of money to pay Karl off in full before he carried out the dirty deed. Hopefully that would ensure I'd never need to see or contact him again. Out of respect for the heartbroken daughter journalists were persuaded to keep the tragic news of faulty electrics causing the fire that claimed my parents' lives out of local newspapers so hopefully Karl would never know the truth that he had committed manslaughter by fire yet again. I knew I was lucky to have escaped being rumbled and quickly left the area after receiving the insurance money. I had heard rumours Karl had moved back to Newark and now lived with his mother. Did he know by now the whole thing was no accident?

Male voices outside the cubicle intrude into my dark memories. Whoever is there probably doesn't know me as Sandra or Amanda and shouldn't pose a threat, but I feel edgy and reluctant to leave my safety net. I lift my legs and curl them underneath me as I sit precariously on the toilet seat. I attempt to calm my runaway thoughts with some quiet deep breathing before leaving.

'Did I see you talking to Julia? Didn't you go out with her for a while at school?' an unfamiliar voice enquires accompanied by the sound of unsteady urinating.

'Yeah. I really liked her, but she threw me over.'

'Did you ever...?'

'No, she made it clear she wouldn't go that far. I was such a prat back then. All hormones and random erections. I should have stuck with her and brushed aside the jibes from the rest of the football team. She was a decent girl and I messed up just because they thought I should be shagging her. If I'd respected her wishes and ignored those pillocks who knows how the future would have panned out with her.'

'Well, there was always Randy Mandy if you were just desperate for sex.'

'Never that desperate, mate.' Their chuckling stabs me in the gut and puts an end to my calming breaths.

'You shouldn't have given up. You could have got back with Julia if you'd tried.'

'Maybe, but the awful thing is I believed all the rumours about Julia and Butterford and now I know none of it was true.'

A deeper stab paralyses me, but I'm all ears. Images and questions begin to swirl in the attic of my mind.

'Really? You mean he didn't get inside her Tank Girl knickers after all?'

'Julia's told me all about it and I believe her. God knows why we all worshipped him and believed his stupid lies. If he turned up here I'd be tempted to bash his perverted lights out. Sick bastard.'

'Didn't he wind up with that Stacey Grey? Last I heard he'd married her, though...' Their voices fade as they make their exit.

Stunned by what I've just heard I cast aside worries about Ascot, beauty spots, singing, Karl and my breathing techniques. I remember Julia, though I never really had much to do with her. She was one of the few I didn't resent despite her coming across as academic, well balanced, popular and everything I wasn't. I was out of school at the first opportunity and had my own battles to fight. I never gave a thought to those like Julia who returned to school for the sixth form destined for successful entry to university and high flying careers. Most of them I was eager to get away from and would only remember them for their snide remarks, unrelenting judgement and cruel mockery. Julia wasn't like that and I'd never witnessed anything negative from her. It seemed to me she was a genuinely lovely girl who'd never caused any problems for anyone. Neither would I have believed anyone would cause problems for her.

Is it true I'm not the only one then? Did something happen to her with that monster after I'd left school? Sandra has left any decisions regarding my actions up to me tonight, impressing looking at things from all angles and not jumping in all guns blazing are both worthy precautions. But she did make me promise not to reveal my true identity to anyone no matter what circumstances evolved, but this is one thing I'd never have contemplated.

I need to talk to Julia. I need to find out what happened to her at school while I was going through my own personal hell away from it. Maybe she has her own reasons for being here tonight and maybe she too has an ulterior motive, a desire for revenge and justice. She needs to know who I really am and hear my story. I leave the cubicle, rearrange my crumpled clothing, touch up my make up, close my eyes, chant a couple of calming mantras then head off back to the main hall hoping against hope I've finally found someone from school who will believe my past and understand my actions since then.

Iain Wilson, *"Legitimate Businessman"* – 8:15 pm

I TRY A DOOR back into the main block and I'm grateful when it opens. I don't want to have to slog back around to the main entrance and I'm not quite ready for the hustle and bustle of the hall. I slip inside and slowly saunter down the corridor. It still has that same slightly institutional smell that comes from bulk-buy floor cleaner but the lights are new; energy efficient things that cast a brilliant white light, adding to the evening's sense of 'the same but different'.

Strolling past what used to be a humanities room where I learned about the bloody Tudors (again) I realise that it's now a dedicated IT resource, black keyboards, mice and monitors stretching around the circumference, small amber lights telling me that, no matter what the school's policy on the environment, these buggers are still on standby, steadily nibbling on the electricity that we're all paying for. I dunno. Maybe I'm just being cynical because it's all new and different. *It were better in my day; I can remember when all this was (playing) fields.*

I'm slowly heading back to the hall, noticing that there's now a CCTV camera pointing at the entrance to the toilets. At least it's not inside pointing at your arse while you stand at the urinal, or watching from above a cubicle. I wonder if that's the way things are going. I also wonder how many times someone is given a bunk up to stick chewing gum or blu-tac over the lens. The camera is a good ten feet off the ground but, in an age of acrobatic routines on *Britain's Got Talent* and local cheerleading classes, never underestimate the ingenuity and unexpected athleticism of a teenager once you give them a challenge.

There's the sound of a hand drier and then the door opens revealing a guy in a shirt and suit with a face that used to be complemented by near-terminal acne and a mullet. The complexion's now fine while the hair is a formal short back and sides. I tap him on the shoulder and say hello.

'Ey-up, it's Iain. How you doing, mate?' He gives me a slightly damp but firm handshake.

'I see you got a sensible haircut in the end.'

'You too. No more indie mop top then? Stopped listening to the shoegaze stuff and those other moaning buggers?'

'The hair went when the suit arrived but the sounds never die. What about you? Still rocking out?'

'Aye, although it's Royal Blood and the Black Keys now; I try and keep up to date with new music but it's difficult when work is so busy.'

'Awesome. Not like when we were kids, eh? Hanging around outside Blockbuster, getting a bollocking from the guy at Tallis autospares. Long evenings of doing nothing.' I'm getting quite into this reminiscing lark. 'So, what you doing with yourself these days?'

My stomach churns with anxiety as Andy 'Willy' Wilkins tells me that he's a bloody Detective Inspector for Nottinghamshire Police, based out of St Ann's. 'Starting a secondment with EMSOU in October,' he explains.

'Em-Sue?' I ask, wondering if this is some oblique reference to having an affair.

'East Midlands Serious and Organised Crime Unit. They go after all the gangs that run drugs, handle firearms, that sort of stuff. You'd be amazed at how many players there are, but we're picking them off one at a time.'

'Really?' I need another drink and say so. We amble back to the hall as my mate explains more about how the police are closing in on criminal gangs. Closing in on me.

Pam McPherson, *Coordinator of Events* – 8:15 pm

'HI AGAIN,' I say as Kim and I get together again. 'Interesting night?' I enquire.

'Sort of. It's a weird mix of familiar and strange.'

'Hey, you haven't told me what happened to you after we left.'

She gives a shrug of her shoulders, her face contorts into a fed up sort of look. 'Not much really. You know I trained as a Primary teacher?'

'Yes, you were unsure of what you were going to do, weren't you? Natural progression really, you were always good with kids. I don't remember you going to teach though.'

'No, I decided it wasn't for me. I ended up working for Lloyds Bank instead.'

'Well that's a side swerve if ever I heard one. You got married, though,' I say, indicating her wedding ring.

'Yeah, no one from school, thank God. Got two kids as well.'

Still looking and listening to Kim I spot someone in my peripheral vision I want to speak to. I grab an arm as it is passing by. 'Hang on a minute, Kim.' I turn and smile at the startled face of Jake Young. 'Hello you,' I say as he swivels round.

'Well I never,' he says, 'two blasts from the past,' as he notices Kim as well.

We begin chatting but something is distracting Jake. 'What's going on over there?' he says. He is watching Ascot make an arse of himself with Gemma. We can't hear what they are saying but it doesn't look a comfortable situation. 'Didn't Gemma have a fling with Ascot at school?'

There is a slight pause.

'I wasn't in her circle, no idea.'

But Kim nods her confirmation, which I think is odd as she wasn't either.

Jake shrugs and turns his attention back to us. Jake had got a lot of ribbing at school because he was so small, only five feet four, but always well proportioned.

'You're still looking fit,' I say looking him up and down.

He is smartly dressed in designer jeans and a checked Ben Sherman shirt. His hairstyle hasn't changed, just combed back and nicely shaped. He smiles at us.

'Not bad, I suppose, but then I am still riding,' he says.

'Did you become a jockey, then?' Kim asks.

'Sure did. I managed to get into the School of Racing at Newmarket. I was there just over a year before being offered a job at Southwell, worked with Dom Steargate who had a yard there. He had a couple of good horses, one of which got me my first win and carried on winning.'

'You two used to go riding together, didn't you?' Kim suggests, glancing between us.

'Yes, we did. In fact Jake and I used to help out at the same livery yard not far from where I lived.'

'Do you still ride, Pam?' Jake enquires.

'Not in the way we used to. I help a friend exercise her two event horses every now and then. She needs to keep them fit. It's great to be able to keep a hand in even if it's only in a small way.'

'Didn't I see you on the telly, Jake?' Kim asks with a frown.

'Crikey, that was a long time ago!'

'What was all that about?' I ask.

'Oh, I was interviewed by Brough Scott for Channel 4. They were doing pieces on up and coming jockeys, me being one of them.'

'That's neat. Did it help your career at all?'

He looks thoughtful. 'I never thought much about it really, but I suppose it did. Doug Withers, who had some cracking horses at that time, approached me but it meant living in Lambourn and I couldn't do that.'

Kim looks confused. 'Where? I've never heard of it.'

'On the Wessex Downs, near Newbury. Lovely place,' Jake says sadly.

'Bloody hell, Jake! Why on earth did you turn that down?' I look at him, shocked.

'It's a *long* story, Pam,' he says.

'Oh, come on, Jake! You can't get away with that,' Kim pleads.

'Okay, okay. Did either of you come across Natalie Dupont?' he asks.

'Who the hell is she?' we ask pretty much together.

'*She*, would you believe, was Sarah Greene's best mate. *She* was her main bridesmaid at the wedding. What's the term, Maid of Honour or something? Sarah might think she's Queen Bee but one thing that Natalie had over her was she passed her exams and went to the Grammar down in Grantham. I only found this out when I first went out with her in '96.'

'Well, well, well,' I say, 'so was she at Primary with Sarah? Is that how they knew each other?'

'No, apparently it was through their parents. I won't go into the details but she is the reason I never went to Lambourn. Bloody wish I had though after what she did.'

'Do enlighten us,' Kim says. 'You're not leaving until we know *everything*.'

He sighs, resigned to his fate. 'It was almost a year into the relationship when Nat asked me if I minded going on an evening out with a couple of her friends. She said her friend was saddled with a very young baby and needed to get out of the house. Dumb me should have put two and two together but didn't. I felt a right idiot though when I saw who it was.'

'Don't tell me - Sarah and Ascot,' Kim interjects, eyes as wide as her grin.

'Indeed it was. What a night. Ascot got plastered and suddenly thought I was his best mate. He then started telling me all about his conquests whilst we were at school. He is such a prat,' Jake says nodding his head at Ascot as he shimmies across the floor of the hall. 'The two girls were on the dance floor and he went on and on about how Sarah got herself pregnant just to be with him. He said he could have had anyone.'

'Well, it takes two to tango,' I say. 'He should have kept it in his trousers shouldn't he?'

'Easier said than done when you get presented it on a plate,' he smirks.

That looks like the face of experience.

Looking from one to the other of us he comments, 'Well, what bloke wouldn't turn it down?' There is no answer to that. He is probably right.

'Anyway, after that night I broke up with Natalie, all because of Ascot. By then I'd wasted too much of my life on her and missed the opportunity to go to Lambourn.'

'Did you see the two of them when you came in?' Kim asks.

'You couldn't miss them, could you?' Jake replies. He turns to me. 'You got bullied by Sarah, didn't you?'

'Indeed I did. It seems Sarah's still a bitch now. I thought I had got over it but tonight is proving otherwise.' Looking directly at Jake, I say, 'But never mind that cow. I am intrigued about what you meant when you said that you split with Natalie shortly after that evening out.'

Jake sighs. 'It was during that night, I caught Natalie and Ascot looking at each other in a way that made me bloody uncomfortable. It got me wondering if anything had gone on before between the two of them. After Nat and I got back to mine I asked her whether she'd ever been with him. She said she had, but it was well in the past. Natalie disappeared into the bathroom but she left her phone on the table. It pinged with a message. I couldn't believe it. There in front of my eyes was a very suggestive text from Ascot. I just assumed something was still going on. After that I just packed her in and threw myself into riding. It didn't help that one of the first places I got a ride afterwards was at bloody Ascot racecourse.' He smiles at the two of us, 'Ironic really.'

'Oh my God! I bet she doesn't know. Her husband and her best friend!' My hand immediately comes across my mouth to stop myself laughing very loudly, giving Kim a sideways glance. She is looking totally gobsmacked. 'I really need that. Thank you so much, Jake.'

He looks at me completely puzzled.

'So,' says Kim, 'you dumped Natalie straight after finding a text from Ascot? That's nice.'

'Yeah, it does seem a bit crass when you say it like that,' he replies. 'But she didn't delete that text. I checked before she left, so as far as I was concerned she was history. A person who is messing with her best mate's husband.'

'How do you know she would have?' Kim asks.

He looks sharply at Kim whilst pausing for some time. 'Do you know, I don't. I never confronted Natalie about it and, yeah, you're right, Ascot was always mouth and no trousers, bragging and lying. Who would – or should – believe him?'

'He should have been called Arse-cot,' Kim says with a grin.

'He should have been called Dick,' I suggest as we all burst into laughter.

'All I know is that I wouldn't buy a car from him and that's for sure,' comes Jake's reply.

'How about a used girlfriend?' says Kim. 'Low mileage, one previous owner...'

'Nice little runner, good bodywork,' Jake continues, 'lovely upholstery and twin air bags.' We fall about laughing again.

'What's so funny?' a voice cuts across our merriment.

'Philip!' Kim exclaims. She comes across me to be at his side.

'Hello, Kim, you haven't changed a bit. If anything, you look better,' he says surveying her and then us. 'Check you out, Jake!' he says, then turning to me with a slight hesitation, 'Pam?'

'Yes, that's me.' I never liked Philip. He always said things without really thinking of the consequences or anybody's feelings; he had no compunction and he really didn't care who he upset.

'So what was so funny?' he enquires again.

'Nothing much,' Jake replies. 'We were just reminding ourselves about past times, and then got onto the subject of Sarah and Ascot.'

Philip looks at us nonchalantly. 'Yeah, I was a mate of Ascot's,' he says with some pride. 'I even got an invite to "The Wedding".'

'Bloody hell, did you go?' asks Jake, with raised eyebrows.

'Bloody right I did. Wouldn't have missed that for the world. Free booze and free food, not the church bit though. Jeez that was a night,' he says partly tutting with the memory. 'Copped off with Alisia.' Smirking again he looks sideways, 'She was absolutely wasted. Pretty cool night.' He's looking for some sort of positive reaction from us.

What a plonker, I think. He isn't going to get anything from me.

Jake just stares at him while Kim raises her eyebrows. 'Well I hope you felt guilty after.'

He laughs mockingly, 'Why should I? It was up for grabs so I took it. There was a lot of it going on that night.' He pauses, then continues. 'Ha! I remember on my way back to the reception I caught Ascot being hauled into a bedroom by a girl looking very like one of Sarah's bridesmaids. I just caught sight of her dress as she disappeared in front of him. He winked at me when he saw me. Lucky git.'

Jake has suddenly become intrigued. 'Oh, really? What a bastard. I always knew he was.'

I sense Jake won't go any further with this so I ask Phil if he knew her.

'No, I didn't know their friends that well. Mind you, when I got downstairs it wasn't rocket science as the table where they were sitting was short of one bridesmaid. She was Sarah's top girl, you know the one that looks after her.'

I glance across at Jake and just raise my eyebrows. The penny drops and he shakes his head ruefully.

'Do you think Sarah knows?' I ask Phil.

'Huh, I doubt it. Would you stay with a bloke that did that, and on your wedding day?'

'I would hope not,' I say. 'Mind you, she was pregnant so may have stuck by him even if she did find out.'

Phil thinks about it. 'I still don't think she knows. By all accounts she has spent her life bragging about the two of them.'

'And you never told her?' asks Kim.

'Not my place to, love. Well, I was on my way to the bar, I had to stop by to check out all the hilarity.' He just nods, walking away with a swagger as he always did.

My head is spinning. It's weird how circumstances play into your hands. I hadn't thought anything more about a story that was told to me while I was doing some work experience during the summer holidays. The event was something to do with helping small local businesses. As I always did I got chatting to the exhibitors and that's when I found out the story about their wedding: one of the cleaning staff had walked into a room to find a bridesmaid straddling another member of the wedding party. How on earth this guy and I got on to that subject heaven knows but now it's proving to be priceless.

We are back to our threesome.

'You okay, Jake? Kim asks.

'Yeah, actually, yeah I am. That makes me feel a whole lot better for dumping Natalie the way I did. What the hell did she think she was doing?' He looks at me for some sort of answer.

All I can think of is, *Oh my God, this is making the evening worth the trip.* I finally look back at Jake replying with a grin.

'*No*, do you really think that Sarah doesn't know?' says Kim.

'Well, it seems that way,' Jake replies.

'God, Ascot is a prize prick,' I comment. 'They deserve each other.' My mind is racing; I need to get to see Alfie. I have some explosive ammunition now, Alfie and I could really put the cat amongst the pigeons. I start scanning the heads to see if I can see him. There he is on the far side of the hall chatting with some other guys.

I am just about to make my excuses when some commotion breaks out. We all turn to have a look. Sarah is having an animated talk with Gemma, her voice becoming louder and louder causing the immediate vicinity to become hushed.

Gemma walks away when suddenly Sarah shouts after her calling her a sad bitch. The silence is palpable; those around look embarrassed. We turn back to each other and continue our conversation while everyone else slowly follows suit.

'I need to see someone. If you will excuse me, I'll see you later,' I say to Kim and Jake as I turn heading to the other side of the hall where Alfie has also gone back to his conversation.

I wonder if Sarah had ever eaten mud because it is going to be dish the dirt night.

Phil Morris, *The Man, The Legend* – 8:25 pm

THAT WAS AN interesting day, I muse as I walk back to the bar. It was a fun wedding as weddings go, not your usual stuffy do. I was quite surprised to get the invitation as I didn't really know either of them that well.

It was brilliant when I saw Ali. She was there alone too, lucky for me. We were friends at school, and I used to go out with her. Well, I took her out a couple of times. She was adorable, and it was a big bonus being able to spend the evening with her. We naturally paired up and chatted about this and that; what a great couple Sarah and Ascot were and what great babies they would make – all that stuff. She was a bit put out when I tried to snog her, which was a shame. I thought I was being really romantic. That's when she told me she was 'seeing someone'. Oh well, if she had been single, I'm sure we would've got together. She had been expecting her friend to get an invitation, having given his name as 'significant other', but he never got one. It's funny. She said his name was Pippa Norris. Odd name for a bloke. Sounds more like a female version of my name.

Sarah was quite cool. She and her bunch of mates were real pranksters; they loved winding up some of the other girls. I heard they got Alfie's sister to strip down to her undies in the park and then ran off with her clothes so that she had to walk home nearly naked. Brilliant. I wish I had been there to see that.

I feel a stirring in my CKs as I imagine Tanya in just a low cut bra and tiny white panties. I redden a little and glance around as I discreetly adjust myself with a swift hand down my trousers. I'm pretty sure nobody noticed.

Ascot was the man. We could've been good mates if we'd got to know each other better – probably. He was quite the Adonis back then. Slim and good looking like me, but fitter, sportier-looking with pecs and abs and whatever – if you like that kind of thing. He seemed surprised to see me when I congratulated him at the reception. I asked him if there was a shotgun involved and he sort of laughed. He gave me one of those 'matey' punches on the shoulder – obviously a bit harder than he meant to. It left a bruise that lasted a week!

It was later on, after the cake cutting and speeches and stuff, I had gone upstairs for a pee and saw Ascot following a girl into a bedroom. I'd seen her earlier. I think she was one of the bridesmaids. She was pulling him by the hand and giggling, and he was putting up token resistance. Lucky bastard. What a stud, just got married and now he's shagging the bridesmaids. What a legend! Anyway, I paused and winked at him as he quickly went inside and closed the door. I couldn't wait to get downstairs and tell Ali all about it, but I couldn't find her. It seems that her friend Pippa had come and given her a lift home. Anyway, I didn't stay much longer. The room was spinning, and I kept bumping into people, so I called a taxi and left. *Happy days*, I grin.

I wonder if Ascot remembers that I was there that night, on that corridor in the hotel, that I saw him being pulled into that bedroom. Obviously, I never told anybody, apart from a few of my closest friends of course, Neil, Willy, Chunk – oh, and Barry, and maybe a couple of others. Obviously I made them all promise not to tell anybody.

Gemma Robinson, *Business Queen* – 8:30 pm

SNEAKING BACK AFTER my indulgent cigarette, I scan the hall. One of the main reasons for coming tonight was because of a suggestion from "Hippy Dick" Boult. "Hippy Dick" was a nickname bestowed on him by a group of particularly childish boys, including Ascot and Iain. Rich Boult had been my Computer Sciences teacher, joining the school straight from his PGCE. I enjoyed his classes and his teaching style. He was younger and less formal than the other teachers, and, he was a genuinely nice person. Over the years we've kept in touch, especially after he took up a university post in Nottingham. At that time, I was living near the city centre and getting my business up and running. The premises I was using were not far from his college; we'd meet up now and then for coffee or a drink. For a while, I sort of hoped our friendship might become something more. It never seemed quite the right time, or place, or whatever. In the end, I realised that it was best to stick to being friends. I really didn't need the complications of a romantic entanglement. He has always been someone I could talk to and I value that. I can remember telling Rich about the situation with Iain and how I'd had to break off our professional association. He agreed with me that once you've lost trust in someone, it's rarely possible to regain it. Over the years, from time to time, he has recommended a few of his best students to me. All but one of his recommendations are still working for the company. More recently, Rich's interest in the company's development of specialised computerised diagnostics and micro-surgery led to one of his protégés joining us who is an absolute genius in the field. So, when Rich told me over the phone that he would be attending and was bringing along "someone you might be interested in", I decided to put aside my reservations about school reunions. If the "someone" has potential, I usually support them through university and employ them during the long holidays, or alternatively, pay off their student debts if they've already graduated. I pay well and all I ask in return is a commitment to work for the company for five years. It's a practice which has worked well in the past and pays dividends in finding talented youngsters to keep the business driving ahead.

Before I can even start to wonder where Rich and his "someone" have got to, my worst fears come true. Ascot is wending his slightly unsteady way across the hall towards me. It's too late to pretend I don't see him, and he can move surprisingly quickly for an overweight forty-year old. He makes a grab for my hand, but I start to fuss with my shoulder-bag and he misses.

'Gem, why are you avoiding me?' I notice that his mock public school accent has given way to the pathetic whine of his sixteen-year old self. The one he had used when I fended off his increasingly amorous intentions.

'Don't call me Gem, please, Ascot. You know I dislike it.'

'But it was my pet name for you. My Gem – more beautiful than diamonds.'

I roll my eyes at him. 'And you know that such soppy talk made me want to throw up then, and it still does now, so stop.'

'I've never stopped loving you, you know. You look great, still the tall, slim girl I fell for. We should find somewhere quiet to be together, get to know one other again.' Somewhere in that little speech he has managed to slink an arm round my body and is now pulling me closer, one hand sliding under my breast.

I shake my head in despair. 'Oh, Ascot. Please! We split up after three dates, if you recall, and I've not looked back with any degree of fondness to those occasions, believe me.' I wriggle free.

He looks crushed. 'I could never understand why you didn't want to keep seeing me. Dad gave me tons of pocket money. You could have had anything you wanted.'

'Perhaps I could, in material terms,' I say. 'But nothing about being with you appealed in the slightest. And now, on my own terms and without having to pay the price of losing my self-respect, I have what I want by my *own* efforts. And your creepy behaviour after I dumped you - turning up everywhere I went - was weird, to say the least. What was that about? It took months before you finally seemed to get the message. And what did you do then? Made a beeline for another "love of your life". Another poor girl, trying to fend you off. Grow up Ascot.'

'But...'

'No, Ascot! You don't still love me. You're married to Sarah and you have kids. It's probably boredom. So, just drop it. We are never, under any circumstances whatsoever, going to have any kind of relationship. Are we clear?'

He nods, discontent clouding his face. I can see that he isn't going to give up, despite the nod. Back in the day, when Ascot got an idea in his head it was almost impossible to shift it, and he doesn't seem to have changed. *How much nastier have I got to be before he gets it?* I wonder. This bloody evening is turning into a nightmare. Rich had better have another genius in tow to make it all worthwhile. In fact, if he doesn't turn up soon, I'm going to find Liza and get us back to the peace and quiet of the hotel and console myself with a large drink.

Unable to think of anything to say to Ascot that won't encourage him to think I'm being nice, I avoid his eyes. We stand in silence for a few moments, awaiting rescue. Gazing about, I can see that some effort has been made to make the place look cheerful. The hall's been decorated with old school photos and highlights like various sports days and team shots. Drama Club and Science Club are prominently displayed. There's even bunting and a few balloons. Although the lighting has been dimmed in an effort to achieve a more intimate feel, it still feels like the school hall it is. In fact, the whole place looks scrappy and sad, rather than festive. The buffet is inadequate and worse even than the wine. Money down the drain as far as I'm concerned. Nevertheless, most of the other people I can see seem to be enjoying themselves. Faces are flushed and the talk is animated. I can't help wondering if Jamie and Ryan are the only ones to have brought in additional alcoholic supplies. The noise level is high but, thankfully, there seems to have been some improvement in the music, not that the improved quality is much to my taste anyway. Even so, it's better than what was being played when I first arrived. As I glance towards the music decks, it looks like relief is at hand, the DJ is about to take a break. And I can see Jamie heading in my direction. He takes me aside. I'm more than happy to be parted from Ascot, who seemed about to launch another appeal.

'Gemma, I'm not sure where Liza's got to. Anyway, Ry and I have had enough so we're off home.' He smiles, 'Ry's had a bit too much of the old vino collapso. He's still quite shy underneath it all.'

'Okay. Take him home to sleep it off. I'll keep an eye out for Liza. She's staying at the same hotel as me and I was thinking of getting away myself.' I glance around again, 'I was hoping to see Rich Boult before I left. He's got someone he wants me to meet.'

Jamie raises an eyebrow, 'With a view to – what exactly? Business? Or, a date perhaps?'

'Business, Jamie, always business. Anyway, I have no idea who it might be.'

'Okay,' he abandons the teasing tone. 'We'll be in touch about the meal. I'm glad we've all met up again. Maybe Liza could come too?' He's waiting for me to signal agreement or not.

I nod, 'Yeah. Ask her, I'm sure she'll come. We're going to stay in contact now. I don't want to lose her or you and Ryan again.'

Standing alone near the bar – such as it is – I wonder if Rich is going to show at all. Then there's one of those strange, inexplicable moments that seem to happen at some point in most large, noisy gatherings, when the volume drops suddenly. Into the relative quiet a woman's voice shrieks, 'Apple juice!' followed by screams of laughter. Clearly, the punchline of a joke which the group of women standing with her find hilarious. Chuckles and giggles fill the room as the noise level rises yet again. Not one of them looks like any of the girls I knew at school. Who are these people? I take one last look round the hall, hoping to see Rich materialise with whoever it is he's bringing.

Not expecting to want to drive home from Newark, I'd already booked into a decent hotel for the night, a short taxi ride away. My tolerance for this school reunion is now officially at an end. I decide to get out while the going is good. First, I need to find Liza. Of course, no sooner have I made up my mind to leave, than Sarah comes striding up to me, her face twisted with anger.

'You – Gemma,' she says, pointing at me so that there can be no mistaking that she means me. 'Stop hounding my husband. Leave him alone – and me. Leave us both alone.'

I look at her, one eyebrow raised. Now I'm "hounding" Ascot? Is she serious?

'I think you've got things a bit arse about face here, Sarah,' I say. 'If there's any hounding going on, it's Ascot creeping me out, not the other way around.'

'Oh, you're not putting the blame on him. He's a soft as a...' Invention runs out as Sarah struggles to find a suitable analogy.

'Marshmallow?' I offer, thinking the comparison works on so many levels.

'Anyway,' she continues, ignoring my contribution, 'he's over you and has been for years, so stop trying to take him away from me.'

'Sarah!' I smile into her tight, furious face. 'Give me a break. I went out with him three – got that? *Three* times when I was fifteen. I dumped him, he stalked me. He moved on to some other poor girl, and a few years later you made a play for him and got pregnant. He *is* soft, so he married you. Remind me again how old you both were? Eighteen? This is the first time in years that I've been in his company for more than a few moments, and I can assure you, hand on heart, I am *not* trying to take him from you.'

'Well, you say that now to my face, but I saw you together and Ascot said you came onto him and he had to make it clear he was no longer interested. Hadn't been for years.'

'Okay, Sarah, believe what you want, whatever. I can't be bothered to argue with you. We're in our forties not our teens. I have a good life away from here, and that's where I'm heading right now.'

I walk away as she screams, 'You're a sad bitch who can't get a man, so just stay away from mine.'

A few heads turn and a ripple of nervous laughter breaks out among the nearest bystanders. I'm out of here and heading for the hall door. Another quick fag break before I go. It's an ironclad rule that I only smoke outside. I make my way back to the courtyard and take a deep drag of nicotine. Yes, I know it will kill me, but for now I need it. Stubbing out the butt I decide that I'm not waiting on Rich any longer. I shall find Liza and we'll head back to the hotel where there's a good bar and a plentiful supply of drink to be had. I shall follow that with an early night. I pull my wrap tight, the temperature has dropped and I'm feeling the chill. Walking back to the hall through corridors leading to rooms where I spent seven years of my life, happily for the most part, except for "the incident" and all its repercussions, I realise that, despite it all, I'm glad I came. Liza and I are closer than we've been since school, and I've met up again with Jamie and Ryan, who seem set fair to becoming good friends again.

The hall is warm and noisy. According to my watch, and to my amazement, it isn't as late as I thought. I can't see Liza. I sigh. Now I shall have to go looking for her again when all I really want to do is get back to the hotel. And yet, once again, I am thwarted.

Iain Wilson, *"Legitimate Businessman"* – 8:45 pm

I'M BACK IN the hall with another plastic glass of red wine and finally free of DI Andy Wilkins and his buddy Chunk who now runs the gym that Jason goes to. They were telling me about the whole thing, that Andy is on standby for a murder investigation if the worst happens. I forced out some platitudes and drifted away when another bloke came up, Martin somebody, I think, and started talking about 'the problem with the police these days'.

I'm scanning the room for Katy, hoping that Neil doesn't collar me again. I spot her on the periphery of a crowd watching some woman calling Gemma a sad bitch. It's wotsername, the missus of that twat Ascot. I'm willing Gemma to punch her but she just carries on walking out of the hall.

The group starts to break up into smaller clusters of conversation, picking over the choicest morsels of the gossipy feast. Katy is with one other woman, someone whose face I vaguely recognise but can't put a name to. I'm fairly sure the other woman has piled on several pounds (if not stones) in the years since we were last here.

Katy, though, well she hasn't changed that much, really. Still has the shoulder length brown hair, the dark brown eyes surveying the room above subtly defined cheekbones. Perfect complexion complementing a classy navy dress. Everything I had admired from afar as a kid but wrapped in a heart-stopping mature sophistication. My feet, however, seem to be fourteen again: nailed to the floor, unable to move. She'd always had this effect on me, ever since we started school back in 1989, fate delivering us into a shared orbit, but with the cruel twist of making me invisible to her. I guess the fact that, for most of those early years, she was a good four inches taller than me didn't help. But the longer we were in the same class, the more difficult it got to pluck up the courage to properly talk to her. I remember there was one time when Madame Dasoult mixed us all up and got us to tell our new partners about ourselves, in French. By some stroke of luck she put me next to Katy. She patiently ran through the details of the house she lived in, her family, the music she listened to, what she liked to eat. I was so hot and flustered that I couldn't remember a thing of what she'd told me. I mumbled something about me, all the while aching to use the most famous of French words, 'je t'aime'. If I was invisible before, I had just proved my irrelevance. We didn't really speak again until the end of our GCSEs and a series of parties to celebrate the fact that the two most stressful years we had encountered so far were complete. Some of us, myself included, were also leaving, determined to escape the claustrophobia of school. I remember that we had got hold of some White Lightning and were well on the way to a final destination of Vomit City, although at that moment happened to be passing through the pleasant countryside of Warm Buzz. I had put my arm around Katy's shoulders (I was now an inch taller than her) and told her that she was the only thing I was going to miss.

'That's so sweet,' she had said. And she turned and kissed me. Maybe, if some of her friends hadn't arrived just at that moment to drag her off somewhere else, just maybe something might have happened. I've replayed that moment in my mind so many times. What if? It seems like my life is full of them. What if my sister hadn't died, would my parents still be together? Would I have stayed on and done some A Levels? Would I have got together with Katy at that point? What would I be doing now?

Probably not running a drug gang in Nottingham.

I could've looked her up at any time after leaving school, but I didn't. If I couldn't bring myself to talk to her when I saw her every day, how the hell was I going to manage a completely contrived situation?

And so I buried my childhood infatuation, occasionally digging it up when feeling maudlin. I hadn't really thought about her at all in the last couple of years so perhaps I'm finally getting over her now that I'm forty. But that email has disinterred everything with all the subtlety of a JCB, scattering painful memories like windblown lilies after a funeral.

I glance down at my plastic wine glass to check there's still some courage left and take a gulp. I fix a smile on my face and walk over to her just as the person she'd been talking to turned away to find her plate of nibbles. Perfect timing.

'Katy! Hi, so good to see you again.' I project a confident and positive veneer, despite my stomach churning like a cement mixer.

She smiles back – that's good. 'Hi!'

And then she looks at my name badge – possibly not so good, although it's hard to say; I'm not the shy little lad I used to be.

'Iain?'

'Hi, yes, how are you?'

'Good, really good. How about you?'

'Yeah, not bad, thanks.' We stand awkwardly wondering what else to say. It dawns on me that although we had key years and locations in common, we didn't exactly share those experiences together. I decide to concentrate on the present. 'So, what are you up to these days?'

'Oh, you know, being a mum and all the hassles that brings.'

Christ. It never crossed my mind she'd be married and a mother. I am such an idiot, so wrapped up in my own circumstances, chasing an avatar that had been on pause for twenty five years. 'A mum? Wow,' I eventually manage to reply.

'Yes, I can't believe it myself sometimes. He's just about to start his final GCSE year, at this school too. Funny how life rolls on, isn't it?'

'Blimey, yes, you're not kidding.' I take a sip of wine. 'So, are you here with your other half?' I hope that it doesn't sound like I'm prying but I'm clearly prying.

'No,' she smiles, 'divorced and single again.'

Get in!

'Oh, sorry to hear that.' I'm really not. I can't remember a time I have been less sorry.

'Well, you know how relationships go, especially if you marry young and your husband turns out to be a useless little shit. He ran off with a blonde bimbo from work.'

I can tell she's probably had a glass or two of the old vino. 'That's awful. I can't believe anyone would do that to you.'

'Yeah, well, shit happens. What about you? Married?'

I shrug. 'Nope. A few girlfriends over the years but no-one particularly special.' *Not compared to you.*

'Well, you never know. There's bound to be someone out there for you.'

This is it. Carpe diem, Iain. 'Well, to be absolutely truthful, I did have a bit of a crush on you back then.'

She gives a tight smile and looks down at her plastic glass. I realise I might have played my hand too early, too crudely. 'Do you remember that time in French? God, I've never been so tongue-tied, trying to talk to you in a foreign language.'

She shrugs and shakes her head. 'No, sorry.' It's clearly not ringing any bells for her. I try a different tack.

'The last time I saw you was at Steve Milton's party just before I left school. We were down near Balderton lake getting pissed on cheap cider. I told you how much I was going to miss you.'

She smiles again. And then re-checks my name badge. I can feel a weight falling inside my stomach. 'Iain. We were just kids. I wish I could remember more about those days but they're long gone.'

I force a smile to match hers. It probably looks like a grimace. 'Yeah. Here's to the present.' I raise my wine glass.

'And the future.'

'Especially the future.' I need to keep calm. I very nearly made a total cock of myself. *Just be natural, don't force it.*

'So, what do you do these days?'

Don't say drug dealing and hospitalising teenagers.

'Oh, just some business consultancy down in Nottingham. What about yourself? Full time mum?'

'No, I'm a supervisor at Vodafone up on Northern Road, yeah?'

'Oh, right,' I say, nodding. 'Enjoy it?'

'It's alright, pays the bills and stuff.' Another lengthy pause. 'So,' she says when I can't think of anything else to contribute, 'have you met up with any old mates?'

'One or two. I see we're also graced with Gemma's presence. Talking of which, what was all that commotion...'

Before I can finish a guy comes up to us. 'Katy! You look amazing!' He puts an arm on her shoulder and turns her towards him. Away from me.

'David! Wow, you too. How are you?'

'Good, good. Well, great, to be honest. Hey, you've got to come over and see Mark and the guys.'

And with that, she's gone. Didn't say 'Catch you later, Iain'. Didn't even look back at me. David Hancock and Mark Hill. A couple of the infamous Footy Lads. Bastards.

I feel hollowed out. First the news about Jason, then an unexpected brush with Plod and now this. I look up at their little group, already kissing some greetings, touching arms, laughing. *Face it, this is a disaster*. But at least I know now. I can get on and live my lonely pissing life without having her face taunting me with what-might-have-beens.

I turn away from my old obsession and stomp away from the hall down the opposite corridor to the one I explored earlier. I pause after a few yards and lean back against a wall, wondering why the hell I thought it was a good idea to come here. I'm usually wary of acting on impulse and this is why. Logically weigh up the pros and cons before committing to anything, is my standard operating procedure, not getting all *totes emoshe* and chasing teenage dreams.

I take another sip of wine. Can't have too much, especially with a cop hanging around. Don't want to get into a situation where I get breathalysed and then have the law prying into my business. Manage that risk. Get back to what you know. People you can rely on.

Yeah, 'cos that's working out well, isn't it? Bloody Tweedle-Dum and Tweedle-Dee and their cack-handed beating are not helping my tenuous grip on sanity.

I run a hand through my hair and brush some paper pinned to the wall behind me. I prise myself upright and glance at what it is. It's a notice board with various things pinned to it. At the top is a sign written in silver on black card:

Class of 89 – English Work

I scan the board and see short stories and poems by kids from my year, throughout their time at school. I vaguely remember the teachers taking copies of the work they thought was worthy of praise for putting up on boards at the end of each year. I had a poem selected once.

And then I spot it.

My poem, picked from all of the things produced by all these kids for five or more years. I'm stunned. I haven't thought about that poem in years, certainly haven't read it since the nineties. I wrote it about Ella. To my cynical adult eye it feels a bit crass and simplistic, but I'm back in a school corridor reading words that really *meant* something to me. Apparently, they still do because my eyes are filling up, making it hard to read any more.

I've got a horrible sense that I'm feeling sorry for myself. I should grow up. An inner voice shouts back that *it's alright to feel bad*. Perhaps if I showed more *emotion*, listened to what I *wanted*, *empathised* more with others, I wouldn't be in this position. *Don't be so fucking repressed!*

Ah, bollocks. There's definitely a tear on my cheek. I blink and wipe it away, conscious of being exposed as an emotional wreck to any passer-by.

I walk over to some nearby steps that lead to the first floor and sit down. And it all comes out in a barely audible sob. My sister, my parents, Danny (who will forever be on fire, screaming, in my nightmares, barely an hour after he saved me from a kicking). And now Katy, the girl I've wasted my dreams on, and Jason and his daughter, hoping that the person I've put in hospital wakes up from his coma. What the fuck am I doing with my life?

Amanda Shaw, *Woman Reborn*
– 9:00pm

BUTTERFORD. It's staggering just how one little word can bombard all your senses in the worst possible way. Images of his dirty fingernails, his yellowing teeth and flabby, hairy belly make me want to vomit even now. The smell of his unwashed body, sweaty armpits and greasy lank hair, the taste of his foul breath on my face, his sour spittle invading my mouth force forgotten wounds to open and bleed afresh. I can still hear his raspy grunts and the obscene filth spewing from his slobbery lips as he rammed into me from behind, his filthy, sweaty palm clamped tightly over my trembling mouth...

Stop it. Stop it. Stop it. It takes every ounce of willpower and self-control to avoid the terror overwhelming me. My steps falter and I have to lean against the corridor walls to prevent myself from collapsing into a heap of screaming torment. Flashbacks assault me like muggers in the darkness. The confidence I believed I now possess is wavering and I obviously am not as in control as I thought. I rummage deep into my consciousness to find the techniques Sandra has instilled in me over the years to deal with these moments of sheer panic. I visualise a signpost in front of me. There is no point looking back I repeat; what has happened cannot be changed. It's over and can no longer do me harm without my own permission. It was not my fault, not my choice and I have to bury it deep. The road ahead is the one that matters. The one I can control and make a success of. Sandra has taught me so many coping methods, has eradicated so many of my complexes and boosted my self-esteem, but I know I cannot always rely on her and need to take control when facing my own demons. My breathing eases and I continue along the corridor determined to find Julia and hopefully seek some consolation in whatever I discover.

Julia Forest, *Tank Girl to Child Protector* – 9:00 pm

I GIVE MYSELF A shake in time to catch up with the conversation and hear the name Karl Stamford. Jamie saw him lurking outside, apparently.

'What's he doing here?' I demand and then wonder at myself. That pathetic specimen probably needs sympathy rather than condemnation but I doubt any of us will have the patience to give him that tonight.

I put him from my mind though as I spot one of Miss Summerfield's former colleagues who looks as old as Methuselah and is still wearing his teacher's uniform of faded tweed jacket. However, he might know if she's coming tonight.

'See you later,' I say to the group and make a beeline for Mr Bloom.

'Hello, sir,' I say. 'Do you remember me?'

He must have been put on the spot so often, struggling to remember one of the hundreds of students he had taught. He's looking at me and searching his memory so I take pity on him.

'It's Julia, Julia Forest. Miss Summerfield taught me at A level.'

'Ah yes,' he says, possibly none the wiser.

'I was wondering if she'd be here tonight.'

'Miss Summerfield?'

'Yes. Do you know if she's coming?'

'I'm sorry, I have no idea. She left Hercules Clay a long time ago.'

'Oh. Do you know where she went?'

He pauses, tapping his bottom lip with a gnarled finger. 'Now where was it? I know she went for promotion. Somewhere down south, I think.' He looks at me again. 'But as I say, it was a long time ago.'

He's not wrong. It was. Although some memories refuse to fade.

'Oh well, never mind. I would have liked to thank her. She helped me a lot.'

He smiles vaguely and I excuse myself. So, no witness at all then.

I turn away from him to see someone else watching me intently. I stare back at her unsure of who she is and shake my head as if to say, 'What? What do you want?'

She glances out into the courtyard and heads in that direction. As I follow her out into the cool, still evening, I'm reminded of another girl by her walk. We pause well away from the music and chatter.

'Amanda?' I say into the silence.

Helen Walcott, *Proud Single Mum*
– 9:00 pm

THE HALL HAS really filled up now and people are pressed on either side of me when I notice the hands of the person on the left of me reaching to take two drinks; beautifully manicured, sparkling, painted nails with long slender fingers and then that voice! The same after all these years.

'Helen!'

I look up and glance at the woman who is standing close to me and a shock like a thousand volts hits my body and takes my breath away. HIM! Except it's not. HE has become someone else, someone different.

'I was hoping you'd be here!' He says smiling that beautiful broad smile, the eyes still exactly the same in a body that most definitely is not.

'Oh my God!'

I'm trying not to stare and I'm vaguely aware that my mouth is hanging open. I swallow and smile back, a lop-sided pissed smile, a smile that says, *What the fuck?* and then he squeezes my hand with his own beautiful ones and says, 'I know! It's unreal isn't it?' It's not really a question, just a statement of fact and as he says it he waves his hands down his body as if to point out the evidence of just how unreal he is.

I laugh and reach to hug him. 'I missed you, Charlie,' I say and he nods, tears in his eyes.

'I missed hearing you say my name.'

'I'm sorry, I...'

'It's fine. It's okay. I'm Hannah now.'

I nod and repeat the name aloud, 'Hannah. I like it.'

'I missed you. You were there and then you weren't.' He clicks his fingers in the air, 'Boof! You just disappeared...' He looks sad then.

'I had no choice,' I say quietly. 'Mum and dad, they...'

He nods. 'I kind of guessed. What happened to...'

'What?'

'The baby?'

'Is here!' Chloe says appearing at my side and sticking out her hand. 'Chloe.'

'Hannah.' He smiles at her and there is a silent moment between us all while Chloe stares at him. I stare at her with a lump in my throat and I can feel him staring first at me and then at her over and over again. Then he breaks it. 'You always did have fabulous style,' he says, laughing at our identical dresses.

'Thanks, but you wear it far better than me.'

'All surgically enhanced, darling!' he laughs. 'I literally picked what I wanted. These tits are Pamela Anderson's, my ass is Beyonce's. What's not to love?' He laughs loudly then and I realise I don't care whether he's a man or a woman on the outside because on the inside it's still the same old Charlie but I will have to start thinking of him as she because Hannah is definitely all woman.

'Come,' she says. 'Meet my friend, Lucy. She's mental. You'll love her.'

'I will, but first come and say hi to Julia and Jamie and Ryan. Remember them? I'm sure they'd love to see you after so long,' and I pull her over towards the table where Ryan and Jamie both sit with their mouths hanging open like they can't believe the vision before them.

'Remember...'

'We were chatting earlier,' says Julia.

Ryan is staring hard at Hannah and I see the penny drop. 'Charlie! Fucking hell! I don't fucking believe it. You look fucking amazing!' Ryan jumps up and hugs Hannah hard.

'Three fuckings!' exclaims Hannah gleefully. 'I am overwhelmed at your response, old friend!'

'I often wondered what happened to you,' says Ryan shaking his head. 'You remember Jamie? We're an item now.'

'Of course I do! Jamie! You always were the best-looking lad in school.'

Hannah is laughing and smiling and relaxing as she talks to them both and Julia nudges me, whispering in my ear, 'Didn't you and Charlie... you know?' and she looks at me and arches an eyebrow, searching my face. I don't answer her just punch her playfully, but I wonder if she's worked out that Chloe is his child.

'I always knew you were gay!' Hannah tells Ryan.

'You could have told me!' laughs Ryan. 'Took me long enough to realise. I can't say your transformation was expected though. When did it happen?'

'A few years ago now. Do you know much about transvestitism?'

Ryan laughs, 'Can't say I do! I've been in a few tranny clubs in my time, but it was never really my thing, you know?'

Hannah nods, 'Well, I dabbled for a bit, but I knew it wasn't enough. I didn't want to dress like a woman. I was a woman screaming to get out!'

'Did your mum and dad ever suspect?' asks Julia interrupting. 'Was it a shock?'

'Course it was a fucking shock!' says a voice and we glance up to see Philip who has appeared at the edge of our group. 'Your folks thought they had a Billy and he turned out to be a Lily!' He roars with laughter at his own joke.

Hannah smiles at him, 'Something like that, yeah,' she says. 'I'd like to say you've changed as much as me Philip, but I think that would be a lie.'

'If it ain't broke, why fix it?' says Philip, supping his pint and nodding to himself in that self-satisfied way he's always had. 'What's with the dresses anyway?' He looks at me and then Hannah. 'It's a bit confusing. I nearly pinched your arse earlier, Charlie, gave me a right shock when you turned around, I can tell you.'

'Now you!' He turns back to me. 'I wouldn't mind squeezing your arse anytime soon!'

I cough and splutter, the wine sticking in my throat, swallow and glare at him. 'In your dreams, Philip.'

'Well, the offer is there if you change your mind,' he says totally oblivious to my horrified face. Julia is glaring at him and Chloe is looking at Philip as if he's crawled out from under a stone.

'How can you refuse?' says Jamie arching an eyebrow.

'The *MeToo* movement has obviously passed him by,' mutters Chloe to Julia who smiles, but I can see it irks her that he's here and she looks away from him pointedly.

'Has anyone been up to the science lab yet? Only I heard it's open if you want to have a look,' says Ryan deliberately changing the subject.

'I'm not sure I want to go up there,' I say, 'bad memories, you know.' I shudder, thinking of the fire and Danny Griggs who never got the privilege to be here tonight, preserved in all of our memories as a pimply teenage boy. I feel a melancholic sensation in my stomach.

'Liza's here,' says Hannah, 'have you seen her? She looks really good. Happy.'

I haven't, not yet and I feel a sense of dread at the thought of it. I don't know what I'd say to her. We were never close friends.

'I thought I saw Karl Stamford earlier, lurking around outside.'

We all stare at Jamie shocked.

'No! Are you sure it was him? Surely he wouldn't come here. He must know he wouldn't be welcome!' Julia's voice is angry and I can't say I'm surprised. Karl wasn't a friend to any of us here. The thought of him makes me feel light-headed and I remember my parents accusing me of sleeping with him.

'I need some air,' I say getting up, the wine making me feel nauseous now, the noise and the lights and the heat suffocating me.

'You alright, mum?' Chloe says across the table, looking concerned.

'I'm okay. I just feel a bit hot that's all.'

'I'll come with you,' says Hannah taking my arm and we leave the hall together.

When we arrived the air was still warm outside, the orange sun setting in a pink sky; it's cooler and darker now. I breathe in deeply and we walk around the side of the school towards the sports field.

'He's still a repellant little shit, isn't he?' says Hannah with a grin.

I smile, 'Philip? You could say that. People don't really change, do they? Not as much as they like to think they do.'

We're quiet for a while as we walk, the sound of jangly music drifting out from the hall and following us. 'Jeez! The Stone Roses! Takes me back!' Hannah does a silly dance and I laugh feeling a bit better to be out here. Then Hannah speaks. 'She's mine, isn't she?

I stop, the breath knocked out of me and nod.

She turns to me and lifts my chin and smiles. 'She's lovely. You've done a good job.'

'How...' I start.

'It's like looking in a mirror,' Hannah says. 'I knew the minute she came to find you at the bar. And I always thought that ship had sailed.' She looks wistful then. 'Guess I wasn't as inept as I thought.'

'Do you mind?'

'Mind? Why would I mind? You've done the hard bit and I get a fully functioning grown up daughter.' She turns to me, 'Do you mind? I mean, did you want me to know? Does Chloe know?'

I shake my head. 'I haven't told her. Not yet... Just lately though, she's been asking more questions. I didn't feel ready. I guess I came here tonight to see if you were here, to see if it was the right time, you know to tell her...' I look at her then say, 'To tell you.'

Hannah nods. 'I can't speak for Chloe but I'm glad I know. I'd always wondered about you, about the rumours. You know people thought it was either Karl or a teacher! I always knew it was neither, but I daren't hope it was me. Didn't we used to think it was impossible to get pregnant the first time?'

'Yes, but we also thought that rubbing raw potato on our zits would cure them and standing up as soon as we'd had sex would stop a baby too. Seems we were wrong about a lot of things.'

She laughs sadly and is silent for a while. 'Do you regret it?'

'Regret Chloe? Never for a second. She's been the making of me.'

'No, I meant, do you regret that it was me? Your first time and then...'

'Being Chloe's dad you mean?'

Hannah nods and I take her hands in my own and look her in the eyes. 'Never.'

'I'm glad. If you don't want to tell Chloe that's your call, I won't interfere with your decision, but, if there's a chance that you do want to, well, I would love the chance to get to know her, and you again...'

'I never forgot you. We were kids but you saved me some of those nights when my parents were, well, you know. I'm sorry I never told you, but I didn't want you to feel that you had to step up to the plate. It was a fumble, a nice one, but a fumble nonetheless and I was caught out. I wanted to deal with it in my own way and when mum and dad sent me away, it seemed easier to let you get on with your life.' I'm crying now, warm tears slipping quietly down my face and Hannah wipes them away tenderly.

'I'm not sure I would have been much cop as a dad back then anyway. Do your mum and dad know?'

I shake my head.

'Bloody hell! So who do they think it is?'

'They suspected Karl. Why, I have no idea. I couldn't stand him, but he lived near me back then. Do you remember?'

Hannah nods. 'He had a shit life, didn't he?' she murmurs lost in thought.

'Yeah, he always seemed to have a black eye or a cut lip. I'm not surprised at the way he turned out, he never had a chance.

We'd hear his parents screaming at each other and beating him, you know?' I remember the terrible fights and the sounds of crying and shouting and slamming doors that would drift across the fences of our back garden.

We're quiet again for long moments, the music getting further away as we reach the far side of the school grounds that back onto the housing estate where us rough kids lived.

'Do you think... do you think Chloe will mind? About this? About me?' She gestures to her body, an anxious look on her face.

I laugh. 'Are you kidding? She's generation LGBT! It won't phase her I'm sure.'

'When do you want to tell her?'

'Not tonight... Soon though. Let's enjoy tonight and I'll talk with her and arrange a coffee or something. Did you say you're in London now?'

Hannah nods.

'Well, it's not so far from Bath. We can meet up. Or arrange to meet back here in Newark. Chloe's at university in York so it would be okay for her.'

'A coffee with my daughter. Oh my God, I can't believe I am saying that!'

'Me neither.' I smile tenderly. 'It sounds good, doesn't it?'

She nods.

'You know what though?'

'What?'

'If we are going to start seeing one another again and be back in each other's lives I have got to stop thinking of you as Charlie.'

'He's still here,' says Hannah gently touching my hand to his heart. 'He's alive and well. He just needed a different shell. You know? I didn't take this decision lightly. I mean, I know I come across as blase, but it's been bloody hard. I finally feel like me and I hope you grow to like the new me as much as you liked the old one. I'm sure you'll agree it's an improvement.'

I smile. 'You were always wonderful to me, but I can see you have much more confidence as Hannah and it's obvious you are happy and that's great.'

'Will you be able to call me Hannah, do you think?'

'I will try, but just let me have tonight with Charlie too? Will you do that? I haven't seen him for over twenty years and I really would like the chance to say goodbye properly.'

Hannah nods, her eyes damp.

'Do you mind if I kiss you? Kiss Charlie just one last time.' It's a kiss that reminds me of that teenage fumble in a different time and place when we were different people, a kiss that says hello and goodbye and when we break apart the past has been laid to rest.

'I'm not a lesbian you know,' says Hannah, winking at me and taking my arm.

'I didn't think you were. Thank you, Hannah.'

'Thank you! That's the best snog I've had in ages!'

I punch her gently and we hug again, me and this lovely, lovely person that I've missed.

'Have you got a man?' she asks.

'No. I've not really bothered. The odd date, but I've thrown myself into my work really. I have a cleaning business.'

'As in proper cleaning? Not sorting out dead bodies or anything?'

I laugh. 'No, the boring kind.'

'Successful?'

'It does okay. You?'

'I'm in recruitment. It's savage, but pays well.'

'Isn't that a really male environment? I mean, you know, how do your colleagues treat you?'

'On the whole they're okay. We have policies in place that I know the company would not be afraid to use if I did have a problem. I guess I found my niche there and, well I guess I'm respected. I do a good job, so the fact that I changed my sex doesn't really come into it. I've had comments of course, but Charlie is still there and he normally knows how to deal with it.'

'So being a man once helps?'

'In that environment yes, I guess it does. I know how men think and behave and react, so I'm always one step ahead.'

'You sound like you enjoy it.'

'I'm manager now, so I hope so.'

'I've only ever worked for myself. I employ a team of ten and we have a lot of big company contracts in and around the Bath area. And to think mum thought I'd never get a job after I fell pregnant.' I shake my head remembering her words.

'Do you get on now?'

I laugh bitterly. 'Not really. The damage was done when she sent me away. I think dad would have come round and he adores Chloe, but mum, well, the shame of a teenage daughter who had obviously had sex was too much for her Catholic sensibilities. Do you know she's never apologised for how she treated me? I was just a girl. I needed my mum and she wasn't there for me. There's no coming back from that.'

We've walked back to the entrance, the music, the chatter of people catching up and the laughter is louder now.

'Hannah!' A very pissed woman is shouting and waving to Hannah.

'Looks like you're needed.'

'That's Lucy. You should meet her.'

'Definitely, but I need to find Chloe first. Another half an hour and and then we're going to head off.'

'You sure you don't want to come and see the lab?'

I shake my head. Hannah shrugs and then gives me another hug. 'I've loved seeing you. Both of you. Another drink here and then we can discuss meeting up for that coffee. My shout.'

We smile at one another and I head off back into the hall to find Chloe.

Amanda Shaw, *Woman Reborn* – 9:05 pm

I REACH THE HALL and scan the figures interacting in the dim light. Along with laughter and inebriated conversations there are angry, raised voices emanating from one corner of the room. It seems there are others with scores to settle and axes to grind which is reassuring and disturbing at the same time. I pick out Julia easily; she's barely altered and still radiates the aura of kindness and calm I always associated with her. I approach her rehearsing my words, but once in front of her where she's chatting amicably with others my voice deserts me. She stares at me with a mixture of confusion and vague recognition, but thankfully interprets my gestures correctly and follows me outside to the courtyard.

'Amanda?' I don't know whether she's noticed my false name badge or not, but obviously has seen beyond it and recognised me despite not ever really communicating at school.

'Yes,' I squeak. 'How did you know?'

' I recognised the way you walk. It's an individual trait we all have.' She smiles.

'Really? I'd say I was just a walking disaster.'

'Hey.' She places a soft hand on my shoulder. 'We all have our skeletons. We've all made mistakes, all have regrets and all suffered at the hands of others. Don't be so hard on yourself. You've obviously come good over the years.'

Her assurance acts like floodgates and it all comes spilling out.

I tell her everything. How that Friday afternoon I'd skipped games and just hung around the courtyard kicking up the dust as I wallowed in my bitter view of the world and cursed everyone in it. How Butterford caught me smoking as he brought his adoring football team through the grounds. How he scoffed and sent me to clean the toilets as a punishment, sneering about how a filthy environment was where I belonged from what he'd heard. How he crept into the cubicle, forced his clammy hand across my mouth and raped me, threatening me with worse to come if I didn't comply. I tried to scream, to kick and bite but his bulky force was too much for me. Sex was just part of my life and held no fear or mystery, but never in adulthood had I been forced against my will or assaulted in a way I can only describe as sick and violent.

Julia doesn't interrupt or show any signs of disgust. Her face shows only concern and tenderness which encourages me to relate the rest of my story.

I tell her of the pregnancy which could only have been a result of Butterford's actions, my enforced abortion and how I was responsible and involved Karl Stamford unwittingly in the death of my parents. How after claiming the insurance money I moved away, but couldn't live with the guilt or misery of my own emotional state. The money soon ran out as I sank deeper into the mire, relying on drugs and alcohol to survive so I reverted to what I knew, working the streets to gain the income I needed to feed my habits. But now all I wanted was that lost baby, so I took no precautions, caring not who would be the father of my child as long as someone made me pregnant and filled the empty longing deep in my soul. But it didn't happen and eventually I was forced to see a specialist who confirmed my whole reproduction system had been permanently damaged by the unlawful abortion and I would never be able to conceive a child.

'That's when I lost it completely. I was no use to anyone, had no one to turn to, no hope for the future and nothing to live for. I'd made a mess of everything and done so many bad things maybe I deserved all the consequences. What life I had left broke up like some great river's ice at the touch of spring. I tried to end it all, but couldn't even get that right, ending up sectioned on a psychiatric ward for a very long time.'

I end my sorry story and am surprised to see tears rolling down the cheeks of my very attentive listener.

'Oh you poor, poor girl.' Julia enfolds me in her arms. I've received so few hugs in my life, but know this is the warmest, most genuine one I've ever experienced. I believed my crying days were behind me, my emotions under control, but I find myself sobbing uncontrollably on Julia's shoulder. She strokes my arm gently until the release I obviously needed so desperately is complete.

Julia tells me about her experiences with Butterford and the effects it had on her. I'm shocked and ashamed I never considered he'd still be pursuing innocent girls back at school. Maybe if I'd reported his attack on me it would have prevented anyone else suffering, but back then I doubted anyone would have believed me anyway. We can't dismiss the idea that maybe we weren't the only ones to suffer abuse by that awful man.

'My parents were to blame for so many things, but I dealt with them in the wrong way and have lived with the shame ever since. Butterford is ultimately responsible for my barren state. My life has changed significantly and I'm no longer the person I was at school, but I still can't shake off the feeling I need to do something to avenge myself.'

'I understand. Come with me.' Julia takes my hand and leads me back into the hall and over to the table at the entrance. She writes my name in big, bold letters on a fresh name tag and replaces the fake one on my jacket.

'Wear it with pride,' she whispers reassuringly.

Heads turn as she takes me over to a group of women clustered around a table. Expressions vary; some unreadable, some unfazed and others obviously consumed by distaste. But what does it matter? Those who still judge and condemn are of no importance and can no longer influence me or hurt my feelings.

Julia introduces me to the group of women she'd been chatting to previously who all greet me with friendly smiles. They share their past, their memories and their present lives and I start to realise they've all had tough times over the years. Not as extreme as my own admittedly, but I was so wrapped up with my own troubles it never occurred to me others at school had their own issues to deal with.

It must have been very difficult for Hannah in those times when there was little or no understanding of transgender matters, yet look at her now. Stunning, confident and obviously enjoying life. It can't have been an easy road, but she's proof we can survive against all odds if we believe in ourselves. Her friend Lucy has obviously had a few too many, but has us all laughing with her cryptic observations and dry wit. It's a new experience for me to feel welcome and comfortable amongst a group of virtual strangers.

Julia points out Pam, huddled with a small group who are casting furtive glances at Sarah, and explains how she was often on the wrong end of Sarah's spite. 'I wish I could have done something but back then I didn't want to get involved. These days my job is all about getting involved.'

I'd never mixed with these girls at school so didn't realise Pam had been bullied or that Helen had also been pregnant when she left. The love and pride Helen obviously has for her daughter Chloe has erased any criticisms and difficulties they've endured. Chloe is certainly a precious daughter and I'm proud of myself because I don't feel jealous or bitter about it, just pleased for her and hopeful for myself.

It's not too late for Sandra and I to raise a child and we'd have choices in these times of donor insemination, surrogacy and adoption. I can't wait to get home and discuss it with her and tell her all about these new friends I'll now have in my life. I must remember to give them all my phone numbers and offer them reduced price treatments at our clinic.

This evening has turned out completely differently to how I anticipated and I'd never have believed I'd be standing here as Amanda Shaw enjoying the company of others and being accepted. But, there's still that one thing niggling at me that would make the event complete. I turn to Julia.

'I've not noticed anyone resembling Butterford. Do you think he'll turn up?'

She takes my hand again. 'Excuse us ladies. We have some unfinished business.'

Pam McPherson, *Coordinator of Events* – 9:05 pm

WALKING ACROSS THE hall towards Alfie all I can hear are snippets of conversations, mostly about Sarah's outburst. I decide to stop and grab an orange juice from the bar before finding a sneaky place to add my own gin from my bag.

On the move again, I recognise more and more faces. Christine looks good, very smart in her new dress, at least that's what it looks like. Fashion isn't my thing, it doesn't need to be. There are so many of them that were on the periphery of my school days. Of course I know my classmates but with at least a hundred in the year it is hardly surprising that so many of the faces are unrecognisable. In the group where Christine is I spot Martin; someone I definitely am not interested in. He was Am Dram, not my scene then as it isn't now.

Reaching Alfie's group I hover on the outside. They are talking Notts Forest. I can't think of anything more boring. I used to like football but once Sky got in on the act they all became overpaid prima-donnas as far as I was concerned. Give me rugby any day, a real man's sport. Alfie sees me and acknowledges me so I slightly move away not wanting to engage with their conversation. A face I remember is Brian just to the left of me. He was a lump at school and hasn't changed much although his belly is now overhanging his trousers. T-shirt and greasy hair; some people never change. For all his faults he was a bright kid. Wonder what he has done with himself.

Alfie appears next to me. 'You okay, Pam?'

'What do you think of that outburst then?' I ask.

'Yeah, don't know what it was about,' he says, scanning the room. 'All I could see was Sarah making a bee line for Gemma, there was an exchange of words and then as Gemma walked away Sarah vented her callousness as usual.'

'Are you still up for some retribution, Alfie?' I ask.

A smile grows on his face. 'You bet!'

'Okay, how much do you know about Sarah and Ascot?'

'Not a huge amount. I was more concerned for my sister than what that pair got up to.'

'How is your sister these days?'

'Bless her heart, she managed to get into uni and studied History of Art; she got a Doctorate in the subject. Considering how scarred she was psychologically, I take my hat off to her for achieving so much.'

'Remind me what madam actually did to Tanya.'

'It wasn't just one incident,' Alfie continues, 'right from the start she picked on Tanya. Why I will never know. Once, she caught her in the corridor and deliberately tripped her up. Tanya fell to the floor awkwardly and hurt her leg. Sarah apparently just laughed, walked past her and kicked her in the shin. Of course her cronies laughed too, throwing more abuse at her before walking off. There were other similar types of physical abuse as well as verbal. I couldn't be with her and protect her all the time. Tanya at one point wouldn't go into school and mum had to intervene.

The worst episode culminated with Sarah catching Tanya on the way back from school one night. I felt so guilty as we usually headed home together, but that night I had after school work. Anyway Tanya was crossing the park, Sarah and her gang were there waiting. Sarah stripped Tanya down to her knickers and bra and left her there taking her clothes and dumping them in a bin.'

'Bloody hell, what a bitch,' I exclaim.

'I guess everyone else thought it was highly hilarious. Although Tanya and mum reported it nothing ever got done because it was out of school. And the police were next to useless.'

'Poor Tanya. This must have been kept very quiet, unless I have wiped it from my memory with what Sarah was doing to me. I knew she moved schools but never thought of asking you why. Sorry, Alfie. No wonder Tanya never came back to the area after uni. How the hell did that cow get away with doing so much?'

'God knows,' Alfie replies. 'I just want to get back at her.'

'Well, our time has arrived. You're not going to believe what went on at their wedding reception.'

Alfie looks at me intently. 'What happened then?'

'Let's go somewhere a bit more private. I don't want anyone to hear because this is going to be good and it's ours.' We walk off heading to one of the classrooms where we can close the door.

'Come on, come on,' insists Alfie, 'I am dying to hear this.'

I tell him everything, although I keep the sources anonymous for the time being. And then I fall silent just watching Alfie's reaction.

'Bloody hell.' You can see the cogs working inside his head. 'Oh. My. God!' he says. 'That's dynamite. But come on, surely she knows?'

'Seems not,' I reply. 'Why the hell would she stay with him if she did? My source was saying that Ascot also boasted about other girls he had conquered.'

'What a sleaze ball,' Alfie comments, raising his eyebrows. 'Phew, that's going to blow her mind. Serves her right.'

'Yep, fate, divine retribution, call it what you want, it's finally arrived after all these years. So, how do you think we should do this?' I ask.

'Do you want to get Gemma involved?'

'No I don't, but she's free to join in if she feels the need to get her own back.'

'Okay,' he says. 'When do we go?'

I look at my watch, he at his. 'It's as near as damn it 9.05. I have had enough so I am quite happy to go with it now and walk as soon as it's out in the open.'

'I'm fine with that. I don't think I will leave though, I want to watch the aftermath.'

'Before we go back can we exchange numbers?' I ask. 'I would love to find out what happens after I leave.'

'Yeah, sure,' he says, 'but why don't you stay to watch the fun? Seems like you're running away.'

'Yeah, I suppose I am. I guess I'm a bit scared of the repercussions. Look at what she has just done to Gemma, can you imagine what she might do? No, I don't want to stay, sorry.'

'Okay, it's up to you,' Alfie replies with a shrug.

'Let's go. But if you don't mind I would like to collect Jake on the way through.'

'Let's do this!' Alfie grins, taking my arm as we stride back towards the door of the classroom.

Re-entering the hall, everything seems as it was before we left. A new group is surrounding the Thomsetts, all of them intent on their every word. It makes me feel sick just looking. I glance around finding Jake, Kim and now Samuel talking together.

'Stay here, Alfie, I just need to go and have a quiet word with Jake,' I say as I stride off.

'Hello, Samuel,' I say as I join the group. 'Sorry to break you all up. Jake asked me to let him know when I had found Alfie. He is on his own if you want to come over?' I suggest, giving Jake a look, which says *You have to come now!*

'Thanks for finding him. Please excuse us Sam. It was good to catch up. Kim, are you coming?' asks Jake.

'Yes,' she nods, 'see you later, Sam.'

As we walk back towards Alfie, Kim leans in towards me. 'Thanks for that, Pam. It seems after all the trouble he got himself into at school and the grief he gave his parents, Samuel has only gone and become a Vicar.'

'Really? That's the last thing I expected.'

We arrive at Alfie's side. He looks at me alarmed because I have brought both of them across. 'Don't worry, Alfie, they know all about it. Jake has his own agenda and Kim is just here for the ride. She was my best mate at school.'

I turn to both of them. 'What is going to happen now will give you closure, Jake. However, I intend to leave straight after. Sorry to leave you all with the aftermath. Kim, if you have had enough it would be great if you want to join me at the hotel for a *quiet* drink but if you don't that's fine.'

Kim nods happily.

Turning back to Alfie I take a deep breath. 'Okay. Ready for it?'

I glance over to check that the bitch and the beast are still in the same place. We quietly make our way over to the circle, standing on the periphery having our own quiet conversation. Jake isn't too comfortable being so close to Ascot; I whisper to him to just give us time.

We listen to the conversation. What a surprise, it is Sarah holding everyone under her spell yet again. We just bide our time, until lo and behold one of the group starts discussing their history. Sarah leads herself right into it. 'Oh our wedding was such a beautiful day. You know we married at Delacourt Manor,' she boasts.

Alfie and I look at each other and turn into the circle. I smile sweetly at Sarah, who looks surprised and puzzled. As she is just about to launch into something else, Alfie pipes up, 'Oh, yes it was a *splendid* day, Sarah, wasn't it? Especially for Ascot.'

'Well, yes it was,' Sarah begins but then realises that Alfie means something else. She grabs Ascot's arm, looking at Alfie. 'What do you mean? It couldn't have been more perfect, isn't that right, darling?' turning to Ascot who by now has gone very pale as he notices Jake in the background.

'Are you alright?' Sarah says looking at Ascot. He is beginning to squirm. There is muttering around the group as if some of them know his past.

'Well, I don't know what you're implying but this isn't the time or place,' Ascot blurts out looking directly at us.

'Oh, I don't know,' I reply. As I stare intently at Sarah taking a small step forward to get maximum impact. 'So Sarah, it doesn't seem you know what *really* went on at your own wedding.' I am practically in her face as she goes from pink to red.

'You!' she exclaims pulling back slightly. 'Well, what do you know, Pammy?' as venom exudes from her. 'You weren't invited.'

'Oh, word gets around,' I smile at her, revelling in the power I have over her. She is beginning to lose her grip.

'Let me get this right: your best mate, Natalie...'

'What's she got to do with anything?' Sarah interrupts. 'She never came to this school.'

'Oh, that's right, yes, she was better than you wasn't she? Got to the Grammar school. And maybe your new husband realised that she was better than you, too.'

Sarah's mouth is as tight as a duck's arse. Ascot begins to look really panicked. I can see he is about to try and shut me up somehow. It is now or never for the knockout blow.

'That's right,' I say vindictively, 'your WONDERFUL Ascot fucked your best mate during the reception.'

The silence ebbs further out, even the background music is stopping. Sarah has gone completely pale, Ascot bright red. After a few shocked intakes of breath the group are now tittering and smirking.

'Perhaps it's karma for being an utter bare-faced bully at school,' Alfie chips in. 'There are plenty of people here, including Pam and my sister who got the back end of you. You are a prize bitch and you deserve every nasty little thing you get.'

Sarah suddenly galvanises herself, turning on Ascot. 'What the hell have you done?' she spits at him. 'Is this true?'

He doesn't know where to look.

'Well...?'

He hesitates and then tries to smarm his way out of the situation, as usual. 'Oh, come on Sarah, that was a bloody long time ago. And we were all drunk. Don't spoil the party.' He goes to grab Sarah's hand but she yanks it away with a looks could kill expression on her face.

'You despicable shit!' she yells at him immediately slapping him very hard around the face.

Ascot's hand goes straight to where the slap has landed.

'What did you expect?' he slings at her as she storms off. His voice is now very loud as he shouts after her. 'You were the one that got pregnant. I would never have married you otherwise.'

Sarah never stops, just carries on marching across the hall with her head held high, moving the crowd as she goes.

Ascot turns on Alfie and me with a dark look. 'Oh, fucking thanks for that,' he throws at us. 'She never knew until now.'

'Well, I can't say I'm sorry,' chimes in Jake behind us. 'You need to keep your mouth shut and fly zipped especially when you're bladdered,' he retorts.

Ascot glares at Jake.

'Don't you dare blame Jake,' I fling at him. 'From the reaction you got here your indiscretions are widely known.' I start to walk away but can't resist a parting shot.

'Good luck. The both of you deserve each other.'

The four of us join together.

'Thanks for that, Pam,' Jake says.

'I couldn't have done this without Alfie. He reminded me of what Sarah did to Tanya and that gave me the determination to see it through.' I glance at the entrance to the hall; I am getting nervous, needing to get away before Sarah comes back. Turning to Kim, I say, 'Sorry, but I need to go. Would you like to join me?'

'Yes, I think I will, thanks. We still have so much to catch up on.'

'Jake, are you staying?' I ask.

'You bet. I want the next instalment. There may be violence,' he says hopefully.

I turn to Alfie and kiss him on the cheek. 'How are you feeling now?'

'So much better, you wouldn't believe. I hope you do as well. I'll give you an update tomorrow.'

'Look forward to it.'

Kim and I head for the door, where Gemma is grinning at us. I smile. 'Guess you caught that, Gemma, hope it helps you as well. We all saw how vile she was to you earlier.' We don't stop for a reply.

Out in the fresh night air, we walk through the gates heading towards the hotel. 'How can one evening's reminiscing turn into something so vengeful?' I ask as we approach the hotel foyer. 'I never turned up with revenge on my mind. In fact I hadn't even given Sarah a thought until I saw her tonight.'

'To be honest, I have no idea,' she replies. 'I know it's the biggest reunion number wise that they've organised, that's probably got something to do with it. You forget just how much went on in our little lives all that time ago. And it's packed deeply inside without us knowing.'

'Well, I doubt the evening will see anything more dramatic than that,' I laugh as we enter the bar.

Gemma Robinson, *Business Queen* – 9:05 pm

COMING THROUGH THE hall doors is Rich, with a stocky, dark-haired man in tow. The face is one I know from the past, but haven't seen for several years. We're both in the computer software business but different fields.

'This is Nathan Garcia, CEO and sole owner of RealPlay, the virtual reality company.' Rich makes the introduction.

'I know.' I turn to Nathan, 'What's going on?'

'I didn't want to make any assumptions about how welcome I might be. I told Rich to keep it low-key but business-like.' Nathan has the grace to look a little shame-faced.

'Okay. So coming to my old school reunion is keeping it businesslike is it?' My tone is distinctly hostile, but only because I feel hostile – and ambushed.

Rich looks from Nathan to me and back again. 'What's the background here, then?' he says. 'I'm not sure why you asked me to introduce you to Gemma, Nathan. I thought you didn't know her. You said a relaxed situation with no pressure. This doesn't quite seem to fit that bill. And, Nathan, I don't like being played.'

'Neither do I. Didn't Nathan explain?' I say. 'He and I had some dealings some years ago when he tried to engineer a takeover of Digital Health Services. Thankfully, I got wind of what was afoot and stamped on it before the media got hold of the story, but I did *not* take kindly to it at the time and...' I turn back to Nathan, 'and, I still won't let you have my company. If you try to set me up again, I'll give you the fight of your life. So, I suggest you get straight back on the plane to California and take up surfing!'

Nathan grins. 'So, still coming out slugging, eh, Gemma? I'm not here to try to wrest your company from you. I have a much better plan this time. I apologise *again* for back then. I behaved badly, and it was a stupid idea and I'm glad you fought me off. We can do so much better than that!'

Despite his words, I am not reassured. I'm still angry with him. He isn't always straightforward in his business dealings and he did make a big mistake with me back then. It seems he wasn't upfront with Rich either. So, I'm not about to forgive him on his say-so that he's a changed man. What I do know for sure is that he's single-minded once he decides on a path to take his business forward. And I do not intend that my company will be next on his list of acquisitions. I need to make sure that he's clear on that. Rich is looking pissed off, as well he might, given the circumstances.

My company is my heart and soul. I built it from the ground up. And while the last couple of years of Brexit uncertainty isn't killing us, it is making life more difficult. The last thing I need now is an American partner sticking his oar in. Any partner would be a problem, but Nathan takes a very hands-on approach to the businesses he's involved with and I don't want him poking his nose in. Her Majesty's Government wouldn't like it either. To say that some of my contracts are sensitive would be to understate the case. I make a mental note to let my contact know that Nathan is sniffing around again. HMG might have some background information that will help me fend him off.

'Do you wanna hear my idea, Gemma?' Nathan is looking determined. I know that expression and it does not bode well.

'Not especially,' I reply, 'but I have no doubt you will tell me anyway. Not here though and not now. Ring my PA and he'll organise an appointment.'

'Oh no, Gemma. You're not pulling that one on me. I'm wise to your moves. We agree a cast iron date and time right now, or I'll make my pitch here, in public, at your reunion. My guess is that we'll have an interested audience in pretty short-order.'

Checkmate. He's got me and he knows it. I can't risk this getting into the media, and someone here will certainly Facebook or Twitter the confrontation. Looks like I have to make a firm commitment to meet with him privately.

'Okay,' I give in as gracefully as I can.

Spotting Liza, I beckon her over. Having Liza here might distract him for a while. She looks at Nathan and then at me with a lift of her eyebrows.

'Liza, this is Nathan Garcia owner and CEO of RealPlay. Nathan, this is my good friend Elizabeth Chastain – Liza.'

Nathan gives her his full wattage smile and I can see she is not impressed, neither by who he is nor by his rather smarmy charm which he then proceeds to turn up several notches. I move away and take Rich's arm, drawing him aside.

'What the hell, Rich? Did you really not know?'

'I'm annoyed at Nathan, but I'm hurt that you think I would deliberately deceive you and bring someone I know you don't want to be involved with.'

I hold up a hand, 'Okay, sorry. I'm just totally knocked sideways here. He's a shark when it comes to getting what he wants, and I feel like an unsuspecting seal, happily swimming around thinking I'm in safe waters and then *snap*, I'm dead in the water.'

Rich smiles. 'Please don't hold me responsible. He said nothing about knowing you, or having had previous dealings with you. And I'm sorry I was taken in by him.'

I look towards Nathan and Liza. He's talking a mile a minute and she is looking mildly interested. I shouldn't have left them alone, it's not fair on Liza to leave her in shark infested waters. I steer Rich back. 'Time to rescue Liza,' I say.

'Does she need rescuing?' asks Rich.

'No, but I'm going to rescue her all the same.'

I interrupt them at a point where Nathan seems to be telling Liza about a new plan he's hatched. I wonder if it's anything to do with his ideas for my company.

'Right,' I say, 'you and I have a firm date for our meeting, Nathan. And I'll catch up with you another time, Rich. I think that's it for tonight. Get your things together, Liza, and we'll get off back to the hotel.'

Liza looks me straight in the eye, her face taking on the "Oh really?" look that I know from our school days. 'What are you? My mother?' she smiles. 'I'm not quite ready to go yet. I've seen someone I want to catch up with. But you get off if you've had enough. I'll text you later.'

I back down. I'm not going without her and it's clear she's not ready to leave while Nathan is still outlining whatever it is he's trying to sell her. As I turn away, Nathan gives me a big wink. No. I'm not going anywhere, he's up to something.

Wandering off to see if any of Jamie's wine is left, I discover there's none to be found. Thankfully, Rich has a hip flask. Watching the other ex-pupils and sipping our brandies, I realise I hardly recognise any of them, and, if I'm honest, it doesn't bother me. Turning back to Rich I ask how his latest intake of students is doing.

'No-one among them I'd recommend to you,' he replies. 'What happened with you and Nathan, Gemma?' Rich knows nothing about that particular episode. Nevertheless, he is a good friend, and I trust him not to blab to the media.

'Nathan and I met during a big virtual reality conference in Silicon Valley. I had some unformed ideas about using V.R. in training and thought he might be a useful contact. Then I found out he was planning to buy me out, having had the same ideas about the use of V.R. that I had. He used some questionable tactics. I took exception to his underhand methods and we parted on bad terms and have steered clear of each other since.'

'What do you think his intentions are this time?' Trust Rich to get to the heart of the matter quickly.

'No idea – yet. But I'll do some research when I get back to my hotel. It's been a while since I followed his path of business acquisitions. There might be a clue to his thinking in the companies he's been involved with over the past year or so.'

I must admit I'm curious as to what Nathan has in mind. Not interested, exactly, but cautiously intrigued. I certainly didn't expect him to come up with another idea involving my company after last time. Whatever he's thinking, I shall have to listen carefully and make no commitments. One sign of weakness and he'll go straight for the kill.

Rich goes off to talk to a couple standing over by the ravaged remains of the so-called buffet table. He says who they are but I'm not really listening.

Liza hurries over to me, Nathan following like an American pit bull on a tight leash.

'Gemma, Nathan has come up with an amazing idea for our two companies.'

'Oh, yes?' I say, giving Nathan a hard look. 'And how much of your company will you still own when he's done with you?'

'Aw, Gemma,' Nathan protests. 'Gimme a break! It's a genuine deal.' He looks at me sideways, as if trying to assess how I might react. 'Y'know, if you're interested in bringing your digital medical expertise into the equation, we can make it a third of the company each. Fully owned and operated by the three of us.'

What *is* he thinking? He's got the light of a man possessed by a brilliant concept. I think hard about our three skill sets. Then I get it. Liza's camouflage make-up business and her contacts among scarred women and men and their medical teams; my computerised medical diagnostics and surgical work; his virtual reality set-up. Put them together and you get a company which offers a full range of worldwide diagnosis, V.R. training in delicate burns/scarring microsurgery, and individualised avatars on which to practice and experiment with different concealing makeups after the medical treatment is done. I have to hand it to him. It is a genius idea and despite myself, I find I am interested. He's gone a lot further in his thinking than I did. I wonder if he came here with this intention, or is this one of his lightening switches – grabbing an opportunity when he sees it? My shark analogy of earlier seems even more apposite. I suspect this is Nathan seeing a profitable move into a new area and taking a chance on making it work. I can make quick decisions, too, and make one right there and then. It would be good for both Liza and me, too, and we just have to be sure that, if we go ahead, everything is watertight. I shall also have to ensure that I keep any new company completely separate from Digital Health Services. I need to keep HM Government sweet and they wouldn't like any crossover.

'Okay. I suggest the three of us discuss this at the meeting Nathan and I set up for next week. I assume you can make it, Liza?'

She nods.

I continue. 'In that case, we'll need a feasibility study to ensure that the concept is a sound one and I'll get our legals on board as well; they'll need to be involved from the outset.' I give Nathan a hard look. It pays to make my position clear from the start.

Liza looks pleased, Nathan looks resigned. If he thinks Liza and I are going to take anything on trust with him, he is as wrong as he can be. Any deal the three of us end up making is going to be shark proof and watertight.

'This is a way better idea than the one I came to sell to you, Gemma,' Nathan says with a big smile. 'And I've gotten to meet Liza as well.' He turns an apparently admiring face towards her. She rolls her eyes at me. I take it her bullshit radar is in good operating order.

There seems to be some kind of screaming match going on. Oh yes! And it involves Sarah again. This time she seems to be having a major bust-up with Ascot. They're at the centre of quite a crowd. Wow! She just landed a good right-hander. He's yelling at her now. They both storm out past me. Okay. I'm leaving before he comes back looking for solace and sympathy. There's a woman walking towards me looking pleased with herself. Is that Pam? Well, good luck to her! I can't help but smile.

The evening is ending on a better note than I expected when I saw Rich come into the hall with Nathan. I don't know what the outcome of our discussions about a new business will be and I can't help being a little concerned, but if Liza and I decide to go for it, we must be as hands-on as Nathan and constantly vigilant. Nathan is no slouch when it comes to getting what he wants and I have no doubt he will use every trick in the book to use us and then sideline us.

Rich has ambled back. Nathan is still trying to beguile Liza and she's having none of it. He seems to take it philosophically, says his goodbyes, tells us how much he is looking forward to working with us. Liza does another eye-roll. Yup, that's my girl.

'Are you ready to make a move now, Liza?' I ask.

She shakes her head. 'I've seen someone I want to talk to,' she says. 'You and Rich go, I'm okay to hang on for a while. I'll catch up with you at the hotel.' She gives me an impulsive hug. 'I'm glad we're tight again, Gemma. I've missed you so much.'

I nod and hug her close. 'Me, too.' I say. I can feel myself getting emotional and teary. This won't do. I'm the buttoned-up business woman with a reputation to uphold. Even Rich is giving me a "What?" look.

The music amps up another notch. People are hugging, dancing in small groups, swaying and getting sweaty. And I definitely want to be elsewhere when the drunken "last dance" gets going. Now that Nathan's gone, I can't see any reason to hang on. Liza doesn't need me here to get her back, she's fine. Rich tips his head towards the dancers and nods towards the door. Time to go. We decide to share a taxi back to the hotel. Liza will come when she's good and ready. I wonder briefly who this mysterious person is that she wants to catch up with. I expect she'll tell me when she gets back. Rich and I intend to spend what's left of the evening together. As long as it includes several large drinks, I'll leave worrying about the future for another time.

Phil Morris, *The Man, The Legend* – 9:05 pm

WHERE DID THE lads go I wonder? They both vanished when I was chatting up that girl. Shame her friend dragged her off cus I was definitely in there! Never mind, I'll probably bump into her later.

I finger the e-cig in my pocket and decide to go outside for a smoke. There had been signs at the front forbidding smoking of any kind on the premises. That was probably there for standard school opening times, but better play safe and find somewhere more discreet. I walk down the corridor and take a left, through the new build part, and slip out into the old quad and behind the bike sheds. Ha, just like old times, except the galvanised metal structure has gone, replaced by a couple of poles and a slanted transparent roof structure. Oh well, there's a couple of others here. I join them and take a draw from my plastic fag, nodding in acknowledgement of my fellow addicts.

'Hi Phil,' says one of them, 'long time no see.'

'Uh, hi,' I say as I struggle to place the face and end the long seconds of awkward silence.

'Rodney,' he says, 'I was...'

'Oh my God! Rod! You look so different. Not as different as some I might mention, but - how ya doin'? When did you become a Mormon?'

Rodney grins. 'Ha ha, very funny. I'm a solicitor, so all the hair had to go. Don't want to frighten the clients.'

'Shame, so what's new? I've been talking to Chuck and Willy – and Charlie – you'll never guess...'

'I just saw Karl,' he half whispers. 'Spooked me a bit. I haven't seen him since that day, and this is the last place I would've expected him to appear.'

'Huh, I haven't seen him since then either. Last thing I heard of him was a rather unnecessary mention in the local rag when his brother died. Poor bugger. Did you talk to him? How is he? Did he go into the hall?'

'No, I just saw him in the car park. He was getting something out of the back of an old Vauxhall van. I thought about waving and saying hi, but I never knew him that well and, you know...'

I eject a billowing cloud of white smoke and think back to those times. He was always a good mate, well, up until that day when everything changed. He always had the best jokes and the funniest pranks; if anyone was gonna put a fart cushion on the form tutor's chair, it would be Karl. I remember once when he and Pete had been on a lunchtime shoplifting spree, they came back with a load of alphabet sticker sheets and covered the Head's car with swear words, hilarious. I grin at the memory. I feel sorry for Karl. Everyone blamed him for what happened. Well, I guess it was mostly his fault, but he didn't bring that hairspray into class and how could he have known what would happen?

I remember it pretty well. It was just another boring chemistry lesson, and Karl and Danny had been messing about most of the morning, blowing rice at people through biro tubes when Hendry was writing on the board, and making fart noises when he bent to pick up the chalk.

Things kicked off when Hendry was doing something sciencey with sodium in the smoke chamber. Karl grabbed the hairspray from Liza's bag – bloody big can – size of a fire extinguisher! Obviously, she shouldn't have brought it into the lab or she at least should've kept her bag closed or something, but it was hilarious watching Karl keep shooting jets of spray at Dan. It was mostly directed at his hair, but he was pretty much covered in no time. He'd got a couple of blasts in his face, and the stuff was dripping off his chin. All the time he was doing it Liza was screeching and trying to snatch the hairspray back off Karl. Dan was pulling at Karl's blazer and calling him all sorts of names. I don't think Karl intended to light the spray with the Bunsen burner – or maybe he did, but he couldn't have known it would act like a flame thrower. Suddenly there was this ball of fire and people screaming. Well, Liza mostly, and Hendry rushed into the classroom. He obviously had no clue what to do, bloody idiot! Danny's head was a fireball, well the whole top of his body really. Karl was obviously mortified 'cus he was frozen to the spot – he must've felt awful. It was all just an accident and could've happened to any of us really. Poor old Karl. I think Danny died in the ambulance, or at the hospital. Wouldn't want to live with the burns he must've had, it was a mercy really...

Liza got burned on the side of her face too. Her hair was on fire, and some hero patted the flames out while somebody else totally failed to operate the fire extinguisher on Danny. I wonder if Liza is here? It would be nice to see her again and see what she looks like now. I always quite fancied her. After the accident she was off school for a while, then when she came back, she'd grown her hair longer and always kept one side of her face covered, like Gabrielle. Quite cute.

There was a hell of a fuss, and Hendry's feet didn't touch the ground. It was all his fault really. He shouldn't have left the lab unattended for so long. He was off with stress for ages, probably on full pay, then took early retirement soon after. Huh, alright for some. I never saw Karl after that. He got expelled and spent some time at that detention centre. Must've been awful. Poor old Karl.

Iain Wilson, "*Legitimate Businessman*" – 9:05 pm

I WIPE MY FACE with my stupidly expensive suit sleeve. I wish I had a tissue.

The sound of voices off to my left makes me poke my head forward to grab a quick look; a couple of women are walking down the corridor from the hall so I try and pull myself back together. I take another peek to see if they're heading towards me, but they've stopped at the notice board, pointing out items written by people they know.

I need to leave. Get back home to the flat, fix this punishment beating shit with Simmo, get back on track. I stand up and stride down the corridor, back towards the hall and the main entrance beyond when one of the women says something.

'Oh, look, here's that poem by Iain Wilson. He wrote it when his sister died. It's so beautiful. I cried when I read it.'

My footsteps falter and my legs stop working. I slowly, jerkily, turn around to look at the women, as they turn to look at me. One is short, a little overweight in a tight black dress, with a shocked look on her face. I think her name is Debbie, Denise, or something.

The other woman has blonde hair cascading over half of her face and looks like she wishes it would cover the other half too. 'Oh, Iain, hi,' she manages to say eventually.

'Liza. Hi. Um. How are you?'

'Good, thanks.' I can tell she's dying with embarrassment.

'You look...' I begin and then mentally kick myself. After the fire that killed Danny and scarred her forever, Liza was understandably self-conscious about her looks. But she does look amazing, so I carry on and tell her.

A man appears to our left and gestures to his watch. I guess this must be Debbie-Denise's partner and he wants to get off home. She turns to Liza, says how lovely it's been and promises to keep in touch and then scuttles off with Unrefined Alpha Male Exhibit A.

Liza watches her go and then looks back at the poem on the board. 'I suppose you heard me talking about your poem, then?'

'Ah, yeah.'

'It's true. What you expressed about losing Ella was really touching.'

My mouth hangs open. 'You... you remembered her name.'

She looks up at me. 'Yes. She was your sister. She was a couple of years below us. I remember the assembly after she died. They had a picture of her on the stage.'

I don't remember any of this. I was probably off school.

'The teachers said,' she continues, 'that we were to be sensitive to how you and her friends were feeling. I would have offered to help if I could've thought of anything to say to you. But in the end I just decided to give you some space.' She looks back at the poem. 'I guess you worked it out in the end.'

And now I look at the poem again. 'I think I was getting there.' *Slightly off the rails since, though.*

'Shall we go and get some air? she says, and suddenly we're slowly walking down the corridor to the exit that looks out at the new sports hall. She slips her arm through mine. 'I hope you don't mind me saying, but you looked a bit emotional back there.'

'Yeah. Old ghosts and that.'

We're both silent then and we both know we're both thinking about Danny and Ella, two young lives snuffed out while we get older. I feel the guilt about Danny come swirling back like charcoal fog. But I keep walking and we push through the doors to a cooling summer's night. The bright exterior lights are on, illuminating the paths and roadways around the school but the distant trees are now black shapes against a deep navy skyline.

'It's funny,' she says, 'and you're probably going to think that I'm an idiot or something, but I've had a couple of glasses of wine, exorcised some of my own demons, so what the hell.' She takes a breath and announces quite brazenly, 'I used to quite fancy you.'

For the second time in a few minutes my jaw drops.

'Not in any pitying kind of way,' she carries on, 'in case you were thinking that. This was before the fire and before Ella. You always seemed so happy. And not taken in with all that bloody bravado from the sporty lot. A happy, free spirit, with a cute face and a floppy fringe.' She laughs, briefly. 'I kept wishing that you'd ask me out.' She stops walking and looks down. 'And then after the fire I knew you never would.'

I am such an idiot. I was so obsessed with Katy that I didn't spot Liza, the lovely, caring, thoughtful Liza, waiting for me to sweep her into my arms. What is it with shyness? How the hell do two shy people ever get together?

I look down too and sigh, not knowing what to say and so an awkward silence lingers around us like a bad fart that neither of us wants to mention.

'I'm sorry,' she says, quietly. 'I'm a bit drunk and tonight seems the night for getting things off my chest.'

I glance at her chest. Hey, I can't help that I'm a shallow bastard.

'After the fire,' she continues, 'you sent me flowers. It helped me get through the worst of it. You were so thoughtful.'

Christ, I'd forgotten that. Thinking back, I'm pretty sure that they were Flowers of Guilt. I need to tell her. 'Look, Liza, I'm not the person you think I am.'

'Yes, I know. We're all older, wiser. You're probably married, three kids, dogs, holidays in the Alps and the Algarve.'

I laugh. 'Well, you got the holidays right. But you're way off on the others.'

She stares at me. 'You're gay.'

'What? No! Of course, I'm not bloody...' I catch myself. 'Not that there's anything wrong with that. But I'm not gay. Or bi. Or anything.'

She smiles. And for a second I'm looking at myself talking to Katy and I can tell she's thinking '*Get in!*'

'No, look. I'm...' I scrabble for the right words. 'I'm not a nice person. I'm not thoughtful or kind.' I can see she's going to interrupt so I crash on. 'Maybe I was, back when I was a kid. But you need to know something else.'

'Don't tell me, you're a murderer.'

Ouch. That's a bit close to the bone. 'No, of course not.' *Not yet, anyway.* 'But I do have someone's death on my hands.'

'What do you mean?'

'Danny.'

'What about him? You didn't do that, it was Karl.'

'Yes, but I'm the reason Karl did what he did.'

She looks suitably confused. To be honest, now that I try to explain it to someone else it does sound a bit weird. I do my best in a rambling, shrugging, flapping way.

'So,' she says eventually, 'you hold yourself responsible for Danny's death because he stopped Karl from kicking your head in while you were grieving for your sister.'

'Um. Yeah. And that means I'm responsible for what happened to you.'

'Iain Wilson, you are the stupidest, sweetest twat I've met in quite a while.'

I'm definitely not sure about 'sweetest' but the rest is fine.

She takes my arm again and we carry on walking around the school. 'You didn't cover Danny in my hairspray. You didn't mess about with fire in the science room. It had nothing to do with you.'

'Yes, but...'

'But nothing. It was Karl. Now be told.'

'Yes, mum.'

She laughs, and I feel a weight lifting off my shoulders. Not much of a weight, granted, given the fact that it feels like I'm carrying a double decker bus full of problems, but just one of them getting off is better than nothing. We carry on walking.

Hannah Parker, *was a proper Charlie* – 9:25 pm

AFTER MAKING OUR way inside, I offer to get us both a drink. I think we need one. The queue isn't too long, and I'm soon taking a large sip of the crap wine. I find a corner of the room to hide; I need to be alone with my thoughts to process the last hour with Helen. The wine is awful but still much better than the concoction Lucy managed.

We'd been dragged into a group chat along the way to get our drinks. It had been nice to catch up with people but all the time I'd wanted to get away so I could think.

I shake my head; it's struggling to take in everything that's just happened. The wave of emotion is so overwhelming, I'm surprised I kept it together during the revelation from Helen.

A daughter, I have a daughter. I'd always wondered if the rumours were true about the pregnancy and I might have once thought that I could be the father, but it seemed so far-fetched. We'd never even known what we were doing. Becoming a parent is something I've obviously thought about over the years; doesn't everyone? I know a lot of people adopt nowadays, for all sorts of reasons and not just because they don't possess the right parts to get the job done, as Lucy would say. I know it isn't the route I wanted. My dream it seems has come true. A daughter.

I tried to play it cool with Helen. I didn't want to come over as too keen, but I really hope that Helen tells Chloe. I know I won't put any pressure on her. Chloe seems like a bright kid. She will work it out, but maybe it would be better if Helen told her first. Arranging to meet for a coffee would be a start. What a night, and the kiss! That was unexpected, but oddly unsexual for a kiss. It celebrated a past shared, and what I hope to be a bright future. A future that includes a child. MY child. Suddenly, I feel emotionally drained and lean against the wall for support.

There had been others I wanted to see tonight, other people that I'd felt I needed to make amends with. But, I don't know if

I have the emotional strength, and anyway I reason, I've made amends with Julia, and she was really the only one I felt bad about over the years. She hadn't deserved the rumours I'd helped to spread about her. The other people probably did deserve it.

Looking around the night is in full swing, although it looks intense in some of the groups. More than one person has turned up to make amends for past encounters it seems, and earlier in the night I'd heard a few raised voices. I wonder if Julia has caught up with the sleaze bag teacher yet. It was nice seeing Ryan and Jamie and the others. Phil was his usual self – he will never change and I kind of love him for it. Where would the world be without people like Phil?

Feeling calmer I take the drinks back to the group. I smile at Helen as I pass her a drink. Just as I'm about to talk Lucy turns up.

'Oh my life, my legs are tired,' Lucy says breathlessly, leaning on me, her blonde hair spilling down my shoulder.

I sigh. 'I'm not surprised. You've been dancing for ages, Lucy. Let me introduce you to Helen, we were friends at school.'

Giggling, Lucy embraces Helen. Much to her surprise.

'Lovely to meet you. Fab dress. Bet you couldn't believe it when you met Hannah again? She's smoking hot in this dress isn't she? Much better as a girl I think.'

Helen smiles at Lucy. I can see she's not sure how to take her. Helen's daughter, my daughter I remind myself, holds her hand up to her mouth trying to hide her smile.

'Right, is that drink mine, Hannah?' Lucy holds out her hand for the glass.

'Yes, here is tomorrow's hangover, served up in a beautiful plastic glass,' I say, winking at Chloe. I hand over the glass of wine.

Lucy grabs the glass and downs it. Helen and Chloe are catching flies.

'I love a free bar,' Lucy says wiping her mouth. If she didn't buy the most expensive lipstick money could buy, her lipstick would be smeared all over her face.

'Okay then. We're going up to the science lab. I'm desperate to see THE ROOM. Have you two been up there yet?' Lucy asks.

'No, I'm not intending to take my daughter up there,' Helen says.

'Oh, don't be daft, everyone wants to see a room where a murder took place,' Lucy says.

'Right then, Lucy, I think it's time we got you a glass of water.' I turn to Helen and Chloe, 'It was lovely to see you again, Helen, and nice to meet you, Chloe. You have my number. Let's make sure we meet up next week for that coffee.'

I embrace them both, trying not to linger too long on the first feel of my daughter. I feel tears threatening as I reluctantly let go and walk away.

Lucy links arms with me, noticing my eyes she says, 'Are you okay, sweetheart?'

This endearment nearly sends me over the edge. I take a deep breath and sigh, 'Better than okay. But, I will tell you later. Let's get you a glass of water and to that lab, you crazy death chaser.'

'As long as you're sure? If anyone has upset you, I WILL fight them.'

'Honestly, Lucy, you brighten up my life in every way possible. I'm so glad we are friends.'

'Don't be getting all soppy on me, Hannah. We can only push our waterproof mascara so far. I think I'm going to be sick.'

Thankfully we are near the toilets.

After being sick and sipping some water, Lucy declares she's back on form. I've always marvelled at the way she can be sick and carry on partying straight after. I feel sorry for myself days after drinking too much. I reapply some of her make-up, tidy her hair back in place, and give her a mint to freshen her breath.

'There, almost human. Now, do you still want to go to the lab?'

'Yes, of course I do, Hannah.'

We negotiate the hall and stairs and make our way back to the science lab. Lucy barges straight in and I follow her in. She stumbles slightly and grabs the side of one of the tables.

'Good, no-one is here. You get inside and I will go and close the door, so we're not disturbed. Then you can tell me all about it,' Lucy says, while I move further into the room, running my hands over the tables and remembering a day I wish I could forget. I don't know how I let her talk me into this. Lucy is a force though.

I'm surprised the room is empty. Maybe not everyone is as macabre as Lucy then – even though she didn't attend this school. I'm surprised more people haven't ventured up here. Curiosity is a powerful instinct.

Iain Wilson, *"Legitimate Businessman"* – 9:30 pm

I COULD GET USED *to this*, thinks one tiny part of my brain. The romantic, emotional, impulsive part. The rest of me looks on in horror. Just because I came here with stupid, sappy intentions to reconnect with someone I had no real connection to in the first place, I shouldn't just rebound into the arms of any woman who shows an interest. I have responsibilities, commitments, meetings. Organised crime doesn't run itself, you know. The clue is in the title. Otherwise it's just crime. Rambling, risky, unpredictable theft, violence and chaos.

A door bursts open on our right and a figure in a grey tracksuit steps out into our path. He looks up at us in surprise and staggers slightly; that's when I notice the vodka bottle in his hand.

'What you fuckin' lookin' at?' he spits.

I can't believe it. The hair is close-cropped and receding, the lines on the face more pronounced and there's greying stubble on his chin, but this is definitely him. 'Karl Stamford.'

'Yeah, what's it to you, dickhead? Look at all you fancy wankers, coming back to school to show off who's got the biggest car or the fattest wallet or the sluttiest woman.' He leers at Liza. 'Don't think much of yours.'

That's the thing that does it. Liza gasps and I feel her begin to reel; he's just ignited a spark inside me and the pain and frustration of the last few hours join forces with decades-old guilt, fear and impotency. He sees me stepping forward and opens out his arms inviting the fight.

'Come on then, if you think...'

I sway around a flailing punch and slam hard with my left fist into his abdomen, just below his right ribs. He drops the bottle and it smashes onto the pavement. He tries to punch me with his newly freed hand but the blow is weak and poorly aimed, skidding off my right shoulder. I'm not executing perfect martial arts moves but to be frank I don't need to. He's drunk, out of shape and easy pickings. My main problem is that I like hitting him. Over and over again. That one's for Ella, that one's for Danny, and another for Liza. But there's more. All of the rejection, angst, loneliness, self-loathing – they're all queuing up for a swing too.

I'm holding him up against the wall with my left hand while my right fist works him over like a meat tenderiser, body then head. It's getting harder to punch him and it takes a few seconds to realise that Liza is pulling at my arm.

'Iain! Stop it! You'll kill him!'

I let go of him and stagger backwards, gasping. He collapses onto the ground, moaning slightly.

'Shit, Liza, I'm so sorry.' I can't look at her so I keep my eyes down and see that I've got blood on my knuckles. Neither of us knows what to do or say. I can hear Karl sobbing and it gets louder.

'Why me?' he suddenly wails, through cut and swollen lips. 'Why does everything bad happen to me?'

'What the hell are you talking about?' Liza shoots back at him. 'You killed Danny! You scarred my face, ruined my life! And now you're drunk and feeling sad that you've been beaten up by someone you bullied at school.'

'My boy...' he mumbles.

'What? You have a son? Bloody God help him, that's all I can say.' Liza stands near him, leaning over, arms folded, clasped as if protecting herself from the cold.

Karl sobs again and amongst the moans we hear, 'He's dead...'

Liza glances at me and I shrug. I know nothing about Karl other than the fact that he finished his education in a youth detention centre after being found guilty of manslaughter.

'James is dead, now Kyle's dead.'

James? That name rings a bell in relation to Karl. 'Your brother, James?'

'Yeah. Little bruv. Joined the army. Got killed.'

Liza and I look at each other again. 'And Kyle?' she asks him.

'My boy. Tried to tell him.' Karl snuffles and coughs before carrying on. 'I came back to Newark, I got clean. Got a job, yeah? Told him that smack was bad news. Didn't listen. He was still in Skeg with his mum. He OD'd last week.'

The three of us are silent for a little while. I can see Liza trying to reconcile this situation with her natural empathetic nature. Her entire adult life has been moulded by what this pathetic loser inadvertently did to her, but I'm not surprised when she says to him, 'Do you need a tissue?'

He glances down at his blood-stained top and gingerly wipes his face on his sleeves. 'Nah, I'm alright, thanks.'

As for me, Karl's dealt me a bigger blow with those words than anything he managed to throw in our brief dance of violence. I run a small County Lines operation into Skegness. Mainly heroin. I could have supplied Karl's lad with the batch that killed him. My head spins.

In all probability, it is unlikely to have been my boys, but even if it wasn't the fact remains that I'm part of the industry that's killing people. And just look at Karl himself. He's an ex-junkie by the sound of it and that doesn't come as a stunning piece of news. He sits slumped against the foot of the wall, bloodied and bruised, drunk and crushed. He disgusts me but I know that part of why he's in this state is because of the actions of people like me. It wouldn't surprise me if I was actually one of the cogs in the machine that kept him in the gutter and then killed his son.

And now I've given him a brutal kicking for good measure. I'm beginning to think that the universe is trying to tell me that I'm a bit of a shit.

I clear my throat. 'Erm, Karl, look. I'm sorry to hear about your lad, okay?'

He glares at me but says nothing.

'So, are you going to be alright?' I ask. 'Do you need anything?'

'Just fuck off and leave me alone.'

Liza looks at me and I shrug. She steps around his splayed legs, tentatively takes my arm and we set off again, glancing back behind us. After we've gone about twenty metres we notice that he's on his feet again staring at us. He makes a big open armed gesture, almost as if he's pretending to be a tree. Or miming the Whole Thing in charades. I frown as we turn the corner and he disappears from view.

'You were, um, a little intense back there,' Liza says carefully.

'Yeah, sorry. Things just came to a bit of a head.'

There's a bit of a pause before she continues. 'Been in many fights, then?'

'No, not many.'

'You seemed to take to it quite well.'

'I do a bit of martial arts to keep in shape. Every once in a while it keeps me from getting hurt.'

Another long silence. Shit. Just as the evening had taken a positive turn I'm now having to justify my sudden violent outburst. I take a deep breath. 'Look, Liza. I'm really not the kind of person you'd like to hang out with. My life is a complicated mess and deep at the core is a lot of...' I struggle for the right word, '... unpleasantness.' I don't think that's the word I wanted but it'll have to do.

We stop walking and she looks at me, those surprisingly dark brown eyes, under the curtain of blonde hair, searching for the real Iain Wilson. 'You're not happy, are you?'

I snort and pull a wry smile. 'I am not overburdened with joy, no.'

'Do you want to stay that way?'

I open my mouth but can't think of what to say so I shut it again and shrug. 'No,' I eventually concede, knowing full well where this is going.

'So change your life. Stop doing the unpleasant things.'

'It's not that easy. I've got commitments, responsibilities.'

'Such as?'

'I can't tell you that.'

She tilts her head and looks at me as if studying a piece of modern art she can't quite work out. 'Are these unpleasant things illegal?'

I screw my face up in an effort not to lie but also not tell the truth and in that moment she knows. 'Bloody hell, Iain, what have you got yourself into?'

'I don't want to talk about it.'

'Is there someone making you do this? Some Mister Big or whatever?'

I break away from her gaze, shove my hands in my trouser pockets and walk a few steps down the path. I've said too much. The events of the day have got me rattled and I've opened up in a way I've never done before. But I can't just walk off and leave her. I owe her some kind of explanation. I turn back and look at her concerned face, the scar almost invisible under the make-up, the high-pressure sodium lights giving her a warm glow. '*I'm* Mister Big. There's no-one making me do this. It's all me. And that's how I like it.'

'Is it, though? Because you seem bloody miserable if this is the way you like it. Do your mum and dad know what you do?'

'No, of course not.'

'And what about Ella? Would she be proud of her big brother?'

Shit. That was below the belt. I say nothing and stare at the ground. She walks towards me and puts a hand on my shoulder.

'What do you *want*, Iain?'

I shake my head fractionally, uncertain of how to respond. I really don't know what I want. She slowly puts her arms around me and gives me a hug.

And it's good. The closeness of another human being, a compassionate embrace, the enclosing pressure on my arms and back and chest. The pleasantly sweet smell of an attractive woman who seems to actually care about me. I put my arms around her, pressing into the small of her back.

That's what I want. It's definitely what I need right now.

And tomorrow? Do I go back to the clinical, logical, emotionless life of a shady gangland supremo, calculating supply and demand, working out at the gym, laughing with a few faux friends in a bar before returning to my empty flat? I already have more money than most people could ever hope to earn legitimately, why do I feel the need to make more?

I feel Liza loosening her embrace. 'Iain, your life is what you make it.' She's staring into my eyes. 'I found that out the hard way. Years of feeling sorry for myself, too afraid to face up to reality and deal with it. You're in a rut that you can get out of, you just need to make that decision.'

Can I?

'You make it sound so simple.' I've still got my hands on her hips. I don't want to let her go.

'Often, the most obvious solution is the right one.'

Could I really just step away from everything I've done in my adult life? Become an actual ordinary person?

'What would I do instead?' I ask. I know that I'm looking for someone else to make everything alright but the thought of just walking away is terrifying. And exhilarating.

'You can do whatever you want. Whatever makes you feel fulfilled and happy. Give all your money away, work for a charity.'

'Steady on,' I say with a smile, 'let's keep hold of the money for the time being.'

'Money isn't everything.'

'I know, but it helps.'

'Has it helped you?'

'Forget the money. This is about me. What would I do? Where would I go? Sit in a villa in the Algarve for the rest of my life?'

'It doesn't matter. Just do good. Be good. Help people.'

I'm silent for a few seconds wondering who I could help, who I could be good to. I look into her eyes again. 'Do you need any help?'

She snorts. 'Iain, I have a list as long as my arm. Psychotherapist to get me through crippling bouts of depression being the main one.'

I'm stunned. 'Really? You seem, so... together.'

'I specialise in hiding things. You know I have my own company? You know what we do?'

I shake my head. 'I didn't know you had a company.' She's impressing me more and more.

'Cosmetics for burns and scar patients. Makes everything look perfectly normal even though it's still a mess underneath. Just like my life.'

'Join the club.'

'The company's doing fine but sometimes I just can't take it anymore. If I relapse it falls on my mum and she's not getting any younger.'

'Is there anything I can do?' I pray I don't sound too hopeful.

She looks at me thoughtfully. 'I don't know. What can you do? Apart from criminal dealings and beating people up?'

'I do actually run a successful business consultancy in Nottingham. Totally legit, proper clients and everything. I know my stuff: marketing, online sales, SWOT analyses, project management, Just-In-Time delivery.' I don't add that much of the knowledge of what really works comes from supplying illegal substances; it would spoil the vibe.

Liza narrows her eyes. 'What do you know about personnel, HR issues?'

'Baseball bats are very effective.'

She thumps me on the arm. 'I'm being serious.'

I choose my words carefully but truthfully. 'It's important for your staff to know where they stand, what are the benefits and consequences of their actions. What you do affects them, what they do affects you.'

'Hmmm. I was hoping you might know a bit more about legislation.'

'I can learn. And I do actually know a colleague who specialises in HR. Also totally legit,' I add before she asks. 'Seriously, I can help you.'

'Iain Wilson, are you asking me for a job?'

'Right now, I'm asking for another chance, another life.' Shit. I think I'm on the verge of going straight.

'With me?'

I swallow and nod, my mouth too dry to continue.

'Iain,' she says softly, 'I'm not sure I can date...' she stumbles over the words and meanings, 'I can't employ a hard-arsed criminal.'

'Technically speaking, I'm not a criminal if I don't have a criminal record. I've never even had a parking ticket. As far as the authorities are concerned I'm as clean as a whistle. And I think I want it to stay that way. You've... well, the whole day has convinced me. I'm done.'

'What about the hard-arsed bit?'

'I can crack walnuts with my buttocks, if that's what you mean.'

She smiles.

'Look, Liza, I don't need to be an employee. Just let me do some consultancy work. Two months' worth, no charge.'

'Hmmm,' she says again, brow furrowing. 'I think, in a professional capacity, there may be an opening for someone with sharp business experience. What are you doing next week?'

I shrug. I don't know what I'm going to be doing in half an hour.

'I've got a three-way meeting with someone you already know and an American businessman. He's a real wolf, all glossy hair and teeth. I don't trust him as far as I can throw him and it'd be good to have someone on my side that can show a fang or two back at him.'

'Sounds good. This person I already know, who's that?'

'Gemma Robinson.'

'Oh.'

'What's the matter? Are you scared of her or something?'

'No, no. Well, yeah, in a way. Isn't everybody intimidated by her? But I think she won't want me anywhere near business discussions. Our last meeting didn't end well.'

'Because?'

'I was high. Never happened again. In a way, she made me the successful businessman I am now.'

Liza smiles. 'I can talk her round. Leave it with me.'

'So have I got the gig?'

'Let's say we'll have that trial period of a couple of months. If you truly want a new start I suggest you get out of Nottingham and find somewhere to live where I can keep an eye on you.'

'And where would that be?'

'Hampshire. Me and my mum have a house on the edge of the New Forest.'

'Sounds perfect.'

I'm mentally moving into a cottage, working normal office hours, seeing Liza every day.

And then my phone rings. It's Simmo. I look at Liza and she raises an eyebrow.

'Look, I just need to take this last call.'

She folds her arms and watches, disapprovingly.

'Hi mate.' Simmo's voice begins telling me that the lad is out of his coma and conscious. I cut across him. 'That's great news, wonderful. Look, can you send his family five grand? Don't ask why, just do it. And one more thing, I'm going away for a bit. Not sure when I'll be back, so you're in charge. Of everything.' He's asking more questions, getting flustered. 'Calm down. Let's just say I met someone, okay? And maybe we're getting too old for all this. Time to settle down, eh?'

He doesn't sound very sure about this. 'It'll be fine,' I say, reassuringly. 'So... thanks mate. You've been awesome. Be safe.' I hang up and look at Liza. 'You better be sure about this because I've started burning my bridges.' I've already decided that I'm not going back to my flat. My escape plan is in operation. Tomorrow I get a new car, a new place. A new life.

She takes my arm and we walk back around to the front entrance of the school. We can hear the music from inside pumping out the theme tune to *Friends*. We join in with the chorus, singing loudly '*I'll be there for you, when the rain starts to fall...*'

We stand there holding each other's arms as if to let go would be to float off into space. She looks up at me with a frown. 'I don't suppose you can give me a lift to my hotel?'

'No problem. Do you fancy a nightcap when we get there?' I probably need to book a room for myself. Or not, depending on how well the nightcap goes.

'Ah, well, the thing is, I promised Gemma that I'd meet up with her there.'

'Oh.'

'I still think you should come along, though. Clear the air.'

I shrug and smile. 'Whatever you say. She's going to go bloody ballistic though.'

'Leave her to me. She owes me.'

I take a deep breath and exhale slowly as I consider what I'm doing. 'I hope I'm worth all of this.'

'I'm sure of it. I know who you are, deep down. You just need to find a way out.'

I'm struck by just how much I trust this woman, how much I need her in my life. And I hope I can convince her that she needs me. I reach up, brush her hair from her face and gently kiss her cheek where the fire had burned and puckered her flesh, twenty five years ago. 'Thank you.'

I pull back and she looks radiant, if a little startled. She swallows and smiles back at me. 'Are you definitely up for this? To take the first steps on a new journey?'

'I am if you are.'

She nods. 'Together, then.'

I'm grinning, partly through the heady rush of new opportunities and the start of a new relationship (however that will turn out) but also through the sheer panic of doing something I would have considered insane when I woke up this morning. 'I'll be with you every step of the way.'

Julia Forest, *Tank Girl to Child Protector* – 9:50 pm

SOMETHING MAKES ME turn from the chatter of our group and I see the ancient culprit being wheeled along the ramp beside the hall to join the throng. He's had a haircut. In fact, he's almost bald. And fatter. Jabba the Hutt springs to mind. His carer appears to be Stacey Grey. So the poor girl stuck it out with him. I know my own complaint against Butterford has faded into insignificance beside Amanda's, but in that moment I decide he is not going to get away with it. Rape of a minor. Regardless of Amanda's reputation at school, his is a serious crime.

We exchange a glance then cross the hall, intent on our unfinished business, but the wheelchair and its occupant seem to have disappeared. However, I hear a familiar guffaw followed by a roar of male laughter. For some reason, Butterford has washed up at the bottom of the main stairwell where he is surrounded by the familiar faces of the school's football heroes. They are paunchier and redder in the face than they used to be, but perhaps the cans of lager they're spraying at one another are partly responsible for the deterioration of the Adonis clan.

'Come on, Stacey,' yells Butterworth, 'pass me another one.'

She reaches into a canvas bag hanging from the back of his wheelchair and hands him a beer.

'So how did you break your leg, Ross?' asks one of the middle-aged lads, although the 'Ross' is still self-conscious.

'Pre-season rugby training,' says Butterford glibly. He turns to his wife, 'Right,' he says, 'get up them stairs and do your stuff for the lads.'

'Ross...' she whines.

'Don't "Ross" me. What do you think I keep you for? Your brain?'

She pouts.

'Get your tits out.' He turns to the lads. 'She needs a bit of encouragement,' he says and starts to sing a well-known stripping melody.

Most of the lads join in enthusiastically.

'Da-daa da-daaa, da-daaa da-daaaaa...'

Just then the Head, like a child at a grown-ups' party, reaches the group. 'Hello, boys,' he says, 'what's going on here?'

'Oh, just catching up, sir,' says one.

Butterford grins at the Head. 'Just a bit of fun,' he says, but Stacey has taken advantage of the interruption to pull her top straight and descend the stairs. She takes a firm grip of Butterford's wheelchair and turns him towards the toilets.

'Toilets still down there, sir?' she asks.

'Yes, Mrs Butterford, although those are unisex now.'

'Thank you,' she says and wheels her husband away from his audience.

Hannah Parker, *was a proper Charlie* – 10:00 pm

I'M INTERRUPTED IN my macabre memories by a gasp from Lucy. I turn to look at her. She's staring at the door. Karl Stamford is standing in front of the door. He reaches his hand behind him and shuts the door, blocking our exit. We're trapped.

Even though his appearance is shocking and he has probably changed as much as me over the years, I recognise Karl. His grey tracksuit is streaked with blood. One of his eyes has swollen shut and blood is smeared all over his face and hands where he has tried to wipe it off his face. He's holding his side. Maybe broken ribs? He's clearly had one hell of a beating.

For once Lucy is lost for words; in shock at the sight of Karl. Maybe a bit more drama than she was expecting. It seems strange to see him back in the science lab after all these years. Memories are flooding back of the terrible incident. I can almost smell the burning flesh and fight to stop myself from being sick.

Karl is breathing heavily and winces in pain. Definitely a broken rib. Who could have beaten him like this? The why doesn't take much figuring out: someone clearly wants to settle an old debt.

I find my voice. 'Karl, what happened to you? Do you want me to call an ambulance?'

As I talk, I step forward trying to get closer to Lucy. She's got her phone gripped in her hand. Before I can register a movement Karl has covered the small distance between us and grabbed her mobile out of her hand. I watch in disbelief as he throws her phone on the floor, the sound of her screen cracking as he brings his foot down hard on the mobile.

Spittle flies from Karl's mouth as he shouts, 'No fucking police. No fucking ambulances. I'm going to blow you bastards to hell. I should have done it at school. Burned you all down to the ground. It's all you deserve for making my life so shit.'

Karl points at me, 'You give me your fucking mobile. Now!'

Lucy stares at me, the fear in her eyes mirrors mine. Shit, I take too long to think about it.

'I said, give me your phone... now bitch.' Karl reaches in his pocket and pulls out a flick knife. At the flick of a practiced wrist, the knife is pointing at us.

'Give it to him, Hannah.' Lucy's voice is shaking.

I take my phone out and slide it across the table. He doesn't manage to catch it and it flies off the end table. Thankfully I don't hear a crack. Maybe we can get to it and get help.

I slowly back away from the onslaught of words. He's clearly mad. His eyes are so wide, he looks like someone infected with rabies. Lucy is behind me now and guiding us to the back of the lab. I can feel her hands shaking. We need to get out, but there is no way out other than through the door. We need to get some help in here, and fast. I glance at the fire alarm which is right next to the door at the front. Why is everything at the front of the bloody room? Who the hell has a science lab with no bloody emergency exit? There is no way we can reach the front without going through Karl.

My eye catches the window at the back. We need to get to that and shout for help. The knot of fear is stopping my brain from thinking clearly.

Suddenly, Karl's words reach the part of my brain not working on getting the hell out of here safely. I thought he said he was going to blow up the school. Chloe. I sway and almost fall, but Lucy steadies me. Chloe. My daughter is downstairs. Helen is downstairs. A feeling I've never felt washes over me. I've heard people describe that animal instinct, that maternal instinct to protect your child. I can feel my face flush as the anger takes over. The anger I carried as a youth. Karl will not hurt my family, not if I can stop him.

I glance at Karl. He's still near the door and seems oblivious to us. He's ranting and swearing about what he's going to do and how we all deserve it. I have no idea how he plans to burn the school down, but I know I need to get everyone out, and fast. I hold on to the anger as sickness and fear try to take over. I think of Chloe and harden myself. I have to save my daughter.

I whisper to Lucy, 'Go and open the window and scream as loud as you can. I will try and distract him.'

Lucy looks scared, 'What if he comes at us?'

I incline my head to the fire extinguisher on the wall. Lucy's eyes go wide but she nods her head.

My stomach is in knots. But, I will protect my family, no matter the cost.

'Karl, why are you doing this? Please let me and my friend leave. We haven't done anything to you. Please Karl.'

Karl stares at me. 'What the hell are you doing in here anyway? Nosey bitches. I wanted one last look at this shithole before I blow this piece of shit school to smithereens. It ruined my life, all for a fucking joke. I didn't mean to do it. I didn't mean to kill Danny. It was just a laugh.'

His vehemence turns into a sobbing whine. I look him over. I cannot see a bomb or trigger. But, then again what the hell do I know about such things? I only know what I've seen on the tv. I have to keep him talking. I have no idea if he really means to blow up the school, or if he has the skills to do it. But, he's clearly gone over the edge.

'You bastards held me back all my life. Judging me at school for a stupid prank. Talking me into doing shit for people. Well this one is for real. '

Karl starts hitting his hand on his forehead, knife in hand.

I know I'm not getting anywhere. I can hear Lucy climbing onto the table. I move to the back, all the while watching Karl. He doesn't seem to notice or care we are there. I pick up the fire extinguisher ready to use it on Karl if he comes for us. I cannot believe the rage I feel. My hands are shaking but it's not from fear, it's from anger. How dare he do this?

I reach Lucy and she's managed to climb on the table at the back and is reaching for the window. She tries to pull it open. For a minute I panic as she cannot open the window.

She mutters, 'Fucking school safety fucking tilting windows.' She stands up and tilts the window yanking it down and screams. I swear for weeks after, I'm deaf in my right ear. Thank God for Lucy's lung capacity.

The scream breaks Karl out of his tirade. He looks at us like he's forgotten we are there. Lucy continues to scream as I watch him, the fire extinguisher ready to do battle. I brace myself ready to attack. Our eyes meet, but I'm not prepared for what I see. Tears are streaming down his face. I see a glimpse of overwhelming sadness.

'I'm gonna blow them to hell.' His last words before he leaves the room. Our relief is short-lived as he locks the door, trapping us once again.

Iain Wilson, *"Legitimate Businessman"* – 10:05 pm

WE'RE WALKING BACK to my car near the main entrance when we hear banging and a voice yelling, loud but kind of muffled. I look around but can't immediately see where it's coming from. Liza's heard it too and points up and right to a window on the first floor. It's the only one with the lights on and there's a woman silhouetted against the eco-friendly illumination, pressed against the window shouting through the narrow gap that allows ventilation in but prevents kids from chucking things or themselves out.

After a second or two we both realise which room it is.

'It's the lab,' says Liza, flatly.

I walk back towards the window trying to hear what the woman is shouting. She seems genuinely distressed although I can't make out who she is. And then I catch some of the words. I turn to Liza with a frown creasing my brow. 'She's saying something about Karl.'

Liza visibly shudders. 'We should go up and see what's happening.'

My frown increases. 'Do you think you should? Considering...'

'I'm fine. I was up there earlier.'

We walk back in through the entrance, past the now deserted reception area and take a right to swing past the hall. A woman in a sparkly green dress steps out of the hall, a younger woman in tow.

'Iain Wilson? Is that you?' says the first woman.

'Uh, yeah, hi.'

'What happened to your floppy hair? You were such an Indie kid.'

I know her but I'm struggling to place her. This evening has completely discombobulated my cognitive functions.

'Helen!' says Liza. 'How are you?'

Helen. Of course, it's Helen. Helen... Walcott, if I remember correctly and if she hasn't changed it through marriage. She copied some Pulp CDs for me after we discovered a shared interest in the early Britpop scene. She was always a bit aloof, though. Maybe that's the wrong word. Wary might be better. Never wanted to meet up after school; I remember her telling me about her parents and how controlling they were. Again, who knows what could have been in different circumstances.

'Hi, Helen, yeah, so the hair went once I had to start wearing suits.'

'You square bastard,' she says with a smile. Not so aloof or wary now. I smile back.

'Are you hanging around for a bit longer?' asks Liza.

Helen looks at her watch. 'Well, Chloe and I were just about to get off, actually, but...'

'Look, you stay and chat with Helen,' I say to Liza, 'and I'll go and check out who's in the lab.'

Helen looks concerned. 'What about the lab?'

'I don't know, just someone yelling and waving at us.'

'Hannah said she was going up there.'

'Who's Hannah?' I ask. I know my memory for names hasn't been good but I really don't remember a Hannah from school. It does ring a vague bell, though. Someone's mentioned that name already tonight.

'Never mind,' says Helen, 'just get up there and make sure everything's okay. I'd come with you but, you know, what with the accident and everything...' She glances at Liza and then down at the floor.

I nod and head for the corridor and main staircase. I'm aware that the DJ has started playing another nineties hit, but even to my twisted sense of humour The Prodigy's *Firestarter* isn't in very good taste.

I take the steps two at a time, accelerating as I hear thumps and more muffled yelling coming from down the first floor corridor. I get to the door and am stunned when it doesn't open. How the hell is this door locked with people inside?

I knock on the door. 'Hello?' I shout.

In response I get a flurry of noise, two female voices yelling at me from inside the lab, then a couple of faces peering through the small wire-reinforced window. One's blonde, the other a redhead.

'Calm down, one at a time. Why is the door locked?'

'It's Karl,' shouts the redhead. 'He's locked us in!'

'And he says he's gonna blow the whole place up!' yells the blonde. Her voice sounds vaguely familiar.

Wait, blow the place up? What?

'When was this? How long have you been in here?'

'About five minutes. We don't have time to talk, just get the bloody door open!'

I press my shoulder to the solid wooden door. It's a frigging fire door, not some shitty pine-framed double glass panelled thing. I'm not going to be able to kick this down. How quickly could I find a key? Probably not soon enough.

'Hang on.' I cast around for inspiration and spot a couple of fire extinguishers a few metres away. The *Fiery Horror* of October '92 meant that the school ensured an abundance of extinguishers of all types in and around the science labs. I heft the large red water extinguisher up and off its wall bracket and lurch back to the lab door. 'I'm going to try and break the lock. Stand back.'

'Hurry up! I don't wanna die!'

'Yeah, and my daughter's downstairs! I need to get her out!'

Jesus, hang on, I'm doing my best. I get into position with the extinguisher horizontal and base aimed at the lock, just below the handle. In my mind I picture the cops using an Enforcer door ram to bust open doors in raids. Never thought I'd be doing something similar. I swing the heavy weight backwards and then slam it into the door. Not much seemed to happen.

I try again, getting a better feel for the swing and blow. There was definitely some movement that time. And again. The door bursts open on the fourth impact with wood splintering from the frame around the lock.

Hannah Parker, *was a proper Charlie* – 10:07 pm

THINGS HAVE BEEN happening fast and my head's spinning.

I grab my phone from the floor as Karl locks the door. Thankfully it isn't broken. Lucy's mobile hasn't fared so well.

'Shit, Hannah, we need to get out of here.'

'I know. The bastard's locked us in though.'

'Someone heard me shouting. Someone will rescue us. Jesus, it's bloody exciting isn't it?'

I stare open-mouthed at Lucy as we pound on the door. Threat gone, she seems to be actually enjoying it. I haven't got time to admonish her before a face appears at the door.

We scream at him to get us out. I shout again about Karl's plans.

'I need to get my daughter out,' I yell in desperation. I can feel Lucy staring at me, but ignore her. There will be questions later, many many questions.

The bloke does a great job of attacking the door with the fire extinguisher. I can hear it starting to give way and I know we are going to escape. As soon as it's open I race to the stairs. Lucy is hot on my heels until I look back and see her swooning into his arms. That girl really is one of a kind.

I focus back on the task in hand. I cannot spare time for what's behind me; I need to make sure my daughter is out.

I race to the bottom of the stairs and smash the fire alarm. I wonder why I hadn't just hit the one in the lab. I know I'll regret this later if anyone gets hurt.

Iain Wilson, "*Legitimate Businessman*" – 10:07 pm

THE TWO WOMEN rush towards me and out into the corridor as I place the extinguisher onto the floor. The redhead is wearing the exact same dress as Helen downstairs and she's tearing towards the staircase as fast as her shoes will allow. Can't say I recognise her though. The second woman turns, a little unsteadily and points at me. 'I's you. Bleedin' 'ell, it's like *Die Hard* or something tonight.'

And now I remember her. 'Lucy, right?'

She swoons towards me and I have to step forward smartly to catch her; I notice that she's still got one eye open as she carefully collapses.

I sweep her up in my arms, grunting slightly with the weight (because human bodies are generally much heavier than you realise they're going to be) and totter off to the staircase. I'm just at the top when the fire alarm goes off and the shock almost sends us tumbling down the steps.

Phil Morris, *The Man, The Legend* – 9:55 pm

ALONE AGAIN, I sigh. Chunk and DI Willy are nowhere to be seen, Charlie and Lucy have vanished, and most of my old mates either don't live nearby or just haven't bothered making an effort to come. I stagger a little and slop my wine as I step away from the bar and look around the room – squinting to bring faces into focus. Bugger, I better leave the van and get a taxi. I've only had a couple of drinks, and it's only wine, but I better stay safe, I begrudgingly resolve.

As I circulate, looking for someone to chat with, my eyes are drawn to a flash of movement. Through the glass panels to the corridor, I see Karl taking several steps at a time down the staircase. He pushes past gathered bodies and barges through the door into the entrance hall. He's in a hurry, it's like somebody is chasing him, but I don't see anyone. It's the first I have seen of him at this gathering – I wonder what he was doing upstairs, it's just classrooms up there.

After about ten minutes of mingling, a few superficial chats and several failed attempts to join what look like more interesting conversations, I decide it's time to call it a night. It's late, and the gathering has thinned – the remainers are gathered in cosy cliques or coupled in intimate pairs.

I slip out and head for the entrance hall. I might as well leave the way I came in, I think as I make my way to the caretaker's door. I surreptitiously open the door and slip inside – pulling it closed behind me. As I turn to the outer door, I have a shock.

'Karl!' I exclaim, what the f... what are you doing?' Karl's hands are inside a big plastic box on the shelf. There are red and green electrical wires hanging over the lip, their stripped ends wound around the clapper and bell assembly of an old, copper, mechanical alarm clock and a strong chemical smell assails my nostrils. His stern face is grim and bloodstained with a deep, bloody graze from his brow to one cheek.

'You okay, mate?' I add with real concern.

He flashes a sideways look at me but doesn't stop doing whatever he's doing inside the box.

'Leave it, Phil, just go, get out, leave me alone!' he orders. 'I'm busy.'

'But – that looks like a – is that – is that what I think it is, Karl? Are you making a – Fuckin' hell, Karl!' I'm getting a strong acid whiff of what I can only guess is highly flammable material. 'Don't do it, mate – seriously, you could hurt people! It's not fair to...'

'Fair? I'll tell you what's not fair! I never meant to kill nobody, I never meant to burn Liza. I liked her. I would never have hurt her, no it ain't fair,' he splutters. He pulls his hands from the box and tears well in his eyes. He starts winding the alarm clock.

I take a tentative step forward to peer into the plastic box. There's a small Gel battery; probably from a motorbike. There's bags of liquid and coloured wires – I don't know how to make a bomb, but it looks like Karl does. Or thinks he does...

Suddenly,

CLANG, CLANG, CLANG, CLANG, CLANG...

The fire alarm bursts into life – but how the hell could they know about the danger?

Julia Forest, *Tank Girl to Child Protector* – 10:00 pm

STATIONED HALFWAY DOWN the corridor like a military check point, Amanda and I finally see Butterford being wheeled back towards the hall. He's still grinning but Stacey has a face like thunder. Presumably, the poor woman has to help him to relieve himself. We walk down to meet them and stand in his path. Stacey looks from one to the other of us uncertainly before coming to a halt.

'Hello, Stacey,' I say. 'How are you doing?'

'I'm okay,' she says, clearly not sure where this conversation is going to go.

'Stacey,' grumbles Butterford, 'why have you stopped? We don't want to talk to these two slags.'

I see Amanda out of the corner of my eye stiffening so I grab her hand and grip tightly.

'Slags, is it?' I say. 'Haven't you retired yet, you old pervert?'

'Nah, I'm still in my prime,' he says.

I grin at him.

'What's so funny?' he asks.

But I don't tell him yet. He's still only in his mid-fifties and not yet ready to retire. As an employee who comes into contact with children, he is far more vulnerable to the weight of the law. Even if any accusation against him is ultimately groundless or cannot be proved, he would be suspended from his post immediately while an investigation took place. I look down at his lower leg encased in plaster of Paris which might be temporarily keeping him off work. 'And how did you do that?' I ask, hoping it was an extremely painful experience.

'He was messing about in our yard,' says Stacey, 'chasing our Bichon Frise puppy and he fell over.'

I grin at her. 'So, not pre-season rugby training, then?'

'In his dreams,' she says.

'I haven't lost it yet,' he resumes as a couple of Sixth formers pass us, armed with more jugs of water. 'Great jugs, girls,' he quips and grins at the five women around him, oblivious of the contempt raining down on him.

'Why on earth do you stay with him, Stacey?' I ask. 'Surely you could do better than this?'

'He was good to me,' she says.

'I was good to you,' he bawls. 'Better than you deserved. You were a slag too at fifteen.'

Boasting of under-age sex. The possibility of viable evidence is growing.

'You don't have to put up with his abuse, Stacey. You're a grown woman.'

She looks at me for a moment then lets go of the wheelchair. She untangles her handbag from the handles and says, 'You know what, Ross? She's right. See if you can find another mug to look after you. I'm going to get a drink.' And with that, she clacks down the corridor, tottering on her stilettoes, even her swaying bottom shouting her disdain.

'So where does that leave you?' I grin down at him.

'Oh, there's always somebody willing to let me into their knickers, Tank Girl.' He leers at me with delight, so proud that he's finally placed me.

'I doubt that...' I begin to say as our conversation is drowned by the persistent shrilling of the fire alarm.

'What the hell's that?' says Amanda.

'Do you think there really is a fire?' I ask. 'Or do you think someone's just set it off for fun?'

We are answered by the sight of people pouring out of the hall and heading outdoors.

'It must be genuine,' I answer myself.

'Yes,' says Amanda. 'Let's be off.'

'What about him?'

'What about him?' echoes Amanda. 'He deserves to be burnt to a crisp.'

'We can't leave him.'

'We can.'

'I can't.'

Amanda looks at me. 'You're right, but it's so tempting.' She looks down at the man in the wheelchair. 'But I'll leave him to you. I'll see you outside.' She walks away from us without a backward glance.

I also look down at the fat, bald, greasy specimen of humanity in front of me.

'Go on, Tank Girl. You walk out too, eh?' And then he laughs.

It's the laugh that does it. He's not getting away with the rape of a minor, sexual congress with a minor, sexual harassment of a young adult, and any other charge we can come up with against him. He's going to face the music.

I go around the back of his wheelchair, flick the brake off and push him out of the school into the cool dark night.

Hannah Parker, *was a proper Charlie* – 10:10 pm

T HE SCHOOL ALARM wailing in the background, I frantically search the confused and excited faces coming out of the school hall. I need to check for Chloe and Helen. I feel sick. Adrenalin has been coursing through my body for what feels like hours, but in reality it's only been about fifteen minutes since we went into the lab. Following the flow of bodies I step outside and scan the crowd. When did it go dark? I hadn't even noticed.

I turn back to the school building and see Lucy in Iain Wilson's arms, my brain finally recognising him. Liza is stomping along next to them and she doesn't look very happy. They spot me and he starts to bring Lucy in my direction, setting her down next to me. I can see Lucy has a massive grin on her face.

Iain Wilson, *"Legitimate Businessman"* - 10:10 pm

I REGAIN MY BALANCE and make my way carefully down the stairs. I can feel the sweat dripping down my back as I get towards the bottom and see Liza's concerned face looking up at me.

'Who the hell's that?'

'Her name's Lucy.'

'Is it?' Liza doesn't seem very impressed. It occurs to me that Lucy is probably ten years younger than the rest of us, has long blonde hair, short dress and impressive cleavage. It also occurs to me that Liza may just be a little bit jealous and I can't help but smile.

'What's happening?' I huff as I get to the bottom of the stairs.

'Some woman came running down, in the same dress as Helen's, smashed the fire alarm and then started shouting at everyone to get out. What happened up there?'

'Karl locked them in the lab and said he was going to blow the school up.'

'What?' Liza's looking aghast. 'Jesus, Iain, I should've let you knock him out.'

Lucy lifts her head up off my chest. 'Did you do that to him, then? The busted nose and stuff?' She stares into my eyes and puts her arms around my neck. 'Cool.'

Liza rolls her eyes.

'Can we just get out of here? She's starting to weigh a ton.'

'Oi!' exclaims the woman in my arms.

We make our way back out to the car park, joining the last of the drunken and confused revellers. Liza spots a sparkly green dress and guides me over to her.

'I think this one's yours,' I say, placing Lucy carefully down onto her stilettoed feet.

The other woman, Hannah, I guess, takes her arm. 'Thanks, Iain. I'm so glad you heard us and were able to get us out. And thanks for looking after this one. Drunken mare.'

'Yeah, no problem.' I still can't place her. But she seems to know me. 'Did you get your daughter out?'

Before she can answer there's an explosion that makes us all jump.

Phil Morris, *The Man, The Legend* – 10:10 pm

I NEED TO DO something quickly. I briefly consider barging out into the night and running as fast as my legs will carry me, but think better of it and step forward. I grab the clock with my right hand and push him hard with the flat of my left hand. He falls back noisily among the mops and buckets. With one eye on Karl I quickly examine the clock. Should I pull out the wires? Should I smash it? No, that sort of thing sets off bombs in the movies. The alarm setting is only minutes ahead of the time. I'll move the hands, but what if I move them the wrong way? Is that the lever that cancels the alarm? I slide it carefully and put the clock on the bench.

I look down at Karl; his face twists, his cheeks concertina into deep wrinkles and tears well in his reddened eyes. I step towards him, offering my hand, which he limply takes. I pull him to his feet and drape an arm over his shoulder, 'Come on, mate – we better get out of here.' I say as I give his shoulders a friendly shake. He hugs me close as I open the exterior door and we step out into the cool night air.

As I begin to close the door behind me I am aware of an electrical crackle followed by bright sparks and a curl of dark smoke. I slam the door quickly and with a fistful of Karl's jacket I push him across the concrete towards the bushes. Suddenly there's a loud WHUMPF and we are both hurled into the bushes in a hail of broken glass.

After long seconds of stillness, the sound and fury of the blazing inferno behind me, and that bloody fire alarm, I look back in horror. The conflagration is in clear view through the now open doorway and empty window frame. The fire door is wide open and clinging on by its lower hinge. I can hear raised voices from the front of the school – I hope everybody is out!

Karl is still face down and worryingly still. I raise to my knees and shake him. 'Karl, Karl! Are you okay? Karl, open your eyes!'

'What have I done, Phil?' he groans.

I shakily stand and pull Karl to his equally unsteady feet. I lead him around the bushes accompanied by the sounds of pops and bangs as various items succumb to the raging conflagration. When we get beyond the darkness of the bushes, I look back to see a few stragglers hurriedly exiting the front doors. Hopefully, the fire will be contained till everyone is clear and fire brigade present.

I lead Karl across the vegetable patch to the school perimeter. I help him through a gap in the wire, and over the low side wall. 'Get yourself home, mate!' I say in a loud whisper. 'Forget about all this. Get in the bath and get that graze seen to. Have you been fighting? Did somebody – never mind, go!' I pull a business card from my top pocket and push it into his hand, 'Call me tomorrow – okay? Promise?'

He heads off down the lane and I make my way back to the main school building.

Maintaining a safe distance, I pass the brightly illuminated caretaker's room. Flames are beginning to lick up the panelling to the upper floor. With great relief I hear the wail of approaching sirens. Keeping in the shadows as much as I can, I make my way up the drive to a place opposite the assembly point, watching with relief as the fire engines turn and head for the main entrance. People are gathered in groups in the car park, watching with obvious fascination as the firemen approach the building, pointing at smoke billowing from the side of the building, from what I know is the caretaker's room, and light flickering in the hall. It's pretty much contained in that one room, as far as I can see.

Hannah Parker, *was a proper Charlie* – 10:12 pm

THE EXPLOSION SHOCKS us all. Every pair of eyes turns to the school.

Oh God, oh God. I haven't found them. Where the hell are they? Please don't let them have been inside. The sound of people screaming, then fire engines, thank God. It's absolute chaos.

Maybe they have already left; Helen's last words were that they were leaving. My stomach flips. Last words are not something I want to think about. Had they left straight after our conversation? I fumble for the mobile I'd put back in my bag, but my hands don't want to co-ordinate. I finally grip my phone. My hands are shaking so badly it takes me seconds that feel like hours to open my phone and select Helen's number. I dial it and it goes straight to voicemail. *Shit. Shit. Shit.*

I start to dial again when the phone vibrates, and I answer with shaking hands.

'Hannah, thank God. Are you okay? Sorry we left. We were in reception when we heard all the alarms go off. And was that an explosion? I had to get Chloe the hell out of there. We are in the car at the end of the drive. Do you want us to come get you?'

'No, it's okay as long as you two are fine. Look, I've got to go, it's madness here. I will ring you tomorrow.'

'Okay, Hannah. Please take care. Speak to you tomorrow.'

Helen hangs up.

I didn't know my heart had this much capacity for love. I've certainly achieved much more than I bargained for coming tonight. What if I hadn't come? Would I ever have known I had a daughter? The emotion, fire and noisy alarms going around me are making me disorientated. I can feel the bile rising at the back of my throat, and feel unsteady on my feet.

'Woah there, Charlie Boy. Well, it's proof if anything that you're a Sheila. Thought you were going to faint then.'

I turn to see Phil holding my arm. He's covered in dirt, and a bit singed around the edges. He goes on to tell me what happened with Karl. I grab him by the face and kiss him on the mouth.

Phil Morris, *The Man, The Legend* – 10:15 pm

I WALK ACROSS THE drive to the car park and see Charlie. Hannah, I mentally correct myself, and Lucy, both with arms folded, standing, watching the spectacle. As I approach, Hannah greets me with a concerned expression – I must look a mess – and asks if I am okay. I tell her about my encounter with Karl and how I tried to stop him blowing the school up, how I nearly prevented him from starting a fire, how I bravely overpowered him, and how I disabled the bomb. Well, how I thought I had, he obviously didn't quite set it up properly. It shouldn't have triggered after I switched off the alarm – or – oh bugger, was it already off and I switched it on? I feel a cold shiver as the colour drains from my face.

Hannah stifles a laugh, 'You daft bugger,' she says. Then steps forward and kisses me, on the lips!

I nearly push her away, I almost rub my sleeve across my lips, but – well – it was nice. She's nice. I smile and put my arms around her. 'Sorry I was a bit of a dick earlier, Hannah!' I give her a squeeze and nuzzle her neck. After several seconds and a lot of thought, I slip a card from my top pocket and press it into her hand, 'If you fancy going out for a meal or something sometime, my treat, no pressure.' I smile. Maybe tonight wasn't such a waste of time after all.

'Come on "nearly hero", you can share our taxi and we'll give you a lift home. You're obviously not fit to drive!' she scolds. She guides me along the driveway towards London Road and I feel somebody touching the back of my head, and dusting my shoulders – oh, it's Lucy – she's picking off bits of glass and other debris. I've not had this much attention in ages.

Iain Wilson, *"Legitimate Businessman"* – 10:15 pm

FIRE AND SMOKE are pouring from the far right hand side of the school, but Hannah is talking to someone on her phone and seems incredibly relieved so I assume her daughter's fine. The Headmaster is running about gathering all of his staff and sixth formers together to do a roll call. Andy Wilkins has his badge out and is striding over to the fire fighters as they erupt from the first vehicle that pulls up outside the school building. He's intercepted by a woman pushing a wheelchair containing that greasy bastard Butterford. He seems angry but the woman, Julia something if I remember right, seems very calm and collected. Whatever it is, DI Wilkins is content to leave the firefighters to do their job while he does his.

'Should we stay, make sure everyone's alright?' asks Liza.

I watch a bloke in muddy chinos and knock-off trainers stagger up to Hannah. I recognise him now, it's that numpty Philip Morris, or 'the Marlboro Man' as we nicknamed him. I don't think he ever twigged why. He used to hang around with that other oddball, Charlie Parker. We used to call him Bird, after the jazz sax bloke. He looked like a bird too, all thin angles and delicate limbs. I haven't seen him here tonight. Philip's talking to Hannah and it suddenly dawns on me who she actually is. Charlie's a... bird! Just as I'm processing that she kisses him which leaves me convinced that I'll never have a stranger day as long as I live. I'm done. I need a quiet sit down and a cup of tea.

I take Liza's arm. 'I think a lot of people have already gone home and there isn't anything we can do. If they need any statements I'm sure they'll be in touch. Let's just go and find somewhere quiet.'

'Like my hotel?'

'Well, don't you want to speak to Gemma?'

'And afterwards? Are you hoping for something extra? Because I don't want to give you the wrong idea. I like you, Iain. A lot. But let's not go too fast, eh? We might be back at school but we're not teenagers anymore.'

I let go of her arm and shrug. 'Sorry. You're right. Let's keep it professional.'

She smiles. 'For the time being. I need to get to make sure I've got the right Iain Wilson before I make a firm commitment.'

I gaze at the burning building and it feels symbolic; a funeral pyre for the old Iain and the birth of another. I'm a phoenix. Phiainix? I grin at the pun. 'Works for me.'

BREAKING NEWS
There are reports of a fire at Hercules Clay Comprehensive school in Newark, Nottinghamshire. The fire service is in attendance – more updates as they come in.

LOCAL NEWS UPDATE: NEWARK SCHOOL FIRE
A fire at Hercules Clay secondary school has been successfully extinguished and seems to have been contained to the Caretaker's office. No injuries have been reported. A school reunion was underway at the time. Early indications suggest a deliberate act of arson with eyewitnesses confirming that they heard an explosion. Witnesses questioned at the scene believe that Karl Stamford was at the reunion and the police are requesting that he contact them as soon as possible to help with their enquires.

Karl Stamford was involved in an incident in the school in October 1992 which resulted in the death of local boy Danny Griggs; another student suffered severe burns.

One of our reporters on site spoke to ex-student Philip Morris who said, 'I didn't see anything, mate. Best thing I've seen all night is a fight between Ascot and his missus in the carpark.'

He was referring to local businessman Ascot Thomsett, who gave no comment to the allegations that he'd cheated on his wife at their wedding some years ago which resulted in minor affray at the reunion. His wife, Sarah, said, 'I will take the bastard for everything he's got.' At this point used car salesman Mr Thomsett confessed that they were in serious debt and she would never see a penny.

Reports of a member of staff being arrested at the school have not been confirmed by the police.

Lucy Longton's Twitter feed:

LucyisLush @LucyisLush - 1h
You will not believe the nigth ive had... kidnapped.... some little #prick DSETROYED my phone Rescued by a tall dark stranger... epxlosions i totes nearly died. I kid you not. Im on my friends phone so dont call me. #whatanight⚑

LucyisLush @LucyisLush - 49m
OMG These #firefighters are hotter than the fire! nothin like this EVER happens to me. You guys won't believe whats happened up north. Who knew Newark was this mad! Makes London seem tame! #exciting #schoolreunion89

C.L.Peache @c_peache - 37m
O M G Lucy. Only you would get a selfie with a fireman! We are sooo booking a night up north in Newark (where is that anyway lol). Cannot believe it you always manage to get the hot men! Are you wearing your big knickers? xD

LucyisLush @LucyisLush - 31m
Can not belive you mentioned my big knickers! Sorry gotta go. My friend is dragging me away from the fit firemen. Amazing end to the night - free booze, tunes, dancing, fights, explosions #bestnightever

Hercules Clay Facebook Page - comments

Matt Jones Dammit! I shoulda gone to this!

Jason Hughes   Would of bin there too if wasn't in nottm at QMC. Too much going on!

Katy Greeves [*marked herself safe*] It was awful. The wine was shit & the sandwhiches were curly

NOTTINGHAMSHIRE POLICE STATEMENT

We can confirm that last night a 55 year old PE teacher at Hercules Clay Comprehensive School in Newark was arrested in connection with historical sexual abuse allegations. The police are in no position to comment on this until further investigations are carried out.

About the Authors

Jackie Leitch has written or told tales since childhood, usually to entertain her sisters, and continued to write throughout her teens (including terrible poetry), twenties and thirties. Her writing skills improved while taking a degree in Literature and History in her forties, but it wasn't until she moved to Newark that she finally joined a writing group. Her writing credits include an award from the National Association of Writing Groups and publication in their 2011 anthology. Two of her short stories were published in 2015 by Dayglo Books and she has contributed to several Fosseway Writers' anthologies. She has been placed in numerous competitions, winning first prize on several occasions. Much to everyone's relief (including her own) she has stopped writing poetry. She has completed and published her family history, which drew on 25 years of research and childhood memories from the 1940s, 50s, and 60s. She has several projects in mind for the future, one of which is to complete a novel set in the 1930s.

Maria Dziedzan was born in Grimsby but grew up in Nottinghamshire. She spent several decades teaching English in the county's comprehensive schools before taking early retirement. So far she has written three novels in her *My Lost Country* series: *When Sorrows Come* which won the Big Bingham Book Read in 2015 and was shortlisted for the Historical Novel Society's Indie Award in 2016; *Driven Into Exile* followed and led to its sequel, *Bread and Salt*. She is currently working on a fourth novel, although this has been put on hold from time to time as she has worked with the Fosseway Writers on their collaborative novel. She plans to work on book number four full time over the next months... and possibly years.

Janey Harvey grew up in Lincolnshire and as soon as she was old enough escaped. She attended university in Leicester and then London where she trained to be a journalist at The

London Institute. She worked in publishing for, amongst others, the BBC and after having two children decided to leave London behind for Newark where she has been ever since. She has had many jobs including collecting eggs in a chicken farm, serving in bars, as an English teacher, teaching yoga to pregnant women, but currently works in Holocaust education. She is studying for an MA in Creative Writing and trying to write a book based on memoirs and CB Radio that may one day - with the Fosseway Writers' support - see the light of day. She has written for a number of magazines including *Juno* and *The Young Telegraph* about being a mum to a daughter with Special Needs. Janey's character, Helen is not based on any one person but an amalgamation of many girls that Janey knew at school.

N. K. Rowe spent his formative years in Coventry before finally settling down in the Newark-on-Trent area in the early 90s. Past jobs include B2B advertising, police intelligence analysis and working with EU legislation, all of which helped bore people at parties. Nick currently works for a speech analytics software company and has completely given up on parties. He has written scripts for a youth theatre company, took up blogging (by accident) and then joined Fosseway Writers. Three years later and he's the Chair (also by accident). He's had a couple of second places in competitions which made him realise that he might not be terrible at this writing lark. In 2018 one of his poems was selected for the collection *Diverse Verse 3* and he shoe-horned six of his short stories into the Fosseway anthology *Gobstoppers, Shrimps and Sour Monkeys*, which he also edited (not by accident). He's currently working on his first novel (very much accidental because it's not the novel he expected to be writing).

C. L. Peache, a.k.a. Clair Robshaw, also answers to CRob and other names that shouldn't be in print. She chose a pseudonym because she hangs out on social media a lot, but also to honour the memory of her late father; Peache was his birth name before he was adopted. She was born in Wakefield and moved to the Yorkshire Dales at fourteen. Village life was a little bit too quiet and didn't allow maximum networking opportunities, so she moved to York. She's glad that mobiles were not available during these years! She then moved to Derby, before settling in Newark (for now). After winning third place in the Fosseway writing competition in 2018, she joined Fosseway Writers and somehow ended up being voted in as the Programme Secretary at the AGM. She's had too many jobs to list but is extremely proud of self-publishing her first books in 2018.

Helen Yourston grew up within spitting distance of Hever Castle, leaving school to attend Secretarial College in Tonbridge. Her love of all things second hand took her into the antiques world, from teaching adult education to auction rooms, then becoming a dealer. Seventeen years ago she met her now husband necessitating a move north of Watford (as the southerners say) to Newark. Now the two of them have their own company organising antiques events. Helen always wanted to write but never believed a book was possible and has to thank Fosseway Writers, whom she met at the Newark Book Festival in 2018. She is now on a clear path to believing she may be able to put pen to paper.

Linda Cooper was born in the U.S.A, raised in Nottingham, sentenced to twenty-eight years of primary school teaching in Kirkby-in-Ashfield, finally taking early retirement and eventually escaping to Newark where she was delighted to discover Fosseway Writers. She has been writing since she could first hold a pencil and has won several competitions and been published in a few small press concerns. She has self published a book of Haiku which was never one of her ambitions and is presently working on a complex memoir of immense proportions. Her character Amanda in this book is definitely not based on herself or anyone she knows.

Ric Millen was born in Birmingham, wisely leaving before learning to talk. He proceeded to Bodmin, Bristol and Bingham before advancing to the middle of the alphabet, first to Nottingham and now Newark. With consistent lack of direction, he worked as a window dresser, record shop manager, social worker and computer software entrepreneur before settling at Newark College as an IT teacher/trainer, VLE developer, and following a glitch in the matrix, a library person. Now retired, he is battling inertia and procrastination in his desire to write a book. Perhaps his contribution to this collaboration is a small step in that direction. Ric is keen to point out that Philip's personality is a concatenation of observed attitudes and behaviours, and the antithesis of his own, unprejudiced, egalitarian, right-on, child of the sixties, character.

Printed in Great Britain
by Amazon